Praise for "The Secret Life of Walter Mott"
by
Kal Wagenheim

"Kal Wagenheim brings back brilliantly those mind-deadening days of closed corporate life in America when creative minds worked mostly, and indefatigably, in trying to find ways to escape from it. Walter Mott, lost in the office maze, was brilliant at thinking up a sort of Rube Goldberg scheme as a way to escape, but fate, and his proving all too human, led him into all sorts of misadventures along the way. By turns funny and ironic, it also provides details of what office life was like back then, the way it once was. Wagenheim has written a comic novel that is a tour de force."
--John Bowers' latest novel is Love in Tennessee

"Kal Wagenheim takes us on a hilarious, poignant, trip back to the Fifties, when conformity was the internalized order of the day. Walter Mott is a memorable character, a rebel in his own way, a Walter Mitty as schemer as well as dreamer. This is a wonderfully entertaining comic novel that often zings at the strings of the reader's heart."
--Robert Friedman, author of Shadow of the Fathers, and other novels.

"An imaginative blend of MAD MEN's angst, Cheever's white collar dissatisfaction, and Thurberesque whimsy."
--Bill Mesce, Jr., award winning author of several historical crime novels, including "The Advocate, "The Defender" and "Four Day Shoot"

The Secret Life of Walter Mott

Kal Wagenheim

ALL THINGS

THAT MATTER

PRESS

But by God, it is steady. It is a basic wage. I always
was a timid bugger about that basic wage. Never
understand where you got the courage to walk
out on it.

Letter from Lawrence Durrell
to Henry Miller, January 1958

People are unhappy when they're free. They'll kill
or do anything to get security.

American artist Clyfford Still,
in Newsweek, Feb. 23, 1963

Sing we for love and idleness,
Naught else is worth the having,
Though I have been in many a land,
There is naught else in living.
And I would rather have my sweet
Though rose leaves die of grieving
Than do high deeds in Hungary
To Pass all men's believing.

"An Immorality"
By Ezra Pound

"To my dear, departed pals, Robert Bletter, Hal Burbage, John Cawley and Dave Straus, who shared the Good Old Fifties with me."

The Home Office

"Oh, Walter...Oh, Walter...yes! yes! yes! Oooooh..."

Walter Mott was driving Wilma Tannenbaum wild with ecstasy, when the alarm rang and confirmed his fears that he'd been dreaming.

"Shit," he muttered, as he popped up in bed, his lids fluttering faster than a hummingbird's wings, his pecker aching and throbbing like an old pitcher's elbow on a rainy April afternoon. He groped in the dark for the alarm and murdered it with a squeeze of his thumb.

Fighting off the real world, Walter advanced the timer fifteen minutes, rested the clock on the floor and flung himself back to the pillow. Still tense, he tried to relax, to float back behind that gauzy curtain and mount those jiggly mounds of goose-pimpled flesh that were Wilma. He willed her into various erotic poses; she responded, but her eyes were blank and still, her skin rubbery cold as a manikin, her crotch smelling of stencil correction fluid. Using every trick of mental gymnastics at his command, he tried to sufflate life back into her, but again the alarm interrupted with its metallic shriek, and his arm darted towards the noise like an angered cobra. "Shit!"

Walter sat up cross-legged in bed, gazing numbly at the phosphorescent hands. It was seven-thirty. A Friday.

Well, things could be worse, he thought, recalling those six a.m. wake-up calls during Basic Training at Fort Dix. He chuckled, remembering how Sergeant Sigler would burst into the barracks and yell, "Okay guys! Drop your cocks and grab your socks. Rise an' shine!"

Walter lowered his feet to the floor, hooked his toes into the slippers and stood erect, shivering in the chill dark room. He rested the clock on the pillow, damp with saliva of his sleep-kisses, and reached for the worn damson-colored robe that lay curled at the foot of his bed like a faithful cat. He shrugged it on over his tee-shirt and boxer shorts, groped his way to the window, and pulled a cord that sent the drapes skittering away from each other with a frightful squeak. A tug at the venetians pulled light through the narrow openings in vapory golden bars.

Walter reached for a Pall Mall, lit up, inhaled, and squinted out at the world. The colors of the rooftops were kindled by the sun; several miles eastward, the tip of the Empire State Building glistened like a burnished needle. He stood on tiptoe to look thirteen floors below at the wintry downtown Newark streets.

When he turned on the small radio atop his desk, the station from across the river in Manhattan reported the city had received more than five inches of snow last night, rain was turning it into slush and ice, and then droned a litany of delays on the Long Island Railroad, a smashup on the upper level of the George Washington Bridge, jams at the Holland and Lincoln Tunnels, and further collapses along two stretches of The West Side Highway.

The announcer reported, with great enthusiasm, that President Eisenhower said he would sign a bill next week granting statehood to Hawaii. That makes an even fifty, Walter thought, since Alaska became number forty-nine two months earlier. He made a mental note to ask Mister Furey how this might affect company policy.

The news was interrupted by a special announcement, offered by a familiar voice: "This is Fred McMurray. Civil defense is common sense. Home fallout shelters are available for as little as one hundred dollars. Simple plans for building inexpensive home shelters are available free from your Civil Defense office. Ask for a copy of the Fallout Shelter booklet."

Walter sighed, shrugged. Thank God, he thought, I won't be needing any of that where I'll be going soon.

Up there, not a sound reached him from the gloomy criss-crossing gorges that already crawled with ant-sized pedestrians and cars that jerked ahead like fitful blobs of mercury. He watched with distaste and pity as the faceless dots below hastened to work.

Then he turned from the view and admired the eighteen by twelve foot office that had been his home for the past nine years. I should really take a picture, he reminded himself.

The entire wall to Walter's right was a contiguous olive green mass of metal file drawers. A ladder linked near the ceiling to a greased horizontal bar rested upright in the far corner. The left wall, too, had file drawers and a ladder, but its monotonous surface was interrupted by the bed, which protruded from a hollow rectangle in the wall. By the far wall, a glass front mahogany bookcase squatted close to the beige linoleum floor.

Above it hung a framed black and white photo of President Jennings, mid-fifties, who wore rimless spectacles, a thin-lipped smile, and a mien that exuded importance. The man's hands were clasped harshly together, as though he were cracking his knuckles, or practicing Charles Atlas's theory of Dynamic Tension.

Next to the portrait was a door; its clear upper panel partly opaqued by two rows of neat black letters which, from the outside, read, "Walter Mott - Manager."

Near the window, a gray metal desk and matching swivel chair rested upon a green area carpet. A phone and a three-deck set of correspondence trays perched atop the desk; the "In" and "Out" empty, the "Hold" overflowing, symbolic perhaps of Walter's vacillating nature. A green blotter nearly covered the desk top, pinned flat by a glass of equal dimension, plus an adding machine, and a ballpoint pen set with a black onyx base that bore his name in goldleaf Old English letters; a tenth anniversary memento from the company.

Walter squashed out the cigarette in an ashtray atop his desk, walked to the bed, ran his fingers through his thinning brown hair, then down along an angular cheek, peppered with stubble. A blurry flotilla of books, pamphlets and clippings was scattered about the edges of the bed and immediate floor area. Marr's, *Periodical Essayists of the Eighteenth Century,* lay beside the pillow; it was page-marked by a prospectus for shares in a South African gold mine. An open volume of, *The Plays and Poems of Richard Brinsley Sheridan,* straddled a collage of newsletters about environmental technology equipment, dividend statements and auction catalogues for stamps, coins and autographs. Sherburn's, *The Early Career of Alexander Pope,* and *John Gay's London,* were paperweights for a ream of clippings from *Forbes, Barron's,* the *Times* financial and travel sections, and *Linn's Stamp Weekly.*

Four hours had done little to soothe Walter's burning eyes, but the memory of a fruitful night was balm of a sort. After his visit with Stormy at the Latin Casino, he had spent two hours figuring out Friday's stock purchases and his bids for a rare stamp auction the following Saturday at Harmer and Rooke. Another few hundred in the kitty, he noted smugly. Afterwards, he had read until three-thirty, dozing off midway through stanza seven of Dryden's, *"To The Pious Memory of the Accomplished Young Lady, Mrs. Anne Killigrew."* The book had slipped from his limp hand; the mauve binding peeked out from beneath the bed.

Walter frowned. Work began in less than an hour. Soon, his coworkers would be streaming into the big room just outside his office. Sighing, he gathered all the books and papers in his arms and dumped them into an open file drawer. He opened another drawer and pulled out his shaving kit, as the radio blurted out a cheery musical salute. Whistling the tune, a light classical version of *"Any Bonds Today"* by a one hundred string orchestra, Walter marched from his boudoir into an enormous space, nearly the size of an airplane hangar, furnished with seventy gray desk-chair sets aligned in precise geometric rows. Monolithic pillars, painted a listless mint green, rose at intervals like headless sequoias.

The furniture stood in silent ranks as Walter strode by in his slippers, his robe flapping loosely behind him. When he reached the far end of the room he shouldered his way through a swinging door that, from the outside, read: "ARF—Agency Records File." He padded along the gleaming white marble corridor a few paces, stopped and slipped a key into the door marked, "Executive Rest Room."

Twenty minutes later, freshly shaved and showered, his hair neatly combed, Walter returned to his bed chamber and put the toiletries back into hiding.

He discarded yesterday's boxer shorts in another file drawer and fished out a clean set from the one adjacent. He reached into the drawer below and chose a pair of calf-high, ultramarine socks. What to wear, he thought, peering into the closet beside his bed. Three suits, two sports jackets, a modest spectrum of ties, and three pairs of dark brown shoes. The gray wash and wear today. After dressing, Walter turned off the radio and placed it in a file drawer. He lifted the foot of the bed until it faded into the wall with an oily rumble; its bottom was lined with more than a dozen false file cabinet fronts. He unscrewed two small support legs from the foot of the bed and dropped them into a drawer, after which he closed all the drawers and locked everything tight with his master key.

Walter donned his khaki trenchcoat, which hung from a mahogany rack in the corner of his office, hooked the black umbrella over his forearm and walked out the door; a tall slender man who looked good in business attire. He tripped over a crumpled blue sock — yesterday's — which he stuffed into a coat pocket with haste and, his composure ruffled, backed out of the room like an escaping burglar, scanning the floor for the damned other sock.

TGIF!

1

Walter emerged on the street floor from the dank service elevator, which smelled of discarded coffee containers, stale pastry and envelope glue, and glanced up at the four-sided clock that hung from the lobby ceiling. It was 8:10. He slipped through a side exit and winced at the din of downtown traffic and the chilly March breeze. Seized by an urge to retreat, he looked back at the building where, above the door, buffed brass letters on a dull verdigris background proclaimed, "SECURITY INSURANCE CO." On a second smaller line it read, "Serving the Public since 1883." Below the plaque, a square yellow and black sign proclaimed, reassuringly, "Fall-Out Shelter."

Walter hesitated, then plunged into the swift current of pedestrians, weaving his way through the throng on Halsey Street, inching towards the corner coffee shop. At 8:25 he came back around the corner like one of a hundred corks bobbing in a swollen brook. He bypassed the side entrance, turned another corner and pushed his way through one of the revolving doors at the main entrance. He strode down the marble corridor towards the waiting phalanx of elevators, umbrella suspended from his right forearm, *The Times* trapped between his right bicep and his rib cage, and, in his left hand, a brown paper bag that cradled a buttered toasted bran muffin and a container of Chock Full O' Nuts Coffee, dark, one sugar.

There were fourteen elevators in the main lobby, one for each floor in the Security Insurance Co. building, which occupied much of the city block. During the morning and evening rush period, each car was assigned to a single floor and sped the company's employees nonstop to their offices. Walter entered Car Thirteen and soared skyward with eleven other members of the Agency Records File department--any more was unlawful and dangerous—amidst the usual exchange of nods, yawns, grunts, the rustling of newspaper pages, and a few cheerful smiles of a subversive nature.

It was 8:28 when Walter pushed through the door marked ARF. The Muzak system, on full blast, roared a blood-tingling Sousa march to usher in the day's labors. The seventy desks, deserted just half an hour before, were filling quickly with clerks. .

At 8:29, Walter hung his umbrella and trenchcoat on the mahogany rack, rested his *Times* upon the "In" tray, removed the lid from his coffee, unwrapped his crumbling bran muffin and prepared to gulp breakfast, while his eyes darted about the office. Where the hell, he wondered, is that damn missing sock?

2

The bell rang a minute later, and Wilma Tannenbaum, Walter's secretary, came in with the morning mail and, since it was Friday, his weekly paycheck.

"Morning, Walter," she chirped. "Here's the mail and here's your check. TGIF!"

"Morning, Wilma. You can say that again."

"TGIF."

"Do you have the time cards for the MAD night shift?"

"Yep. Here they are." She plopped the stack of cards on his desk.

"Saaaaay," she said, leaning close to him, "your eyes look like you've been getting too much bed and no sleep."

"No," he said, blushing a bit, "I think I'm coming down with a little cold."

"Well, you take good care of yourself, precious. Would you like me to get you some tea and lemon?"

"No, no thanks, Wilma. I'll be alright."

"Okay, but you better take it easy with the weekend coming up. You bachelors, running around till all hours." She winked and smiled.

Mesmerized, he watched her heaving derriere float out the door. Had the bed been open, she'd be tramping right across the mattress where, only an hour ago, they were co-stars in an X-rated dream.

Wilma had joined SIC more than eleven years ago, just a few months ahead of Walter. In that time, his hair had thinned and turned a bit gray at the temples, but she had retained her youthful features. Above the neck, that is. Nearly a dozen years of sedentary desk work had ballooned her high school cheerleader's figure into a caricature, a Dedini cartoon nymph, with huge pillowy breasts and an enormous pair of hips.

By piecing together Wilma's complaints over the years, Walter guessed that she wasn't getting enough exercise at home either. Her life seemed to be one long yawn, hardly satisfying to a woman of her "sensitivity," a word she often used. Wilma's husband, Morty, the assistant production manager of a brassiere factory in Weehawken, drew the night shift every other week.

Theirs was a childless marriage. When Morty worked nights Wilma sprawled on the living room sofa in her terrycloth robe—cigarettes, rum and Coke and Cheez-its at her side—and was lulled into a stupor by late-late movies and commercials for aspirins, detergents, hit records, discount furniture, and miracle vegetable dicers. When the National Anthem ended, and the screen hissed visual static, she would rise, stiffly, step into her silk pom-pom slippers, click off the set, shuffle to the bedroom and fall asleep with the icy pillow clenched between her ample thighs.

Not long ago, however, Wilma had made the grim resolve to channel her passions towards self-betterment. She obtained a library card, joined three book clubs and the classical music section of a record club, and during her lunch hour took to prowling a used book store near the SIC office.

It was on one of those cultural forays, a few months ago, that Wilma, unobserved, had spied Walter Mott in the rear of the shop, leaning against a book rack, dramatically etched by the naked light bulb as he flipped through a fusty edition of Balzac's, *Droll Tales*. She had no way of knowing, of course, that Walter's critical frown, which so enhanced his features, was prompted by the bookstore owner's passion for stray alley cats; the place reeked of rancid milk, rotten sardines and cat urine.

Wilma had worked with Walter for years, but after this fleeting glimpse through the grimy bookstore window, she saw him in a new perspective. He was tall, passably and passively attractive, and apparently quite cultured; not at all like Morty, whose closest brush with literature came when he wrote an article for the brassiere industry trade journal, *Keeping Abreast*. Wilma had retyped the article in the office, and it was published under the title, *"My Cups Runneth Over."*

Since that day at the bookstore, Wilma had become more flirtatious; she often casually suggested that Walter, "come over some night and pick out any of the books you want. I'll just be throwing them out one of these days. With my book clubs, and all of Morty's magazines, our apartment is bursting at the seams." So, Walter noted, was Wilma's sweater, as he munched his morning blueberry bran muffin.

"Yes, I'll have to drop by one of these nights," Walter always said. Wilma's motives seemed clear enough, but he had long ago decided, quite painfully, that he must remain uninvolved. He was too close now to risk it all. So he mentally filed Wilma's offer in his crowded "Pending" tray. And he dreamed of her.

Walter lit a Pall Mall, and flipped through the stack of time cards from MAD, the Machine Accounting Division, which was down on the eleventh floor, the site in an air conditioned room for a monstrous five-ton UNIVAC computer, which stood eight feet tall, took up 220 square feet of floor space and was powered by 8,000 vacuum tubes. At night, a platoon of part-timers fed the machine, which processed and sorted all insurance policies and claims received during the day. The information was shipped upstairs to ARF the next morning, where it was evaluated and stored in the archives for future reference.

The MAD nightshift, formed more than a decade ago, was directly responsible to ARF. Walter managed its salary and personnel affairs, leaving the actual supervision of the work to a woman he had never seen, with whom he communicated via company memos.

He pulled a time card from the top drawer of his desk and checked it over: *"Nill, Wilbur. Thursday to Wednesday, 6:05 p.m. to 11:05 a.m. Total: 25 hours."* Glancing at the door to make sure no one was watching, Walter slipped the card in alphabetical order with the others and buzzed the intercom.

"Wilma, these cards are Okay. Type up the list and send them down to Payroll." She came in, picked up the stack of cards, and waggled out.

3

With a sigh, Walter towed the pile of correspondence in front of him and tried to concentrate on the first letter, a request for last month's Sickness and Accident sales figures in the Skokie, Illinois office. *Booooor- ing.*

"Excuse me, Mister Mott?"

Walter looked up into a pair of intense gray eyes, so accented with mascara that they upstaged the small, saucy mouth which was bare of lipstick. The girl's wheat-colored hair was swept back in a pony tail which disappeared beyond her gently sloping shoulders. Her small breasts punctuated her sweater rather nicely. Dot ... dot. Those eyes. He looked into them again, deeply.

Walter felt himself plummeting into love. He became enamored of the most unlikely, least attainable girls. Once he had fallen for a young lass who sat opposite him on the train bound for Manhattan. It was something about the sound of her stockings rubbing together as she crossed one leg over the other. He was on his way to see a new Rosselini film not showing in the Newark theatres, and would have loved her company, listening to the gentle friction of nylon in the darkened cinema.

Just the week before, he was flipping through *Reader's Digest* at the company dentist's and was utterly liquefied by an ad showing a lovely lass strolling through a green, out-of-focus glade. The text had said, *"Modess, because..."* But with this young vision standing by his desk, Walter felt the page turning on Miss Modess.

Walter rose awkwardly and executed a quick, silly bow. "Yes?" he said, with an unplanned squeak.

Her smile revealed a trace of condescension. "I'm the new girl, Scar- lett Kosciusko," she said in a throaty whisper which evoked memories of

Dietrich singing *"Lili Marlene."* "Mary Ann, the girl who usually collects for the Sunshine Fund, said it would be good if I went around in her place and got to *know* everyone." There was a deprecative inflection to *know.*

"Well," he said, settling back in his chair, "I'm Walter Mott."

"Yes, I know." She seemed about to yawn. Silence: both wore small, tight smiles.

"You *did* say *Scarlett,* didn't you?"

"My parents were dating back when *Gone With the Wind* premiered in the Cameo Theatre. That's in Wilkes Barre. During the intermission, Dad proposed to Mother. So when I was born..." She shrugged, "... I'm so tired of explaining it."

"How unusual."

"Not really. Just another example of how the mass media influences middle class folkways."

"Yes, of course," Walter mumbled, retracting his antennae a few inches. "Well, how much do I owe The Sunshine Fund?"

"It's a quarter a week."

Scooping a handful of silver from his pocket, Walter dropped three nickels and a dime into her palm.

"Here you are, Scarlett. I'd give you fifty cents, but then I wouldn't have the pleasure of your coming to collect next week."

That was the boldest thing he'd said to a woman in years. This elicited a smile from Scarlett. His heartbeat accelerated and his cheeks felt warm.

"Mary Ann will be collecting from now on," she said. "Thanks Mister Mott. It's been very nice to meet you."

She was about to leave, but hesitated. Still smiling, she asked, "Are you by any chance related to the folks who make Mott's Apple Juice?"

"No," he said. "Wish I *was.*"

"It's absolutely delicious, isn't it?"

Walter was an orange juice fan, so he lied. "Yes. It's marvelous."

Scarlett, turned to leave, but again hesitated. "You know, you have a really interesting name."

"Interesting?" Walter said, as his heart began thumping.

"I'm taking a Contemporary American Literature course at night, over at Newark-Rutgers, a few blocks from here. One of the books they assigned had a short story all about a man with a name almost like yours."

"Really?"

"It's a terrific story by James Thurber, called *"The Secret Life of Walter Mitty."*

"Uh, huh..."

"*Walter Mitty, Walter Mott.* Do you think your parents may have named you Walter, in honor of that?"

"God, I don't know. When was it written?"

"Oh, in the late 1930s, I think."

"I was born way before that." Walter smiled. "Maybe this guy Thurber gave him the name in honor of me!"

Scarlett smiled. "*Touche.* Actually, it's a fun story, all about this mild-mannered guy who daydreams a lot, and lives a fascinating secret life."

"I'll look for it at the library. I go there a lot."

"Who knows? Maybe he did model it after you." She leaned closer, smiled. "Do you lead a secret life?"

Walter felt a bit nonplussed. Did this cute young lady have psychic powers? He shrugged. "Hate to disappoint you, but I'm afraid my life is rather ordinary."

"Well, I think you'll enjoy the story. Who knows? It might inspire you." She reached out, shook his hand lightly and walked out, her pony tail bouncing behind her like a pet puppy.

Walter wanted to be clever and say goodbye in Polish, but the only word he knew was "*dupa*"— which meant "*ass*"— taught to him by his Belmont Avenue childhood neighbor, Joey Visotski. He wanted to stop her and ask about her hopes, her dreams, her aspirations, her phone number, her opinion of large families, of nuclear disarmament. He wanted to cry out, "*Shane.* Come back, Shane!" But she was gone. He hurried to the door and followed her bouncy pony tail to a desk in Irwin Kemp's filing section.

4

Irwin Kemp. That cunning clown, that concupiscent fiend who fondled unwitting girls as though he were shopping at the produce counter; a squeeze here, a pinch there, a playful hug, until before you knew it he was balancing them on his knee like an old grandpa. Irwin was hardly subtle in his approach. Whenever he walked behind a shapely young woman in the office, he couldn't resist whispering, loud enough for her to hear: "Shake it, but don't break it; wrap it up and I'll take it." Hardly original, but already, according to Irwin's "modest" accounts, six of the fifteen file girls had succumbed to his Pepsodent smile. Oh, nothing really serious. A little kiss, a squeeze of the breast perhaps. Of the remaining nine, four were newlyweds, still immune to his sly reconnoiterings; the other four besides Scarlett were so unappetizing that he treated them as though they were pieces of office equipment. Once, referring to the very frumpy typist Joan Lewis, he commented to the guys at lunch, "She's so ugly I wouldn't fuck 'er with *your* dick." Then there were the occasional stray blossoms Irwin encountered on his daily field trips through the labyrinthine SIC building. Shuddering, Walter made a mental note to warn Scarlett about Irwin Kemp, who more than once told Walter that his all-time favorite tune was from *Finian's Rainbow*, a Broadway show he'd seen a few years ago. Then he would proceed to sing a few phrases. "When I'm not near the one I love, I love the one I'm near." But today Irwin was not in a singing mood.

"All right, Silas Marner, hand over six bucks."

Speak of the Devil. Irwin Kemp stood in front of him, his right hand extended, palm up. Irwin was a short, dark-haired, slender man, brimming with energy, flashing a brilliant smile, always impeccably dressed, Florsheim shoes polished to perfection.

"What now, Irwin? I paid you yesterday for the football pool, and the day before for Florence Dalrymple's birthday, and the day before for Ernie Kellogg's hernia operation flowers. What now?"

"Old Johnny Mulligan is retiring."

"Who?"

"Old Johnny ... our messenger boy ... I mean, man."

"He's sixty-five already?"

"Monday. But the party is next Friday night at Glenwood Manor, the place we had the Christmas bash last year. Do you want the Delmonico Steak or the Fried Scallops?"

"Hm?"

"It's a Friday, so we have fish for the Catholics."

"I'll have the Delmonico."

Irwin snatched a pencil from Walter's desk and raised one hand as though it were a note pad. "Gimme your serial number, buddy. I'm gonna have the Vatican check you out in their files."

Walter pulled out a fiver and a single from his wallet.

"Just so you know what you're getting into, it's five beans for the meal, plus all the beer you can guzzle 'til ten p.m. Hard liquor's separate, except the first Manhattan before dinner. The extra buck is for Old Johnny's gift. Dontcha wanna know what we're buying the geezer?"

"If you don't tell me, I won't sleep a wink all night," Walter said, riffling through the papers on his desk.

"You know how he's been running up and down the halls delivering messages all these years? We figured we'd buy him a pair of roller skates."

Kemp doubled over, slapped the desk and wheezed with glee at his own joke. Then, erect and red-faced he said, "Naw, serially, we're getting a wristwatch. With almost a hundred people chipping in we should be able to get one with movable hands. That way he'll be able to wake up on time to water his petunias, or whatever else old farts water."

Irwin glanced outside the door, where Wilma Tannenbaum sat typing away at her large Underwood. He ran his fingers through his close-cropped hair.

"Jiggle, jiggle, jiggle. *Jesus.* She's got the biggest boobs I've ever seen in my whole eye."

Smiling, he turned to catch Walter's reaction. Irwin reminded Walter of the cheerful emcee on those afternoon TV quiz shows where thrilled housewives won electric blenders, or automatic coffeemakers for being able to name the capital of Madagascar. Walter liked Irwin, but he felt in no mood for his antics this morning. He continued to shuffle through his correspondence.

"Well, I'll leave you to your *work,*" Irwin said, accentuating the final word with gentle sarcasm. "And thanks for the dough. I'll send you a card when I make it across the border to Mexico."

Irwin winked and sauntered out. In passing, he plucked Wilma's bra strap, and arched his back as she--without looking up or missing a stroke of her seventy-word-a-minute typing rhythm--swiped at him with a fleshy arm.

Walter gulped down the last few tepid drops of his coffee and flipped the container into the waste basket. The cup had left a tan liquid ring on the glass, which he wiped away with the paper napkin from his bran muffin. Beneath the ring, pinned flat between the glass and blotter, was a saying printed in bold black letters: "One day, as I sat musing, sad and lonely without a friend, I heard a voice say 'Cheer up, things could be worse.' So I cheered up and, sure enough, they got worse."

Other items beneath Walter's desk glass included: a company calendar for 1959 with the holidays circled in red; a typed list of intra-company phone numbers which Walter frequently called; and a homemade greeting card which he had received on his last birthday from Irwin Kemp. The card was severed in two, so that both the cover and inside flap were visible. The cover bore a grisly drawing of two intense eyes and a macabre, gap-toothed leer, below which was scrawled: "Then, too, there's another way to look at it…" On the inner flap, a trail of gory droplets led to the words: "…your life is slowly oozing away. Many happy retoins, Oiwin."

Irwin was a maddening enigma to Walter. He just didn't fit in with the other ARF regulars, to whom Walter felt smugly superior. How the hell, he wondered, did Irwin ever get any work done between his clowning, ogling, daydreaming and shuttle trips downstairs for coffee? Yet Irwin, who was twenty-eight and had been with the company for four years, was more efficient than anyone else in ARF.

Of course, he, Walter, had perfectly sensible reasons for sticking it out. He was simply marking time until … but Irwin? What was *his* game? Most of the others were clods; lucky to have the company to which they could cling. But Irwin was bright. How could he stay so cheerful in so deadly and dull a clime? He actually seemed to *enjoy* his job. Walter chuckled, recalling the balmy afternoon last spring when he, Irwin and several co-workers, walked out of the building for a lunch-hour stroll. Irwin had stopped suddenly, looked up at the sky, and bellowed: "Gee, it's so nice out; I think I'll *leave* it out."

Or the time Irwin sidled up to Grace O'Connell, a painfully shy young lady in the typing pool, leaned over, held out his right hand, and whispered, "Grace, pull my finger." Poor innocent Grace complied, and Irwin let loose with a thunderous fart, causing her to turn red and nearly faint, as Irwin nonchalantly retreated.

Or the time he shocked one of the secretaries, saying in a whisper loud enough for others to hear, "I had a wet dream about you last night." Then, after a pause, "I dreamt we were swimming down the Jersey shore," and walked away, amidst cackles of laughter from those within earshot.

Or the morning when Irwin slipped into the company cafeteria before it opened, and on the blackboard, in huge chalk letters wrote: "Today's yummy dessert special: Dingleberry pie!"

Then there was the lunchtime gathering the other day when Irwin mentioned to the guys, "Hey, have you noticed how in the public toilets now they have two kindsa urinals? One regular height, and other way down, almost touching the floor?"

"That's for little kids who can't pee that high," said one fellow.

"I dunno," Irwin said. "On my high school football team, we had this guy Charlie Lowe. Had a dick more than a foot long. Way down to here. I *swear*. We called him One Hung Lowe. I think they made those low pisspots for really hung guys like Charlie."

That elicited a few questioning glances and an uncomfortable silence about pecker size.

The Latin Casino

1

Walter was a creature of habit. Almost every weekday evening for the past nine years, after supper, fair weather or foul, he would stroll the eight blocks north along Broad Street to the Newark Public Library and read until it closed at nine thirty p.m. On occasion, if an attractive woman were sitting nearby, he would venture a fleeting, winsome smile, but it never went farther than that.

If a good film was playing at the Branford or RKO Proctor's, he might leave the library earlier. The other night, he was gripped by the coming attractions for Alfred Hitchcock's new thriller, *North by Northwest*. Then he sat back to enjoy Billy Wilder's latest, *Some Like It Hot*, and laughed so hard that nearby patrons gave him strange looks.

Some Sunday afternoons he took the Number 31 bus up South Orange Avenue to the old Christian cemetery near the Irvington border. He would stand erect before the modest gravestone of his deceased parents. An only child, he would stare for a few moments at the inscription: "Roger Mott, born April 9, 1899. Lillian Mott, born March 28, 1901. Taken together by the Lord Jesus on August 15, 1944." And walk away, his eyes brimming with tears.

Other weekend afternoons, Walter walked eastward along Market Street, past the shops, bars, pool hall, auction houses and vegetable stands, to Newark's Penn Station and sat in the waiting room, watching passengers carrying luggage, hurrying to trains, buses and cabs, traveling to all manner of exotic (to Walter) destinations.

Perhaps once a month, feeling a bit more adventurous, Walter boarded the train to Penn Station in Manhattan, and walked up Seventh Avenue through the Garment District. On the way he would splurge, buying a tasty hot pretzel from a sidewalk vendor, and then stroll about the theatre district, dazzled by the throngs of patrons streaming in to enjoy the matinees of *The Sound Of Music, West Side Story, The Crucible, Redhead, Destry Rides Again, Sweet Bird of Youth, Threepenny Opera* and other big hits. Late one afternoon, while walking past Sardi's Restaurant, on West 44th, he even spotted Gwen Verdon, the glamorous musical star, arm raised to hail a cab. New York was so thrilling. But there would be plenty of time for all that.

Walter had embarked upon an ambitious self-education program, to prepare himself for The Big Moment, which grew nearer every day, when he, too, would be free to enjoy life and travel the world.

Several years ago, he'd savored the six-volume, *Memoirs of Jacques Casanova*. The world's most famous lover had seduced him with the very first paragraph.

"I will begin with this confession: whatever I have done in the course of my life, whether it be good or evil, has been done freely: I am a free agent."

Last year, Walter had steeped himself in Contemporary Philosophy; this year he was concentrating upon 18th Century Literature. Next year, cramming for The Big Moment, he thought about learning Greek. Or Italian. Or Spanish. It all depended upon which heavenly spot he would someday select to spend part of the year. So many choices.

2

Last night, Walter had remained at the library until closing, fondling the couplets of Alexander Pope like a mad lapidary. Walter checked out the Pope book and took a southward bound bus along Broad Street, then Elizabeth Avenue, to the Pocahantas Diner, his favorite late-night snack spot. Shelly Krantz, an ex-bootlegger, owned the Pocahantas. And since Shelly, tobacco-stained teeth clenched around his ever-present cigar, swore that, "everybody's a *gonnif*, a crook." he handled the cash register personally, or delegated that task only to his wife, Selma, or his bored teenage sons and heirs, Melvin and Davey. It was a clean, well-lit place where horseplayers with squinty eyes and dazzling black shoes—guys with names like Herbie The Hozzer, Normie The Nosher, Bermuda Schwartz, and Cappy Capodanno—sat at the counter, chewing toothpicks and scanning *The Daily Racing Form*, searching for tomorrow's winners at Aqueduct or Belmont.

Nearby, chain-smoking Chesterfields and sipping endless cups of black coffee, sat Rick. No one knew his last name, he never offered; a thin, gray-haired bespectacled man in a dark suit and tie, who looked like an accountant, but who was their bookie, and, it was rumored, if they failed to pay up on lost bets, a ruthless hitman.

Esconced in a corner booth, Walter continued to read Pope's verse while he enjoyed his usual late night snack: coffee, dark, one sugar, and a toasted English muffin topped with orange marmalade. Many other things on the menu appealed to Walter; his tastebuds went into an uproar whenever the waitress served a huge slab of cherry cheesecake to one of the horseplayers; but his nightly choice was tasty, filling and cheap. Sticking within his budget was important; there was plenty of time for cherry cheesecake.

Later, half a block away, near the bus stop, Leroy, a disheveled fifty-ish black man, sat atop a wooden milk crate at his usual post, tootling a jazz tune on his battered alto sax, a tin cup on the sidewalk in front of him, inviting coins from passersby. As Walter approached, Leroy set aside the sax and launched into one of his big vocal hits: "Hey boppa-*ree* bop, yo' mama's in a *tree*-top; yo' poppa's on the corner yellin' *pussy* fo' sale!"

Walter pulled a dime from his pocket and dropped it in Leroy's cup, evoking a wink and a nod. Most passersbys ignored Leroy, and the local cops shrugged him off as harmless since he never sang dirty lyrics when ladies were within earshot, but Walter always dropped a coin into Leroy's cup, partly out of generosity, and partly due to a superstitious fear. *If I stop giving, something bad might happen to me.*

It was after eleven when Walter took the bus back across town. Unable to read during the bumpy trip, he gazed out the window at the gloomy Newark streets, dreaming of being somewhere else. He knew that the exotic vistas, shifting and glittering in his head like the fragments of a kaleidoscope, would soon be his new reality.

3

He stepped off the bus, the small volume of Pope in hand, the umbrella hooked on his forearm, and walked into a dark side street, where he pushed open a metal door and entered a flyspecked, Stygian cabaret located almost in the shadow of the SIC building. An absinthe green sign above the door flickered and buzzed, *"Latin Casino."*

Walter patronized the Latin Casino about twice a week; sometimes to assuage his nocturnal solitude by surrounding himself with people and noise, and occasionally when dreaming of Wilma Tannenbaum became intolerable. Of course, without compromising himself in any way that could jeopardize The Big Moment.

He entered the half-filled bar and saw that Stormy was alone, seated upon a stool and staring into a glass of crème de menthe. He rested his umbrella and book atop the nearby cigarette machine and sat down beside her. She greeted him with a sensuous, closed-mouth smile, dropped her long artificial lids to half-mast, and leaned heavily against him. She rested her right hand on his thigh and gave it a friendly pat.

Five years ago, Walter had struck up a friendship with Stormy, who, at first glance, resembled a Marine sergeant in drag. Her nose might have been clipped from a George Price cartoon. Her black hair was dyed even blacker black, giving it the appearance of a wig. Her mouth was thin-lipped and wide. Her eyebrows were shaved and repainted in a quizzical arc high on her forehead so that—while the rest of her face was calm, almost to the point of lethargy—Stormy's blue eyes seemed to be in a constant state of amazement.

She measured five foot eight, weighed one hundred fifty pounds, and walked past dark alleyways without a trace of fear. Her breasts and buttocks were matched in robustness by an ample gut which received waterings of crème de menthe, her favorite beverage, even with take-out White Castle burgers, her favorite luncheon. Stormy's muscular arms sported identical tattoos on each bicep which advertised her name in a flamboyant blue scrawl. Walter—and a regiment of other lucky males—also knew that she bore identical stigmata on her upper thighs. Despite her intimidating mien, Stormy was eminently feminine; a case, no doubt, of the whole having nothing to do with the sum of its parts.

The sixth of nine children, Stormy was born thirty years ago in a farmhouse near Anniston, Alabama. She quit school at sixteen to sling hash in a highway truckstop where, she explained, she developed her biceps by Indian wrestling with the drivers. If she won, they paid her a quarter. If she lost, they both went into the storage room where, minutes later, they paid her three dollars.

In the early 1950s, Stormy's outstanding bosom earned her a job as a stripper in a Phenix City, Alabama, often described in the regional press as "The Sin City of the South." But this idyll was short-lived. One night, a soldier from nearby Fort Benning got involved in a crap game fracas and the rising sun found him afloat, in the Chattahoochee River, staring blindly down at the fish. U.S. Army tanks rumbled across the narrow bridge from Columbus, Georgia to Phenix City, setting several hundred strippers, croupiers, shills, pimps, hookers and queens off on a mad hegira for the boondocks.

Stormy worked her way northward, supplementing her income by throwing Indian wrestling matches, until she discovered New York City. For several months she veiled her face, bared her umbilicus and adapted her Rebel bump 'n' grind to the exoticism of Arabian belly dancing in a smoky Lower East Side den.

But Stormy's career was nipped in the bud when her belly grew large with the child of the club owner; a man twice-tried—and acquitted—for white slavery, who was affectionately known as "TB" for his lingering cough and his fetishism about putting Christmas seals on his mail all year round. TB paid for the abortion, slipped her an extra hundred to get lost, and Stormy migrated westward across the Hudson River to the Latin Casino, where she lived on a percentage of the drinks she hustled, plus whatever she earned on the side. "Or any way you want me, darlin'," she coyly informed each new prospect.

Stormy lived in a walkup one-room flat with private bath on West Kinney, a few blocks from the Casino. Walter's lovemaking with Stormy was always brief, but thrilling, somewhat akin to a rollercoaster ride, or holding on to a bucking bronco at a rodeo. She would grip him fiercely, moan and yelp encouraging comments: *"Thassit my darlin'! Yeah! Yeah! Yeah!"* Afterwards, they would lie side by side for several moments, panting, staring at the ceiling, hearts pounding. Stormy would then plant a wet kiss on Walter's cheek and jump out of bed, signaling that it was time for him to leave, and for her to get back to "business" at the bar.

There were nights, though, when they never left the bar. Walter would sip his Seagram's 7 rye whiskey and chuckle as Stormy regaled him with a never-ending revue of the trials and tribulations of her life, which she insisted with enthusiasm would make a best-selling novel, "If only I could write." Walter, enjoying his role of Pygmalion, would reciprocate with occasional lectures on, and readings from, whatever he happened to be studying at the time.

4

Walter had a genuine affection for Stormy. Though he knew that she had sex with many men, it was a tribute to her artful diplomacy that he never felt there was any other "steady" for her. He had often stepped into the Casino and seen her at the bar, talking with some stranger. After a few drinks, they would head for the exit. But always, just before the door closed behind them, Stormy would turn and give Walter a conspiratorial wink, causing him to tingle with leonine pride, as though he and she were in cahoots against the rest of the stupid world.

Never in their relationship had there been the ugly moment when money passed from his hand to hers. Of course he often left a few dollars on her kitchen table for grocery money, and occasionally treated her to a four a.m. Sunday breakfast at an all-night diner down the street, but that was different. He was a *friend,* and the others were *customers.*

"I was jus' thinkin' aboutcha, Walter ..."

"Got to leave early tonight, Stormy ..."

"But I *told* ya, honey," she said, mildly vexed. "Ah ain't *got* 'em."

"The incubation period is eight days," he said. "There's always a chance the eggs will hatch."

"Listen, Doctor Casey, I'll letcha inspect me with a *telescope* if ya want ..."

"Microscope. Let's wait a couple days more, Stormy. I *told* you not to go with that Merchant Marine guy. He was scratching his crotch at the bar all night. Didn't you see him?"

Stormy smiled, unveiling a broken tooth. I wish she'd get that fixed, he thought, then reminded himself that he had an appointment with the company dentist next week; another SIC fringe benefit.

"Say," she said, her eyes blossoming wide open, "ah haven't told ya the latest about me 'n that wino guy who lives over in The Goodwill."

"*Which* wino guy?"

"*You* know. The wino with the one leg who's always tryin' to flirt with me? He drinks here sometime and then when he gets a bag on he says whyn't we go *home* together?' Well, I *like* the guy 'n all that, but ah ain't a-*bout* t' crawl in the *sack* with him. Man, that one leg gives me the *creeps*. Well, every time I says 'no' to him, he gets mad at me and I don't like him gettin' mad at me over somethin' like that. So las' week I tried to make up with him. I mean, this wino guy's awful lonely an' I like bein' friends so we can *talk* once in a while, you know? So the other day I'm walkin' down the street an' guess what I see in a garbage can?"

"The wino guy?"

"No, silly. An artificial *leg*. So I say to myself, 'Stormy, here's a chance to really help the wino.' So I grab the leg outa the trash can and bring it upstairs. I wash it off real nice in my bathtub an' then wrap it up with newspaper an' my red hair ribbon. Then I write a nice li'l card an' real quiet like I sneak up t' his front door, lean the leg against it, knocks, and run like the devil. Child, is he mad at me *now*."

"Mad? Why?"

"I never did take notice, but I brought him a *left* leg, and he's …," her voice rose in exasperation, "… missin' the *right* one. Now he thinks I was tryin' t' make *fun* o' him. Jus' goes t' show ya, tryin' t' *help* people. It jus' didn' never *occur* t' me there was a diff'rence in legs. Life sure kin get *complicated*."

"I wouldn't let it worry me, Stormy. You meant well. Say, why're you wearing your overcoat? Cold?"

"Got my *costume* on," she said, pulling her coat open. She was naked except for what looked like a bikini covered with clinquant red sequins.

"Your what?"

"This is my Arabian Nights costume," she said with pride. "Made it myself."

"You mean you're back in show business?"

"Bet your sweet ass I am. I'm gonna earn money *respectable*, like I did before. I told ya how I used t' do my Arabian Nights dance, didn't I? Well, Jimmy—the boss—he's gonna pay me five dollars a night, six nights, plus whatever I get on tips. Ever see one o' those Ay-rab places in New York?"

"No …"

"The customers, they always give money to the dancin' girls. They come right up an' lay it on the girl's forehead, sometimes 'tween her titties. An' then the girl dances with the money hangin' on them. I used t' make thirty dollars a *night* sometimes."

"Is that right?" Walter said, intrigued.

"Got a dollar, honey?" she whispered. "Lend it t' me. I'll show ya how we kin' make more with it." He reached for his wallet. She put her hand on his. "Not now. Later; when I begin t' dance. The folks in this bar, they don' know nothin' 'bout how they're supposed t' give dollars. Ain't their fault; they jus' don' have no *education.* So, when I begin, you kinda *show* 'em."

"Me?" Walter said, his heart skipping a beat.

"It's easy. Wait 'til I get heated up. That's when I lay back on the floor n' start t' wiggle. Then you come up real casual like an' lay the dollar right on my box—right where they kin' see it. Then I'll do a dance with the money, an' you'll see how they're *all* gonna chip in. Okay?"

"Okay," Walter said, gulping. She gave his hand a squeeze and slid off the stool. "Gotta get ready. I make my entrance from the ladies room."

5

In a few minutes, Jimmy, the owner, a bald, no-neck guy with a stubby cigar jammed into a corner of his mouth, walked to the center of the dance floor. Eddie, one of the waiters, pulled the plug from the jukebox. Like magic, it silenced not only the music but most of the conversation at the bar.

"Okay everybody!" Jimmy yelled. "I got an announcement. Quiet. *Quiet,* goddamit!"

He smiled at the silence. "Now, it gives me great pleasure t' introduce dat famous Ay-rab dancer, Stormy ... the Princess of Poontang!" A roar of laughter rose and subsided as Eddie plugged the juke box back in, pushed a button, and the first notes of the scratchy 45 rpm record of *Port Said* swirled out of the loudspeaker.

Stormy's appearance from the Ladies Room door was heralded by whistles and applause. In addition to the sequined bikini, she wore a transparent veil and her ankles and wrists were adorned with tinkling copper ornaments. Standing on a small raised platform, she began with a savage stand-up bump and grind with definite Minskyan overtones. As the record turned, quiet and sensuous, she fell to her knees, arched backwards and weaved her torso from side to side, her long hair sweeping the floor behind her.

This was his cue, Walter realized. Clutching the dollar bill and feeling nervous, he negotiated the ten steps from his stool to where she writhed below him. He bent to put the dollar down, but she presented a moving target. She looked up and hissed "Slap it awn, honey ... *now!*" She arched her hips up towards him, holding them quiveringly in place. Embarrassed over standing there so long, Walter placed the dollar on her bare stomach, between her belly button and the edge of her bikini bottom. He began to retreat, but saw the dollar curl up as though it would fall, so he gave it a gentle slap with his palm and it stuck to her perspiring skin.

His heart tom-tomming, he stumbled back to his seat. But it was *working*. No sooner had he settled down to watch than a pot-bellied giant in a pea jacket lumbered up and put a dollar next to his. Then one wise aleck wearing a suit without a tie folded a dollar bill, kissed it and slipped it *inside* her bikini bottom, which ignited a roar of glee among the patrons.

The record stopped and Stormy hung there until it started again. When it did, she lowered herself to a supine position and commenced to vibrate epileptically on the floor. Up came a grizzled Wallace Beery type who slapped a bill down, then a grinning young fellow who looked like a college student, then a beefy blonde woman with a short, shaggy hairdo and tight slacks.

When *Port Said* was over for the second time, Stormy lay still, waiting for the third go at it. Through some fluke, the jukebox came on with Elvis Presley belting out *Blue Suede Shoes,* but Stormy took it in stride, adapted herself to and mastered the new idiom, bumping away harder than ever. The parade of dollars continued until a garland of green adorned her crotch. When the music stopped and Stormy sprang to her feet, a din of whistles, applause and counter-stomping showered her with appreciation. Bowing and smiling her broken-tooth smile, she retreated to her "dressing room", where she waited at the door until a lady patron was done peeing.

6

"Here's your dollar," she said to Walter five minutes later when she sat down beside him. "Boy, these folks sure learn *fast*." She flashed a neat little pile of dollar bills and said with enthusiasm, "Sixteen dollars; an' on a weekday night, too. For bein' my assistant, let me buy *you* a drink."

"Where's your costume?" Walter said, noting she was fully dressed.

"In my coat pocket." She smiled. "Say … got any new po-et-tree?" She had a way of syllabizing that word.

"Ever hear of '*Rape of the Lock*'?"

"Sound's sexy …"

"It's by that fellow I told you about last week; Alexander Pope."

"The poor li'l guy you tol' me was cripple n' ugly 'n all that? He go rape somebody?"

"There *was* no rape," Walter said, being patient. "Just some girl getting a lock of her hair cut off."

Stormy, wondering, pointed down to her crotch area.

"No," Walter said. "On her head. Alexander Pope was a poet back in the early 1700s and he knew a lot of titled families."

Stormy stared at him, blank.

"The nobles," Walter said.

"Oh," she said, brightening. "You mean th' earls an' th' dukes an' folks like that?"

"Exactly. One young gentleman named Lord Petrie was in a playful mood and he cut a lock of hair from a young lady named Arabella Fermor. The families of the two young people, especially the girl's, were very upset."

"Why?"

"They were very formal in those days."

"Oh."

"So Pope, wanting to calm everyone down—they didn't have tranquilizers back then—he wrote a funny poem all about a young girl who had a lock of her hair cut off. And he dedicated it to the young girl, Arabella Fermor."

"Did she feel better after that?"

"Much."

"Tha's nice. Could you read me the poem?"

"It's very long; almost nineteen pages ..."

"Hell, what'd the pope do, tell how ev'ry cussed *hair* got cut?"

"He wasn't a pope. His name was pope, Alexander Pope."

"Then what about the popes? Ain't their names 'Pope', too? I'm a Baptist, so I don't know much about the Catholics."

"No, Stormy. That's just a title, like president or general or senator. Just like there's President Eisenhower, there's Pope Pius, Pope John, and so on."

"That's pretty familiar, callin' them popes by their first name, dontcha think?"

Walter was getting exasperated. "But Pope Pius isn't his real name. He took it when he became a pope."

"What'd his family think about him changin' his name after he becomes famous?"

Walter was about to make another try at explaining the customs of the papacy when Stormy held up her hand. "That's okay. I was jus' kiddin' ya, honey."

"Kidding me about what?"

She giggled and her voice rose. "That I didn't know 'bout the *popes*. Now when can you read me this po-em by Pope Alexander?"

Walter smiled, which inspired a broad grin on Stormy's face, and they both erupted in loud, uncontrollable cackles. Stormy slammed her hand

23

down so hard that the nickels, dimes and quarters all along the bar jumped half an inch in the air. Walter laughed so much he felt short of breath and his eyes were watery. He wasn't sure exactly *why* he was laughing; he *still* hadn't the vaguest idea whether Stormy *really* understood, but the laughing felt wonderful.

Blinking at the tears, Walter said: "Honest, Stormy, all kidding aside, it's really a long poem. We'd need plenty of time, plenty of peace and quiet."

"Then c'mon up to my room."

He gave her a stern, almost paternal look.

"T' hear the po-et-tree, silly," she said, nearly collapsing his rib cage with a good-natured dig of her elbow.

Walter thought about the bugs. He really wanted her, but not the bugs.

"No, really, Stormy. As I've told you, I've gotta hit the sack early tonight. Big day at work tomorrow."

"Well, suit yourself," she said. "Guess I'll go find me some company then."

"Wouldn't you like to go get a hamburger or something?"

"Oh no, I wouldn' wanna keep you out past your *bed*-time."

"I didn't mean *that* early."

"Tha's alright, Walter. I wanna stick aroun' here anyway. I'll see you around, Okay?"

"Stormy …"

But she was gone, carrying the glass of crème de menthe with her. Walter's heart sank when he saw her circle the bar and sit down almost opposite him, next to, of all people, that damn smart aleck in the suit, who'd slipped her the dollar bill inside her bikini. He looks like a real smoothie, Walter thought with envy. Walter got up, snatched his umbrella and poetry book from atop the cigarette machine, and walked out. Stormy threw him a wink, but he never saw. She probably *is* clean of the bugs, he thought to himself as he approached the side entrance of the SIC building and opened the door with his key.

Contemplating Murder

1

Now, this Friday morning, Walter sat at his desk and flipped through *The New York Times.* A short article on an inner page prompted a chill. The headline read, "It's Friday the 13th For 2d Month in Row." The article said, "The Greater New York Safety Council has issued some advice: Don't walk under a ladder, don't break a mirror, and avoid strange black cats. It appears, according to the council, that you might have a can of paint fall on your head, or cut your finger, or be scratched by an unexpectedly ferocious cat." The article concluded with, "Those afflicted with kaidekaphobia — fear of the figure thirteen — will be sure to get out of the right side of bed, and go through the day warily."

"Kaidekaphobia," Walter mumbled to himself. A superstitious fellow, he desperately tried to remember from what side of the bed he'd risen that morning.

Just then, as the office clock struck nine-thirty, in strode Mister Lindstrom Furey, director of ARF, looking as pudgy as a puffin in his Prussian blue overcoat. Tanned and hatless, his sparse chestnut hair slicked down with a tweedy British pomade, Furey's cockalorum strut hinted that state secrets were tucked in the Moroccan leather attaché case which he gripped so tight that his knuckles blanched. He offered a perfunctory smile to those who looked up from their desks.

Furey ducked his head into Walter's office, said, "Morning, Walt.", then entered his corner office next door. Walter rested his hand on the phone receiver, ready to play along with Furey's Little Morning Game. He snatched it up on the first ring.

"ARF, Mott speaking."

"Walt," see me when you've got a minute, will you?"

Replacing his receiver, Walter headed for Mister Furey's office with part of the morning mail. It was his job to screen all incoming letters and weed out those that required no Policy Level Decisions. Most letters sent to ARF were routine matters, but each morning Walter generously separated a few for Mister Furey, who busied himself a good part of the day by pondering and exploring the ramifications and nuances of the requests.

A typical one, on intra-company memo paper, had arrived yesterday:
"Date: March 10, 1959
"To: ARF, Home Office
"From: Elkton, Maryland Sales Branch

"Please forward info on Group Insurance sales volume for our office November last year as compared with good results by any three sales branches of comparable size that operate in areas where average income of prospects are comparable. Need data as incentive for sales meeting next month. Bill Porter, Mgr."

"Walt," Furey had said, "I want you to recruit three girls to form a Special Task Force to scour the files." The search was begun at nine forty-five. In exactly one hour and ten minutes, all the information was typed out in a letter for Furey's signature, with six carbon copies addressed to company executives whom Furey believed would be interested to know of ARF's sleuthing prowess. His pen poised to add his flourish of an autograph to the report, Furey thought better of it and put in a long distance call to Elkton.

Stubby feet atop his desk, *Lucky Strike* cigarette dangling from his lips, free hand massaging his bulbous midsection, Furey began.

"Hello, Porter? This is Lindstrom Furey, director of ARF in the Home Office. I've got those figures for you on group sales and thought you'd like them right away so you can work on blending them into your pep talk. Yep, we don't waste any time." This led to a discussion of Elkton and fishing in nearby rivers, golf on nearby links, hunting in nearby woods, an invitation to drop by the next time Porter visited the Home Office, and concluded twenty-eight minutes later with, "so long, Bill." Another friendship cemented. Someone else for the Christmas card list, which now had four hundred and sixty-three names.

Furey's wife, Miriam, dictated the choice of the cards, which grew progressively more chic with the passing years. Last season's message, printed on expensive but understated gray vellum, simply said, *"a joyous noel"*, in squat, modern capital letters. On the inside flap, in a smaller type size, it said, *"the fureys"*. Tucked in the lower right-hand corner, in even smaller type, was their address: 14 Whippoorwill Lane, Shangri-La Pines NJ

2

When Walter walked into Mister Furey's office this morning, he had just hung up his overcoat and rested his briefcase on the rug next to the desk, where it would remain until evening, when he took it home on the train. He leaned back in the swivel chair, feet atop the desk, his thumbs hooked through his fiery red suspenders.

"Hi, Walter. Pull up a seat."

It was easy to tell that Mister Furey was a SIC executive. No papers cluttered the smooth surface of his wood desk, which held only a phone, a small silver-plated clock, and a two-paneled picture frame; one-half showing Miriam, an attractive, fragile-looking blonde; the other his fourteen-year-old son Lindstrom, Jr.: crew cut, plumpish, freckled, his wide smile aglitter with silver braces.

The desk was cleared for action; for pondering The Big Picture. Another clue was Mister Furey's suit jacket, which he never removed. Most SIC workers spent the day in shirtsleeves because it was more comfortable. But for a senior executive to shed this garment was tantamount to a major general leaving his stars in his cufflink case.

Then there were Furey's polished fingernails—a must—which concealed the fact that he had been a voracious nail-chewer most of his life. When the minutest problem arose, he would gnaw his fingers down to gory stumps. Several years ago, upon receipt of his promotion to the executive level, Furey nearly went mad during the withdrawal period. But a few weeks later, after an arduous do-or-die struggle to save his career, he swaggered into the barbershop on the street level of the SIC building and nonchalantly requested his first manicure, flashing his new set of claws like a gleaming, spic and span engagement ring. Now, when confronted by crisis, Furey's lone visible reaction was a slight tic on the left side of his face.

A few years earlier, one member of Sac's upper echelon had come to the office wearing suspenders. A harmless enough whim, but the fad spread like fire in an oxygen tent. Belts were "out", suspenders "in" for any executive worth his salt, and Fury took no chances that his suspenders might pass unnoticed; they were blinding crimson.

"Here's today's mail, Mister Fury," Walter said, resting the letters on the desk. Fury flipped through the correspondence while Walter, lightly humming *"Any Bonds Today"*, waited for instructions,

Since the SIC building had more executives than it had corners, Mister Fury was proud of his corner location. More than two-thirds of the company's executives were left to grumble over their single-exposure offices. Corner offices were "inherited" in much the same way as jobs in some trade unions. Last year, in a confidential report from SIC Personnel titled *"How To Retain Key Men,"* one recommendation near the top of the list was that future SIC Regional Office buildings be shaped in an octagon, to provide more corner offices.

Mister Furey's carpet, a bit more plush than Walter's, was Standard Executive Beige, rather than Standard SIC Green. Where Walter had file drawers lining the walls, Fury had only a small cabinet by one wall and a low bookcase by the other. The rest of the wall space was occupied by large, full-color aerial photos of SIC Regional Offices in five U.S. cities, and architectural renderings of two more under construction … both of which were being built with the desired eight-sided structural element. On the wall facing the desk was the same photo portrait of the man trying to crack his knuckles. Furey's, however, was autographed, *"Sincerely, Chiron F. Jennings."*

Furey pushed the letters aside and rested his elbows on the desk. A pained expression contorted his rotund face; he resembled an infant on the verge of a tear burst.

"Walter …"

"Yes, Mister Furey?"

"We've worked together for … what is it, nine years now?"

"It'll be eleven years in two weeks."

"My God, time flies. I remember when I had your job," Furey said, his expression softening. "You were just starting out as a clerk when Mister Jeffries retired and they promoted me up here. Though you were with us for just a year at the time, Walter, your hard work in the office, plus the potential you showed us in your aptitude tests convinced us that you were the man."

Walter wanted to remind Furey that there had been only eight other men in the whole department at the time, all of them complete imbeciles. But he kept silent, wondering what Fury was up to. A cold shiver ran up his spine. Was he in trouble? Had they found out? Had someone run across his other sock?

"In all this time, Walter, have you ever known me to be unfair?" Furey always made a point of mentioning a person's first name when he addressed him. He had read somewhere that it had a telling effect.

"Why no, Mister Furey," Walter said, tensing his neck for the axe. My God, he thought, it's Friday the thirteenth. Bad things happen. *Kaidekaphobia!*

"I'll tell you the whole story and see what you think. I've noticed something very upsetting to me, Walter."

God, it *is* the sock, Walter thought, cursing his sloppiness. *Kaidekaphobia.*

Furey popped up out of his chair. "Be right back. Nature calls. That long train ride." He hurried out the door.

Walter was a non-violent sort, but for a moment he pondered the idea of murdering Mister Furey. I've worked too hard all these years to prepare for my escape from this place, he thought. I can't let a god-damn sock be my downfall. *Yes.* He could ask Mister Furey to stay late tonight, and before Furey reports him to the higher ups Walter could stab him with his letter opener. Or … or strangle him with his tie. He could hide his body in the filing cabinet. Wait a minute. Would Furey's plump body fit inside? Would he have to carve him up into bloody hunks of flesh? Uggh. *The smell.* No. Maybe he could stuff the body in a huge mailbag, drag it out, and drop it in the Harrison River, just a few blocks away.

No, no, Walter thought. Much too messy. Maybe tonight he could approach Rick, the silent guy who hung out at the Pocahantas Diner. People whispered that Rick was ruthless, and would wipe out anyone for a price. *Yes.* Rick could probably handle the job, meet up with Furey at the train station on his way home, and make him disappear. How much would Rick charge?

Furey returned and sat down with a loud, satisfied exclamation. "Aaah, that's better." He assumed his serious expression. "Walter?"

"Yes?"

"When I got off the elevator, 'bout nine-thirty or so, Walter, the lady was out there in the hall as usual, serving her coffee and buns. The company allows our people ten minutes to buy their morning cup and their bun; nobody begrudges them that. But Walter, this is supposed to be from nine-ten to nine-twenty. I pass there daily at nine-thirty and there's always one hell of a line out there, Walter. Just figure it out. Say every one of our fifty-six girls—we won't even *count* the *men*—say every one of the girls takes, let's say ten minutes extra a day for her break. Why that's … wait a minute, I figured it out on the train coming in."

Furey reached for his attaché case and rested it atop his desk. He opened it and Walter strained to glimpse the contents. Scratch pad, copy of *The National Enquirer*, a banana peel, and a paperback titled, *"Thirty Days To Greater Word Power."*

"Here it is, Walter," Furey chirped. He pulled out the pad and snapped the case shut. "Fifty six girls goofing off ten minutes a day. That's 560 minutes a day, Walter. That's 9.3 lost girl-hours a day; 46.6 lost girl-hours per week. And over the year, Walter, it adds up to 2,426 lost girl-hours. Think of it; 2,426 lost girl-hours over a cup of coffee and a …" he smacked his desk with an open palm, "… a damn *bun*."

Furey was so elated you'd think he'd stumbled upon E=mc2. But he simmered down and addressed Walter in an oily purr. "I'm sure the girls don't realize the *portent* of all this, Walter …" he paused to see how *"portent"* went over, since it was the first time he'd ever used the word, "… and if *I* talk to them they freeze up. Why don't you bring it up subtly when you see them, okay?"

"Why certainly, Mister Furey. I'll talk it up every chance I get," Walter said, his heart thumping with relief that murder was off the agenda. For now.

"I know you can do it, Walter," Furey said, patting him on the back. You've always been a real ladies man." Furey grinned at his little joke. Walter returned the grin with a meager smile and retreated from the office.

3

Walter spent the next few minutes digging through a mound of reports and memos, while one corner of his senses soared off with Scarlett Kosciusko. At ten thirty he opened the package of time card envelopes for the MAD night shift, which was sent downstairs by messenger at five p.m. and delivered to the night supervisor.

Walter searched through it and found the one for Wilbur Nill. He opened it and pulled out the paycheck and statement for $50.83 net, after deductions for income tax, Social Security, Unemployment Insurance, Group Life Insurance and Community Fund. He signed, *"Wilbur Nill"* to the receipt and put it in his desk drawer. He would keep it there until Monday, when the other employees' receipts were returned from downstairs and he would forward them to the Payroll Department.

After pocketing the check, he took the ARF envelope and opened the one marked *"Mott, Walter."* He signed the receipt for $147.73 and also placed that check in his pocket. He called in Wilma Tannenbaum, whose job it was to distribute the pay envelopes and collect the signed receipts. After Wilma left, Walter itemized his weekly budget. He knew it by heart, but with a sharp pencil he wrote it out every Friday nevertheless, in neat hand lettering on his company scratch pad:

Wkly Budgt

N.Y. Times (6 daily, 1 Sun.)	.85
Coffee & bun (5 days, .50 ea.)	2.50
Weekend meals	7.00
Cigarettes, 1 pack a day	
@ .20 a day	1.40
Dept. Store Charge Acct.	5.00
Misc. (bus fare, etc.)	13.60

$30.35 total

Including $2.60 left over from the week before, Walter had $201.16. As was his custom every Friday, Walter slipped out of the office at eleven fifteen a.m., cashed his checks at the nearby bank, and walked down the block to the office of Merrill, Lynch, Pearce, Fenner & Smith.

Joe Fortunato, Walter's account executive, rose from his desk to greet him. Joe was a tall, square-jawed fellow with short-cropped black hair and a perpetual five o'clock shadow. He had once been a collegiate football star. Walter had never seen Joe not smiling.

"Right on time, as usual, Mister Mott," Joe said. "What'll it be this week?"

"Hi, Joe. Is General Electric still at 79 and 5/8?"

They looked at the big board on the wall. It was.

"Put me down for another share."

The transaction completed, Walter pocketed his receipt and turned to leave.

"Mister Mott?"

"Yes, Joe?"

"Remember last week I told you about mutual funds?"

"That's something new, isn't it?"

"Actually they've been around several years now … it's a way of spreading the risk. Some of them are yielding great returns…"

"I think I see them listed in the Sunday *Times*. Thanks. I'll take a careful look." Walter waved goodbye and disappeared through the swinging glass door.

"Nicest guy in the world to do business with," Fortunato said to a fellow account executive. "And smart? Started comin' here about eight, maybe nine years ago. Just keeps pourin' in about seventy-five to a hundred every week without fail. Must have a portfolio worth over eighty thou by now. Real shrewd picker."

Fortunato looked up at the big board. General Motors had just climbed to 80 ½.At the bank across the street, Walter deposited $90, leaving himself his allotted $30 for the week. He checked the balance in his little black savings book. $9,830. Soon he would have to find a new bank. He was already up to the insurable $10,000 limit with two others, and now he was coming close on the third.

Then, Walter entered the vault, removed his safety deposit box, and took it into a small private cubicle. He opened the box, and gazed with admiration at his growing collection of rare stamps, already worth a small fortune. His special prize was the 24-cent upside-down "Jenny." This airmail stamp, showing a U.S. Army Curtiss Jenny biplane, had been issued in 1918. The government printed 2.1 million of these stamps, in sheets of 100. Due to a printer's error, one of the sheets showed the image of the airplane upside down. It quickly became a sought after philatelic prize. At a Harmer and Rooke auction in Manhattan five years earlier, after a lively bidding war, Walter obtained one of the stamps for $3,000. This year, other stamps from the sheet of 100 were going for $6,000 or more. *Not bad*.

Walter strode back to the office, feeling content and secure with his stocks, stamps and savings. He scrutinized the people hurrying by that sunless afternoon, especially the middle-aged men, huddled and bent against the whipping March wind, grim and preoccupied, walking without seeing; thinking, thinking, perhaps, of the many more years they would rush along this same sidewalk, back to their offices or shops; back to tongue lashings or subtler, more cruel humiliations, or … *boredom*.

A river of compassion coursed through him. And out of him. Then he envisioned a sunny isle somewhere, anywhere. As he walked through the crowds of harried faceless people, buffeted by the chilly spring gusts, Walter was enveloped in his own warmth. The Big Moment was coming soon.

Tab Hunter's A Fag?

1

At twelve noon a bell rang and there was a scuffle of chairs and feet as the clerks rose from their desks like a flock of gulls. It was time for the free—yes, *free*—feeding.

During his first few years at SIC, Walter ate lunch, along with perhaps eighty-five percent of the employees, in the enormous self-service cafeteria on the second floor. *Nouveau riche* junior management men, who had graduated to more exclusive facilities, referred to it amidst snickers as "the peons' room". Confined to "the peons' room" were secretaries, file clerks, stenographers, messengers, janitors, elevator operators, typists and all others who took orders without having anyone below them upon whom they could vent their own frustrations.

The peons, more than five thousand strong, were served in two forty-five minute shifts; one from noon to 12:40, the other from 12:40 to 1:25. Each workday, they would stampede in, snatch a plastic tray, silverware, napkin, and check the menu mounted in white plastic letters on the wall, which not only described the delicacies but advertised the caloric content of each. There was even saccharine for the pear-shaped. The meals, planned by a company dietitian—salads, stews, omelettes, meatloaf and pasta—were free, wholesome, and dull. The peons sat eight to a Formica-topped table.

After eating, smoking was prohibited; not for safety or health reasons, but so as to herd the workers outside and make room for the second shift, which streamed in just as the first group was downing the final spoonful of dessert. To discourage malingering, the Muzak often played snappy tunes, such as a light classical version of Leadbelly's, *"Pick a Bale O' Cotton,"* with one hundred string accompaniment.

Walter now ate in the much smaller Junior Management Room on the third floor, reserved for supervisors, assistant managers and managers, and featured linen tablecloths. The JM's chose their food—the same free cuisine as in the peons' room—from typewritten menus and were served by matronly white-frocked waitresses who called everyone "dear". Smoking was allowed.

The Executive Dining Room, on the opposite side of the third floor, where Walter had once enjoyed a memorable lunch as Mister Furey's guest, was yet smaller and more Chesterfieldian; oak-paneled walls, thick carpets, and a menu which favored prime steaks and chops. In the Executive Dining Room, a bowl of fruit was placed on each table after dessert, as well as a silver tray stocked with cigarettes and panatelas. Smoking was not only allowed, it was *de rigueur*.

2

Walter always ate lunch at the same table with the same companions. This was the unwritten rule in both the JM and Executive Dining Rooms. When his promotion entitled him to eat with the JMs, there had been two other men at the four-place table: Martin Shaw of the Actuarial Department, and Raymond Lang of Accounting.

Lang—a tall wrinkle-faced man whose sideburns were turning gray—was eager to share the news about a culinary discovery. "On my way home to Montclair yesterday, I drive up Bloomfield Avenue, and there's this Wop neighborhood in North Newark. I usually just keep going, but I spotted this place with a big sign, *"Pizzeria."*

"What's that," asked Marty Shaw, a short, pear-shaped, nearly bald fellow, whose brow was almost constantly furrowed, as though he were in a perpetual state of puzzlement.

"Patience, young man. So I park out front, go in, and they're making these huge—I mean *huge*—round pies …"

"Pies?" said Marty. "Are they sweet?"

"Jesus, let me finish," said Lang. "They're all covered with cheese, and they top it off with tomato sauce, and sometimes other stuff, like sausages …"

"Sounds spicy," said Marty.

"They even sell it by the slice. It was cheap. I had it with a Coke, and it was great. I'm gonna bring the family down there, maybe on the weekend."

"What do they call it again?" Marty said.

"Pizza. It's an Italian word."

"Well is sure sounds spicy."

Throughout the meal, Marty and Ray would gabble about the previous night's TV fare. Both had usually seen the same programs and, via a series of "Didjya see?" and "Howja like?" they would, to Walter's dismay—he didn't own a TV set—argue about the relative merits of Ed Sullivan, Jack Benny and Milton Berle, and recount every detail of melodramas about teen-agers who were always outwitting their simpleton fathers, hyper-intelligent dogs which were always outwitting everyone, and late-hour "talk" shows where nobodies became somebodies overnight by figuratively unzipping their hearts, souls and trousers for the benefit of several million insomniac Peeping Toms in darkened living rooms.

That is, when Ray wasn't describing every step of his infant son's blossoming vocabulary; or when Marty wasn't equating the storm fronts moving in from the southeast with the latest nuclear tests in the Soviet Union, or predicting that the New York Yankees' "lock" on the American League pennant—nine titles in ten years—was fragile, at best.

Today, pointing to a front page story about Cuba in *The Star-Ledger*, Marty said: "Look at this nut Fidel Castro, taking over like that. He acts so cocky ..."

Ray broke in. "Not to worry. I don't give that dumb Spic six months until he's out on his ass."

A year after Walter joined them the quartet was completed by Charlie Phelps, a copywriter with the Advertising Department. Since advertising was one of SIC's "sacred cow" divisions, the copywriters—though they supervised not a soul—were considered part of management. Walter liked Charlie, or rather, he was amused by him. But Irwin Kemp, who sat at an adjacent table, didn't like Charlie at all. Once, while they all sat together in the smoking lounge, Irwin had diagnosed Charlie's condition as "diarrhea of the oral cavity." And, since the diagnosis was made in the patient's presence, Charlie was no great admirer of Irwin's either.

Phelps, whose Monday-Friday "uniform" was a gray flannel suit and conservative striped tie, was forever voicing his plans to move "onward and upward" in the world by landing a lucrative job with a Madison Avenue ad agency. Every few months he updated his resume, mimeographed dozens of copies, and mailed them out. Once, BBD&O actually offered him $1,000 more than his $7,500 annual salary at SIC. But Charlie turned them down, explaining with indignance to his lunchmates that the account to which he would have been assigned—a tomato soup that sold 185 million cans a year—wasn't enough of "a creative challenge."

"I'm no Hemingway or Sean—he pronounced it "Scene"—O'Casey," he kept on repeating, "but *tomato* soup? *Please.*"

Throughout his lunchtime gasconades, Charlie was forever popping his pipe into and out of his mouth; he would then cup the bowl in his hand and stare at it as though it were Yorick's skull, separate the bowl from the stem, methodically clean the stem, reunite the two parts, return the pipe to the breast pocket of his suit and then suddenly pull it out and start the ritual anew.

SIC's ad people were advised well in advance of all imminent policy changes and Charlie doled out the "scoops" to his companions with great gusto. Looking even more priggish than usual today, he strode into the dining room, nodded to the others, took a seat, and dug into his salad. He devoted the next few minutes to industriously munching his food and whistling the latest hit tune, *"Nel Blu Dipinto di Blu,"* until Shaw finally said, "What's up, Charlie?"

Charlie looked up at him, a gob of French dressing adorning his dimpled chin. "Mmm? Oh, nothing special."

"C'mon now. The way you're all buttoned up, something big happened today."

"Big?"

"Don't try to snow us," Lang said. "When you're quiet that means there's something brewing at the top." Lang italicized *top* with an upward jab of his fork, indicating the tenth floor executive conference room, which insiders sometimes called "Geneva."

Charlie, who concealed his emotions about as well as the masturbating chimp at the Bronx Zoo, had been waiting for the invitation. He hunched over and commenced a side-of-the-mouth whisper. "Can you guys keep this under your hat?"

Taking their silence to be a solemn pledge of secrecy, he continued. "We've come upon something that's gonna put SIC out in front within two years. "We're gonna leave old Megalopolitan in the *dust*."

Lang leaned closer, towing his striped tie through the onion soup.

"This morning," Phelps continued, "we had a visitor up there. Ever heard of Doctor Helmut Schwartz, the motivation research specialist?"

Shaw and Lang wrinkled their brows. Walter concentrated on his soup. "Schwartz is a Vienna psychiatrist who came to the States after the Second World War. Since then he's been working under contract to *all* the blue chip outfits. Pulls in about two hundred thou a year. This guy *analyzes* a company's product using Freudian methods. Then he analyzes the potential consumer. Next, he tells the company what it should do about its product to make it more saleable."

Phelps leaned back in his chair and grinned. "Any of you guys got the slightest idea *why* a guy buys an insurance policy?"

Shaw, an avid reader of SIC's promotional brochures, ventured a guess: "Security for his loved ones?"

"That's just the surface reason," said Phelps, blending a tincture of pseudo-Viennese with his nasal Bronx accent.

"To have a retirement pension, I guess?" Lang said.

"Closer. But what's the *real* motivation?" Phelps yanked the pipe from his mouth, replaced it with a forkful of mashed potatoes, popped the pipe back in and continued to chew. He looked around the table. Silence.

"A man buys life insurance," he said slowly, "to...*satisfy his inner yearning for immortality*." He leaned back in the chair and sucked on the empty pipe.

"What the hell's that got to do with it?" Shaw said.

"You're not *digging*, boys," Phelps said, tapping his forehead with the pipe stem. "Tell me the truth, Marty; when you buy a policy, who are you doing it for? For you, or for Sharon and the kid?"

Shaw opened his mouth to speak, but Phelps interrupted with a forceful jab of the pipe stem against Shaw's breast pocket. "You *think* it's for them, but down *deep*, you're saying, 'When I'm gone and Sharon and the kid are living in the house I left them, and eating off the monthly payments I left them, I will live in their memories as a good provider. I will be *remembered*. Therefore, I will be *immortal*." Phelps jammed the pipe into his pocket with a triumphant flourish and continued to eat. Shaw and Lang were silent. Walter swallowed a forkful of mashed potatoes.

"So, this afternoon," Phelps went on, his mouth full, "I got a rush assignment to knock out the text for a sales folder we're gonna flood the mails with." He pulled out a typewritten sheet of paper. "See how this hits you. The front cover shows this ordinary Jane—pretty, about thirty—sitting on the living room sofa. Next to her is a little girl who resembles her, about six years old. And on Mom's lap is this little butchie in a striped polo shirt, about two, who looks sort of like a well-behaved Dennis the Menace. They're all looking in the same direction, towards a photo on the end table. And they've all got this sad, yet thankful, expression on their faces; even little Butchie. And what's the photo on the table? Pop, he's maybe thirty-five, good-looking, Rory Calhoun type, who's smiling, yet looks sort of serious. And the headline reads: '*Dad forever.*'

"Hits you where you live, doesn't it? On the inside of the folder we pour on the stuff about 'No matter what the future holds, your wise planning now can make it secure for your loved ones; a future in which you, Dad, will always be the head of the family, the one who molds your loved ones' destinies, the one they will depend upon and remember with love and gratitude. This SIC insurance plan also has features for the happy day of retirement when the children are raising their own families and you and Mom can bask in the perpetual sunshine of a vacation paradise, all year 'round, carefree thanks to SIC's guaranteed monthly income checks.' Then it finishes with the usual blah-blah in simulated handwriting: 'I'll be calling soon to explain this marvelous plan to you with no obligation on your part. Signed, your SIC representative.' So, whaddya think, fellows?"

"Sounds okay," Walter said, picking at his vanilla custard, which somewhere during Phelps' monologue began to suspiciously resemble vomit.

"Okay? Okay? This guy Schwartz is a *genius*." Phelps said.

"But," Walter said, "what if the guy hates his wife?"

"Hates who?"

"His wife. What if he hates his wife? Why would he want her to get all that money when he's dead? And what if he knows that *she* hates *him*? And that first chance she gets she'll remarry? I was just reading the other day in the paper that one out of every three marriages ends in divorce. That just includes the ones who have the guts to make the move."

"I've got it," Shaw said, excited. "You could print up a special edition for unhappy homes. Show the wife and the kids looking at Dad's picture. And also have the *new* husband sitting next to them. And they're *all* looking at the picture and thanking good old Dad for not falling behind on the premium payments." Shaw's day was made after that rare, for him, *bon mot*. A satisfied grin creased his face. Lang and Walter also smiled, but Phelps bit his pipe stem.

"All right, screw around," he said in a growl. "But this guy Schwartz is talking about the average man. You know, and besides …."

Just then Irwin Kemp yelled over from two tables away, "Hey Walt. This is the worst meal I've ever eaten in my whole mouth."

3

Phelps' rebuttal was muffled by laughter. Walter pretended to listen to the boring Shaw-Lang-Phelps discussion, but kept an ear open to the wisecracks at the nearby table, where Irwin held court among a group of young co-workers.

"What's faster, or a bullet?" Irwin asked, to puzzled expressions. Then, as though teaching a group of slow learners, he said, loud and with emphasis, "The higher the fewer." Next, he said, "What's the difference between a duck?" More befuddled expressions, a few hesitant smiles. "Each leg is both the same," Irwin exclaimed. And, finally, "If all the girls at Vassar were laid end to end in Yankee Stadium …," he raised both palms in the air with a sly wink, "… I wouldn't be a bit surprised." This evoked howls of laughter.

Irwin followed with another question. "*Quick*. What's black and white, has three legs, and three eyes?" Bewildered looks. "Cole Porter and Sammy Davis Junior."

He then said, "Has anyone read the latest Harold Robbins novel? My God, it's the first time I ever read a book where on one page you're in tears, and on the next you've got a hard-on."

Before his lunch buddies could react, Irwin held up an invisible microphone and said to one of them, "I'm taking a poll for the Gallup Organization. When you take a dump, what hand do you use to wipe your behind?" The young man pointed to his right hand. Irwin looked at the guy next to him. "How about you? Which hand?" The other fellow hesitated, then raised his right hand also. Irwin said: "You both clean your ass with your right hand? Gee, that's strange. Most folks use toilet paper." This also evoked an uproar of laughter, as the two guys, smiling, pretended to beat up Irwin.

4

After lunch, Walter strolled into the lounge with Irwin Kemp, Charlie Phelps, Ray Lang and Marty Shaw. They sank down in easy chairs which were clustered about a coffee table. Walter unfolded his *Times*, and Charlie studied a typewritten sheet of paper as he smoked his pipe.

The lounge was another of SIC's many fringe benefits. One half was devoted to a small lending library. A wall rack displayed the daily papers and a few dozen popular magazines. The shelves carried all the best sellers, and an ample supply of standard tomes, the majority of them self-help manuals on such diverse subjects as photography, gardening, carpentry and raising tropical fish. In the "Philosophy" section a volume of *The Power of Positive Thinking* in a cheery vermilion jacket flanked a scowling gray collection of essays by Schopenhauer. Nothing by Sartre, heaven forbid, and the lone copy of a book by Buber had been checked out three years before by a since-departed employee named Meiser, and never returned.

The other half of the lounge, called "The Rec Room," had two shuffleboard games, a dart board and two ping-pong tables. A desk at the entrance was littered with "twofer" tickets for moribund Broadway shows. Travel posters exulting over exotic places festooned the walls. A wall rack held a collection of multi-color travel brochures and a stack of mimeographed circulars announcing the annual SIC Columbus Day Picnic to Bear Mountain. SIC organized numerous bargain-priced trips for its employees, anything from a weekend jaunt to the Poconos, to a Caribbean cruise. Myriad activities were offered to fill the evening or weekend for energetic SIC employees: softball leagues, basketball leagues, bowling leagues, swimming leagues, touch football leagues, handball leagues, ping-pong leagues, chess and checker leagues, a photography club, a philatelists' club, a numismatists' club, an anglers' club, a marksmens' club, an amateur theatre club, and a literary discussion club. Not to speak of the parties, ranging from luncheons at nearby restaurants to less frequent all-night soirees at some suburban country club.

Given the tremendous number of women in the company, each department had a wedding shower at least once every few weeks, and an equal number of "farewell" parties eight months to a year later when the young wife, bloated with imminent life, would sniffle a teary goodbye to her office mates, who had seen her through morning sickness, food whims—the all-time winner was sour cream with cough drops—and, in one case, a burst water in an elevator.

Someone was always getting promoted. The promotee would blow the first week's raise—usually about $5—on a box of candy and/or cigars, which was displayed with pride on his or her desk for those who came to offer congratulations. If not a promotion, it was a birthday, anniversary or retirement which offered an excuse for some good, clean, organized group fun.

Two women in each department served as Sunshine Reps. As soon as a SIC employee fell ill, the Sunshine Girls dutifully took note on an index card which was added to a "tickler" file. If the employee was not back to work within a week, they bought flowers and candy, paid for by The Sunshine Fund's dues of 25 cents weekly per employee, and personally delivered them to the ailing one. If an employee or his or her close relative passed away, a sizeable bouquet—no candy—was always delivered to the funeral parlor.

A controversy had recently arisen concerning The Sunshine Fund, which, after weeks of wrangling, was finally mediated by the Executive Director of Personnel. If an employee suffered a death in the family *and* became ill as a result, one faction felt that he or she was entitled to two bouquets—one for the sickie and one for the deceased—while another faction argued that one bouquet sufficed for both occasions. Personnel magnanimously favored sending two bouquets, causing murmurs of approval throughout all of SIC-dom, and an inestimable boost in employee morale.

On Monday evenings, if the employee had managed to elude some SIC-sponsored extra-curricular activity, that person was urged to tune in the TV at eight p.m., and watch *"To Your Health,"* a SIC-sponsored network series of dramatized medical case histories starring Charlton Heston—who won the Oscar that year for his role in *"Ben-Hur"*—as the family doctor, besieged by a constant parade of seemingly incurable patients and predatory nurses. "Next week's program," read a bulletin on the Rec Room wall, "chronicles the gripping story of how modern science averts a near tragedy in the life of a typical American family. Be sure to see: *'Cancer-Silent Enemy.'* Guest stars: Steve Reeves, Debbie Reynolds. Note to company reps: You'll also be interested in the three thought-provoking Mortgage Insurance commercials shown during the program. Listen carefully and use these striking sales approaches when talking with your prospects."

5

Settled deep in the chair, Walter turned to the *Times* financial section and checked over his investments. He noted with satisfaction that IBM was up to 303 1/8 and a news story on the same page heralded record profits for IBM during the first nine months of the year. AT&T was steady at 53 5/8, and Coca-Cola, Polaroid and Con Ed were all healthy. So was that peppy little anti-missile stock he'd gambled on. What a pleasant surprise *that* had been. His $2,000 original investment had nearly tripled.

Back in 1950, when Walter began investing in the market, the Dow Jones Industrial Average was 206. Since then, despite a few ups and downs, it had zoomed up to 601, thanks in part to the new interstate highways that zipped goods from place to place, and the growing popularity of television, which created an appetite for those goods. Counting his market shares and the nearly $30,000 he had stashed in three banks, Walter estimated his net worth at close to $150,000, enough to retire on. It was now just a matter of time.

Ray and Marty began another "Didja see?" question-and-answer period.

"Hey guys," Ray said, "didja see that movie with Sophia Loren at the RKO?"

"Which one?" Marty said.

"I think it was called *That Kind of Woman.* What a piece she is. Man, I would've loved to be Tab Hunter ..."

"Is that so?" Marty said. "Didn't you read *Confidential Magazine* about a year back? They said Tab Hunter was a fag."

"Tab Hunter? C'mon. You're kiddin'."

"They said he was spotted at some party, dancing with guys!"

"All I know," said Ray, "even if I *were* a fag, one look from Sophia Loren would fix me real quick. I had a boner all through the movie."

"I dunno. Tab does look kinda *delicate,* if you know what I mean. Now you take a guy like Rock Hudson. We went the other night to see him and Doris Day in *Pillow Talk.* It was great. And *he* was great."

"Hey," said Charlie, "didya hear Fred McMurray on the radio the other morning? He says we can make our own bomb shelters for about a hundred bucks. That's about half the going price."

"Not bad," said Ray. "Maybe we can team up and help each other."

"I've got a cheaper solution," said Irwin. "When the Russian planes approach, we can all run down to Bamberger's Bargain Basement and hide under the pillows."

"Irwin," said Ray, "don't you ever take anything seriously? This is not a joke." He scowled and slammed a right fist into his left open palm. "The Commies wanna to kill us."

Undeterred, Irwin said, "By the way, fellas, any of you seen my latest invention?" He produced an inch-thick pile of letter-sized papers from his breast pocket.

"What is it this time," Phelps asked.

"I all it The Jiffy Clutter."

"But what *is* it?"

Irwin brightened. He had been waiting for the opening. "You've all heard of labor saving devices, right? This is a labor *faking* device."

Walter looked up from his *Times.*

"I hold in my hand, gentleman, a pile of reports," Irwin said, brandishing the papers with the slick assurance of a sleight-of-hand-magician. "*Any* reports; preferably outdated and useless reports. You keep this Jiffy Clutter in your desk drawer. The time comes during the day when you've got nothing to do, which is most of the time, and you'd like to goof off for a while, right? Your desk top is all empty, right? Up to now, all goof-off-minded employees have been in a dither, right? But now, with the sensational Jiffy Clutter … *look*."

Irwin dumped the pile of papers atop the coffee table and the sheets fanned out, creating an authentic clutter.

"What's so good about that," Phelps asked.

"Patience, young man. Now, you've got a nice cluttered desk, just perfect for meditating, while from a few feet away it looks like you're up to your ass in work, right?"

"Right," said Ray Lang, as though he'd discovered a new element.

"Comes the bell at 4:40. Time to go home. With ordinary clutters, you lose a few precious minutes getting everything back in place. But not with the miraculous Jiffy Clutter, which cuts work two ways. *Watch*."

Irwin tugged at the corner of one of the sheets of paper and all of them snapped back into a relatively neat pile. He sat back with a triumphant grin.

"What the hell?" said Marty Shaw.

"Elementary, my dear fellows," Irwin said. "All the papers are linked at their corners with tiny bits of rubber band. A quick flick of the wrist and … presto! Everything back in a neat pile, ready for stashing in the desk drawer. This will revolutionize goofing off."

Irwin rose and made a dramatic, sweeping gesture with his hand. "I may even print outdated useless reports in foreign languages for white collar workers all over the world. German, Spanish, Italian, Japanese. No leisure-minded clerk will want to be without a Jiffy Clutter. Plus, I can make a fortune in replacement parts. After all, rubber bands do wear out. Planned adolescence, I think they call it."

"Obsolescence," Phelps corrected.

"What do you think, Walt?"

"As a member of management, I can hardly sanction such a thing," Walter said, smiling. "But it certainly is interesting."

"Ray?" Irwin said.

"Mmmm, yes. I'd say it's definitely very interesting."

"Marty?"

"Yes, definitely."

"Definitely what?"

"Interesting."

"Interesting. Interesting!" Irwin shouted. "Doesn't anyone have a goddamned opinion around here?"

"I think it's lousy and it stinks," Charlie said, popping his pipe into his mouth and folding his arms.

"Oh, I don't know," Irwin said. "I think it's one of the best ideas I've ever had in my whole brain."

6

The big clock on the library wall ticked to one p.m. Walter snuffed out his cigarette in the ashtray and took the elevator back to the office, where he dawdled away at the endless mound of paper. His lack of sleep, the big luncheon, the boring chitchat, and now the column of figures, were making him drowsy. He shook his head, trying to focus upon the statistics, but once more his chin dipped downward. Groggy, he rose, grabbed a few reports and walked out of the office. He called over his shoulder to Wilma, "I'm going downstairs to Statistics to check on a few things."

Out in the hall, Walter entered the regular employees' bathroom, and locked himself inside a toilet stall. His watch read 1:14 p.m. A couple of hours nap will freshen me up, he thought, as he leaned his head back against the cold, hard tile and soon began to snore.

At 3:35 p.m., a loud flushing toilet in the next stall jarred him awake, his neck stiff. He rose, wobbled out to the sink, dashed some water on his face and combed his hair. Refreshed, he returned to the office for the short stretch until the 4:40 bell.

When the bell sounded, the flock rose once more and made for the coat lockers, gabbling like pigeons. Walter rushed to the door of his office to see if he could catch a glimpse of Scarlett Kosciusko. He nearly collided with Wilma Tannenbaum, who was coming in to pay her usual goodnight call. "Don't forget the books," she sopranoed, fluttering her dark lashes in his face like a pair of Spanish fans.

"Yes, some night soon, Wilma. See you in the morning."

Mister Furey stopped in front of his door, attaché case in hand. "Gotta catch the 5:10. Council meeting tonight. See you tomorrow, Walt … and don't forget about those girl-hours."

"No, I won't. Good night, Mister Furey." God, he thought as he watched Mister Furey leave, if things had gone wrong today he'd be a corpse.

7

It was five thirty p.m. when Walter rose from his desk, hooked his suit jacket on the clothes rack, rolled up his shirtsleeves and took the elevator down to the second-floor cafeteria. He fell in line with seventy-five members of the MAD night crew who were filing into the peons' room for their free supper. These were mostly part-time employees: housewives beefing up the family income, students earning their way through college, and the like. Of the fifty men in the group, all wore the uniform of SIC's peon caste: white shirt with sleeves rolled up, necktie slightly loosened. The MAD people supped between five thirty and six fifteen p.m., then worked until midnight, feeding data into the gigantic UNIVAC computer that hummed away in a huge air-conditioned room.

Walter filled his metal tray with meat loaf, boiled potato, green peas, chocolate cake and a cup of hot tea. Since only 200 people in the entire company worked nights, the 2,500 capacity cafeteria was nearly empty and afforded him the luxury of a table to himself in a quiet corner.

At a nearby table, he overheard three MAD coworkers engaged in a passionate argument, but didn't quite understand what it concerned. These computer folks spoke an entirely different language. Something about "Fortran", and "IBM", and "an optimizing compiler", and "quotient overflow", and some fellow named Backus. Walter shrugged and, with his fork, speared a chunk of meat loaf.

Most mornings, Walter read *The Times*, mainly to check on his stocks. He rarely looked at the front page. Politics bored him. At dinner time, he picked up a copy of *The Newark Evening News.* Again, he avoided the headlines, and focused on the bottom of most pages. During his meal, Walter amused himself by searching for odd "fillers", which reported on strange happenings around the world. When he spotted one, he would tear it out of the paper, stuff it in his pocket, and, later, store it in a file folder, which now contained a few hundred of them. Some day, he thought, I'll publish a collection. A few recent fillers he'd collected were as follows:

"LOS ANGELES (UPI). One of the entrants in the 'Miss Los Angeles Press Club' beauty contest was Ruth Hermine, a 3-foot-tall midget. The club stewards ruled she would have to pay only half the $10 entrance fee."

"SAN JUAN, PR. (AP). Fire chief Raul Gándara doused a fire in his house with a garden hose. Flames flared up again and destroyed 300 copies of a book he wrote titled *The Technique of Firefighting.*"

"FARNHAM, Eng. (UPI). Roger the horse likes to play dead, and it is causing his owner, Philip Davies, all sorts of problems. The animal lies on his back with his legs in the air, closes his eyes and opens his mouth. Many are convinced he's dying and call Mr. Davies and the police. Mr. Davies is thinking of putting a notice on the gate, saying, 'This horse is not dead.'"

"VATICAN CITY. — The nun assigned by the Vatican to guard St. Peter's Basilica from women in mini-skirts, see-through blouses and other revealing dress was removed from her post today. The Vatican said Sister Fiorella was suffering from nervous exhaustion."

"ULM, Germany (AP). Struck with an urge to travel, an 86-year-old man got on the West German autobahn Friday and set out for Yugoslavia — in a wheelchair. After pushing himself nearly two miles along the passing lane, he was apprehended by police who explained that, among other things, he was headed in the wrong direction."

"AUSTIN, Tex. (UPI). Studying piano discourages marijuana smoking and rioting, according to Dr. Irl Allison, the founder of the National Guild of Piano Teachers. A poll of the teachers of participants in the 40th Annual National Piano-Playing Auditions 'shows not one of the 76,000 participants has been found to smoke marijuana or to riot,' Dr. Allison said."

"PITTSBURGH (AP)—When Arthur Addison's wife did not come home after 48 years, he sued for divorce. His wife did not appear in Common Pleas Court to contest the action."

8

At six p.m., Walter took the elevator to the 11th floor and waited at the entrance to the Machine Accounting Division, right next to the time clock. He extracted a time card from his pocket, which read "Nill, Wilbur." At 6:05 p.m., when the first cluster of MAD people was disgorged from the elevator, Walter punched in, returned the card to his pocket and entered the department, as though on his way to work. But he walked around a corner, out a side exit and climbed two flights of stairs to his department on the thirteenth floor.

He donned his jacket and scarf, took his umbrella, and was just stepping out when Hannah, the cleaning lady, waddled in with her pail and mop. Since Hannah spoke only Hungarian, she and Walter had maintained a nodding acquaintance for several years.

"Right on the button," he observed. The cleaning crew worked its way from the top down in the SIC building, starting on the 14th floor at five thirty p.m., and Hannah was usually out of there no later than seven thirty p.m. Once, about five years ago, when they stayed up there to give the department a re-painting, Walter was forced to sit through two showings of a Tarzan movie at the Branford Theatre before he was able to head back to the office and get some sleep. Walter acknowledged Hannah's gold-toothed smile with a nod of his head, and went out to the elevators. Down on the street floor, he saluted the uniformed street guard with a curlicue of his umbrella and strode out through the main entrance, ready for his usual night on the town.

Farewell to Johnny Mulligan

1

Glenwood Manor, the site of old Johnny Mulligan's retirement dinner the following Friday, was located on a main street in nearby Montclair. A small cocktail lounge near the entrance led to an ample banquet hall. The Agency Records File division's employees and many of their wives, husbands, girlfriends, fiancés and fiancées—172 people in all—were seated at the linen-covered tables strung around the hall in a giant horseshoe.

In the seat of honor was old Johnny Mulligan, wearing his blue pin-striped suit and a wide tie with a bright floral design. He had gotten a haircut, and even trimmed the white hairs which drooped from his nostrils like Spanish moss. Everyone was eating.

On Monday, Johnny Mulligan would be sixty-five; the compulsory retirement age at SIC. Not even the President was allowed to lift a pin after his sixty-fifth birthday. Johnny had joined the company forty-six years before at the age of nineteen, the same year when Woodrow Wilson took over The White House from William Howard Taft, and Charles Chaplin, a recent arrival from England, was breaking in to American silent film. Too young for World War I, and too old for World War II, Johnny had hardly missed a day at the office throughout those forty-six years. Slight of build and quick of stride, he began as a messenger boy. Six dollars a week. Clear.

Four years later, Johnny was promoted to Letter Sorter in the Mail Department, a task which he ably and officiously performed for thirty-five years, until the age of fifty-eight, when his arthritic fingers could no longer keep up the pace. Then, too, more and more letters were pouring into the Mail Department each day. So Johnny went back on "the road", as a messenger for ARF. Pushing a gray metal cart, it was his job to deliver intra-company mail from one part of the spacious ARF Division to the other, or from ARF to other departments on other floors, or occasionally to nearby buildings where SIC also had offices. Johnny also deposited Mister Furey's weekly paycheck on Fridays, plus his own, which now amounted to $83.84. Clear.

When Johnny's wife Margaret died seven years ago, he sold the small frame house in Kearny—the one they'd bought in 1938—and moved in with the eldest of his three daughters and her husband in their nearby Nutley home. After the funeral expenses, Johnny had $8,000 left from the sale of the house, which he was saving for his grandchildren's college education. Johnny fancied himself to be somewhat of a patriarch, although when he was in the company of his daughters and sons-in-law he could never think of anything very patriarchal to say, and usually contented himself with quietly humming, *"Bye Bye Blackbird,"* reading aloud tomorrow's weather forecast, and nodding "yes" to offers of more mashed potatoes.

In the office, Johnny had a tiny desk all his own near the entrance to the ARF Division. He would sit there and drum his fingers upon the desktop. Then he would get up and chat with one of the secretaries. Then he would sit down and drum his fingers some more. By that time he would usually be asked to deliver an intra-company letter.

If it was an outside trip, he would go to his locker, put on his black felt hat, wrap his magenta woolen scarf around his neck if it were winter, slip on his shiny black rubbers if it were raining or snowing, and finally bound away, clutching the letter in his gnarled, shaky hand. Sometimes, Johnny took an hour to deliver a message two blocks away. He chatted with every elevator man, policeman and letter carrier he spied. He knew them all. His many "pals" and his daughters and his grandchildren were a great source of satisfaction.

2

After scooping out the last of his fruit salad, except for an elusive sliver of pineapple which he didn't dare grab with his fingers, Mister Furey rose, tapped his water glass with the syrupy spoon, and began the formal ceremony.

"We're very fortunate tonight to be honored by the presence of Mister Alan Gibbs, Executive Vice President and *personal* assistant to President Jennings. Mister Gibbs has taken time out from a very busy schedule to be with us. And now, without further ado, I give you Mister Gibbs."

There was mild applause. Mister Gibbs, a lank, clerical figure with a rosy complexion, removed his rimless spectacles and monotoned the unctuous seven-minute eulogy which he uttered at the thirty-odd SIC retirement dinners to which he was assigned each year. Only the names were changed to inspire the innocent.

He handed old Johnny Mulligan a pre-printed vellum certificate that _____ had completed ___ years of honorable, valuable, laudable and insuperable service as a SIC employee. Johnny's name and the years served were noted in an ostentatious India-inked script; the handiwork of a thin, squinty fellow in the SIC Art Department who spent much of his day, year after year, writing names on vellum certificates.

Mister Gibbs then handed Johnny a wallet-sized membership card and gold-plated lapel pin for SIC's Golden Age Group—known as GAG—an organization of retired employees who shuffled into the SIC library the third Monday of every month, snacked on coffee and Danish, and "tsk-tsked" over absent members who had been bedridden or interred since the last reunion.

Next, Mister Gibbs gave Johnny a set of Amelia Earhart luggage. SIC had a standard list of awards and there were two choices for forty-plus years of service. One was a deluxe flycasting outfit and the other was the luggage. Johnny never fished and he hadn't crossed the state line in more than fifteen years, but he was more likely to take a trip, he reasoned, than take up fishing. Then Mister Gibbs, with a nod, and a glance at his wristwatch, ceded the floor to Mister Furey.

"Thank you Mister Gibbs." Furey turned to the audience. "I won't keep you folks long. I know you're all itching to try *The Twist*." Laughter ensued. He cast a quick sideward glance at Mister Gibbs, who responded with a faint, indulgent smile. "But I would like to say we're proud that Johnny Mulligan spent the last seven of his forty-six working years with us at ARF. He was a valuable asset to our team, and no team can function without the utmost effort of each member. And now, Irwin Kemp, our Johnny Mulligan Adios Dinner Committee Chairman, will say a few words. Irwin?"

Kemp sprang up from his chair and responded to the mixture of hoots, whistles and catcalls by clenching his hands together and raising them above his head like a victorious pug. He stuffed a long carrot stick into his mouth, puffed his cheeks, raised his hand in a "V for Victory" sign, and said with ostentatious vigor, "Thank you fellow salt miners!"

Outburst of laughter. Kemp glanced down at the two executives flanking him. Pleasant frozen smiles. Mister Furey's right forefinger was inching stealthily towards that elusive sliver of pineapple.

"Gee, it's nice in here ..."

An uproar of laughter and shrieks.

"I won't keep you long; I know you're all anxious to try *The Twist*." He raised his beer glass. Another roar of laughter. Then he turned to Johnny Mulligan.

"Johnny, we ARFers will all miss you. We know you'll have plenty of time now that you're on the outside," he said, pausing for laughter. "So we just thought we'd get you something to help you keep track of it."

Kemp pulled out the watch from its velvet-lined case and handed it to old Johnny, who rose stiffly to accept it. Kemp sat down. Furey stood up. Beaming—he'd managed to nab the piece of pineapple—he turned to Irwin. "Thanks, Irwin. And now, let's hear from our honored guest. Johnny Mulligan!" The hall shook with thunderous foot-stomping and applause.

This was Johnny Mulligan's crowning moment; the capstone of forty-six years with the Security Insurance Company; nearly two-thirds of his life. He stood erect—a knobby, friable stick—his arthritic hands trembling as he grasped the table. He cleared his throat and his first sound was not the Irish-tinged squeak of old, but a rich, clarion tone, which he had been rehearsing for days.

"Friends …"

"Tell 'em, Johnny!" yelled Gil Horwarth, a man of sixty-four whose time would come in a few months. Laughter. John bared his tobacco-stained teeth in a smile. He started again.

"Friends …"

In a carefully measured tone, he uttered what he had been rehearsing over and over while he walked about on his errands the past week.

"I am deeply honored."

He paused and, for the first time, it was evident that old Johnny Mulligan was a bit tight. He looked around, perspiration spangling his flushed face, his small black eyes watery and bright.

"It's a good feelin' … it's a *good* feelin' to be here like this …."

He fingered his watch in a shaky hand.

"And this watch … I'll … why every time I look at the time, I'll think o' you all, every blessed one o' ya."

Applause and cheers. A few fellow workers dabbed hankies at their eyes.

"A day like this makes me think back to the day when oy first joined Ess-Oy-See. 'Twas back in 1913 and things were mighty rough."

And old Johnny was off on an almost year-by-year account of his eventful career. Twenty minutes later: "Then, in 1930, oy was wit' the Mail Department at the time; old Mister Masters, the Mail Chief, he died, may his soul rest in peace." John licked a fleck of foam from the corner of his mouth.

And on and on he went, at a maddening slow pace as he seemed to wait for each word to come from some invisible prompter on the ceiling. The crowd grew restless. Walter counted the crumbs on the tablecloth. When he finished counting, he crushed a few of the larger crumbs and began a recount. A few girls leaned close to each other and gabbled in a low hiss. Some of the men reached for beer from the big frothy pitchers. Others lit up a second or third post-meal cigarette or cigar.

Mister Gibbs' chin dipped slowly towards his chest, and his eyes were half shut. But he remained awake; worrying about tomorrow's high-level meeting, to discuss what could be a ticklish public relations problem: raising insurance premiums on heavy smokers. The Surgeon General's report a couple of years ago, and the subsequent article in *Reader's Digest,* about the connection between nicotine and cancer, had finally convinced the top brass—most of them heavy smokers—to act.

Walter, who was seated at the far end of the Table of Honor, couldn't take it any longer. He slipped out of his seat, and into the cocktail lounge, which was empty except for the red-jacketed bartender who was popping peanuts into his mouth as he watched Rod Serling's, *The Twilight Zone,* on the TV.

Walter sipped his Seagram's rye whiskey, nibbled the free peanuts and watched the show while the faint drone of old John's voice mingled with the clinking of glasses, scrapings of chairs, and mounting whispers of the audience.

"Hel-*lo,* Scarlett," Walter said, spinning around with enthusiasm on his bar stool.

It was Scarlett Kosciusko, the new filing girl. She wore a clinging white silk cocktail dress with a flare bottom. She looked glorious. He fell in love with her again.

"Hello ... Mister *Walter Mitty,*" she said, smiling.

He smiled in return. "Speeches bore you, too?"

Oh no, I ..." She glanced back at the door marked *"Dolls,"* which was adjacent to another door marked, *"Guys."*

"Like a drink?"

She looked unsure, but nodded her head and formed a faint smile. Walter gestured for her to sit on the stool next to him.

"What would you like?"

"I'll have a dry martini."

Walter ordered it and another rye whiskey for himself. Scarlett sipped her drink and looked at him with her intense storm-cloud-gray eyes.

"Smoke?"

"No thanks. I never touch them."

He lit up. "Since we must all go someday, it may as well be from cancer."

"That's a nice healthy, deterministic way to look at things," she said.

He smiled, foraging the folds of his brain for something clever to say. "How do you like your job, Scarlett?"

"Oh, it's fine, except that everyone keeps asking me to *join* things, and I just don't have the time."

He looked at her. She continued with a noticeable edge of sarcasm. "No, I don't have a boyfriend. How about you, Mister Mott. Do you belong to any of the clubs?"

"No," he said, flipping a peanut into his mouth.

"Wife won't let you?"

"Don't have one. What makes you think I'm married?"

"Isn't that part of the company rules?"

"Rules?"

"You know; that all company executives must be fine, upstanding, stable, drearily dependable citizens; married, kids, mortgaged home in the suburbs, subscriptions to *Life, Time, House Beautiful*, etcetera."

He smiled, wry. "Generalizations can be dangerous. I must say, though, you're rather observant for someone who's only been here a short time."

"Can you keep a secret?"

"I'll keep yours if you don't tell the brass that I'm not married. What's yours?"

"I'm studying the company." Noting his expression of puzzled amusement, she added, "*Seriously*. Remember? I told you I take night courses at Rutgers, over on Rector Street."

"Oh, right," said Walter.

"I used to go days, but my mother and father, they live in Scranton now, couldn't keep up with the tuition. So I have to work days and study nights."

"Bully for you, but I don't get that stuff about your studying the company."

"I'm majoring in Sociology. Since I have to work days I decided to pick a place like this—the epitome of the big corporation—to study what the people are like. Maybe I'll go on for my Masters and use it as my thesis. The theme could be, 'Has the Industrial Revolution caused people to seek security and conformity as it is at SIC, or is the revolution simply an outgrowth of man's innate *desire* for this kind of security and conformity?' Almost sounds like, 'Which came first … the chicken or the egg?' doesn't it?"

"You've got me feeling like a guinea pig," Walter said. "My, you *are* the ambitious little one." Walter felt a rising wave of interest in her; not merely love now, but interest. "Now I understand that lingo you fed me a few days ago about 'the typical effect of mass media upon the middle class mind.'"

"You remembered that?"

"You made quite an impression on me." He suppressed an urge to giggle. How, he wondered, did I ever get up enough courage to say that? She lowered her eyes. There was an awkward silence as they looked at their drinks, then at each other in the mirror behind the bar, then at their drinks again. Walter lit another Camel. He motioned to her glass.

"Like another?" He asked with his best smile; the kind he used only after an exceptionally good joke or in front of the bathroom mirror when he tried to decide which was his most flattering facial expression. Suddenly he felt free and pleasantly uninhibited. He *liked* this girl.

"Just one more," she said. "How about you?'

"Hm?"

"I've told you all about me. What about you?"

"Well, to begin with, I was born ..."

Hardly original, but she threw back her head and expired a little laugh, a lyrical chirp. Well, a giggle. She looked marvelous, he thought, when she did that and her blonde hair fanned out on her shoulders.

"... when I recovered from *that*, I learned to walk, and then talk, or vice versa, and then my career really went into high gear: kindergarten, first grade, second grade—I tell you, it was one promotion right after another."

"No, *no*." she said, laughing. "I mean when did you come to work here?"

"Oh, *that*. More than ten years ago, when you were in pigtails."

She laughed again. Walter hadn't felt this good in years.

"After I got out of the service, I went to college at night for a while."

"Really? Where?"

"Same as you, Rutgers-Newark, down the street."

"And you never got to read about your namesake, Walter Mitty?" she said with a playful smile.

"Too recent."

"What do you mean, too recent?"

"I only read stuff that's a hundred years or more old."

"You've got to be kidding."

"I took this literature course with a funny professor named Doctor Clement Fairweather, a real character."

"That was his name? Fairweather?"

"Yes. And he drove us nuts. He would only assign us books from the 1700s, or 1800s, even though some of the kids were dying to read Hemingway and other modern guys. But Doctor Fairweather said, "If a writer's work is good, it will still be around a hundred years later. Be patient." He was an expert on the work of Alexander Pope, and he got me hooked on the guy."

"But there are all these marvelous authors nowadays. Her voice rose with enthusiasm "Isaac Asimov. Ray Bradbury. Durrell, Leon Uris ... Norman Mailer. There's even a young guy from Newark, Philip Roth, who's just come out with a best seller."

"Well, if they're still around a hundred years from now, I'll give 'em a try."

Scarlett gazed at him and smiled. "You are really strange."

Walter shrugged, sipped his whiskey.

After a moment, Scarlett said, "So. You've been here ten years?"

"Yep. Back in 1949. A year later, the assistant director, Mister Jeffries, died. Mister Furey moved up to take his place, and they needed someone to be manager. Not having anyone else, they chose me."

"You're being modest. You must be very capable, I'm sure."

Walter smiled. What she'd said—about him being capable—made him feel good, even though it may have been polite party talk. Except for his encounters with Stormy, Walter hadn't spent this much time talking with a woman since he couldn't remember when. But now a torrent of tenderness and affection welled up within him. So many years since he'd felt such an emotion, at least towards an object within his grasp. He wanted to put his hand on hers, but held back. She looked at him, her grey eyes filled with what Walter took for compassion.

"It's so sad," she said, shaking her head.

"What's sad?"

"About Mister Mulligan."

"Why is it sad?"

"His retiring, and his wife dead. He won't have *anyone* to spend his last years with."

"What about his children?" He lives with them. And his grandchildren, too."

"No. Young people don't understand."

"Okay, grandma."

She produced a feeble smile. "I remember my grandpa. He lived with us, my father, mother, my brother and sister, and me. Grandpa's wife died five years before he retired, so he took the spare room in our house. He always kept kidding me about how he couldn't wait to retire. But once it came, he didn't know what to *do* with himself. He was a coal miner all his life. First he'd go to the park with the paper. Then to the store. Then walk the dog. Then he'd watch TV from after dinner until all hours of the morning. One Friday night, two years after he retired, I came home from a date about one-thirty in the morning. I looked in the living room and saw him in his easy chair. I remember saying to myself, 'He's watching the *test pattern*.' He must have had the stroke just before The National Anthem. Daddy tried to pry the *TV Guide* loose from his hand. It was so ghastly." She drained her drink. Walter felt deflated. And he had been feeling so good.

"Want another?"

"No, I shouldn't."

"Oh, c'mon. I enjoy talking with you."

"So far, *I've* been doing most of the talking."

"I enjoy listening then." He raised his hand to signal the bartender.

"No, really; I don't want another."

"Would you like to have one someplace else?" His heart beat a bit faster.

"I couldn't. I came with a bunch of the girls from the office."

You could tell them you're not feeling well, and are going home."

Her face hardened into a mask of cool rage. "You've got it all figured out, don't you?"

Walter's heart sank. "Oh no, please, I didn't mean ..."

He was rescued by a chorus of screams from the banquet hall. Irwin Kemp rushed in and yelled at the bartender. "Gimme me some ice in a towel! Got a phone here?"

"What happened, Irwin?" Walter said.

"Old Johnny. Must be his heart."

Scarlett moaned and covered her face with her hands. Walter ran into the banquet hall, which was in a state of chaos. Virtually everyone was crowded around the place of honor. He elbowed his way up front.

Old Johnny, his face ashen, was slumped in his seat, his head resting in the lap of Mister Gibbs, who was frozen with fright. Irwin rushed up with the wet towel. While Walter held Johnny's head, Irwin patted him with the towel. Walter nearly passed out from the reek of alcohol.

Johnny's face twitched, and the color slowly flushed back into his face. He opened one bloodshot eye and his face cracked in a silly grin. He raised his right arm and opened his mouth to speak:

"Then, in 1954 ... I remember it as clear as yesterday ..."

Everyone broke into a loud cheer.

Walter hurried back to the lounge, to reassure Scarlett. She was gone. He ran to the cloak room, grabbed his coat, and bolted out the door.

"Clutch it! Clutch it!"

1

Scarlett was by the edge of the driveway, seated on a low flagstone wall, her shoulders trembling as she silently wept. He sat down beside her and patted her.

"It's all right. The old bugger was stinking drunk. He passed out. But he's wide awake now, and telling everyone about the year 1954, for God's sake."

Scarlett leaned against him, clutching his arm, crying and laughing at the same time. She subsided into a low whimper as he kept patting her back, and thinking to himself that perhaps now she would go for that drink somewhere. He scanned the lonely road, optimistically expecting a cab to pass by. Then he realized that the only place he had seen one pass by promptly was on a movie screen. It was a cool spring evening. Ten chilly minutes passed, silent except for Scarlett's low whimpering. Finally, she turned to him, her eyes swollen with tears.

"What are we doing out here?" she said.

"Waiting for a cab to take you home," she said.

"But I've got a *car*," she said in an annoyed whine.

He shouted, "Why the hell didn't you *tell* me?"

"Why the hell didn't you *ask* me?" she shrieked. She stood up and headed back toward the lounge.

"Where are you going now?" he said, reaching out and catching the sleeve of her overcoat.

She snapped at him. "Back inside."

"More speeches?"

She looked at him.

"What kind of car do you have?" he said.

"A fifty-four Plymouth."

"God, it's *years* since I've driven a car," he said with a sigh.

"You don't have a car?" she said, regarding him as though he were from another planet.

"Nope," he said, grinning and shrugging his shoulders.

"Boy, Detroit would be a ghost town if there were more like you around."

"I know how to drive, though … if I still remember. That last time was in the Army. I was the chauffeur for the chaplain."

"What the devil do you *do* without a car?"

"Take buses. … cabs … *walk*."

She giggled. "You really *are* mysterious."

"Do you think I could try driving yours? Drive, honest, not park," he added with haste. "Please?"

Scarlett reached into her pocket and handed him the keys.

Seated in the Plymouth, Walter fumbled about, trying to put the key into the ignition.

"No, *no*. That's the lighter," she yelped. Finally he turned it on and the car jerked forward with a loud growl.

"Clutch it. Clutch it!" she shouted, laughing. He rested his left foot on the clutch, let it up gradually and the car lurched ahead. He jammed it into second, gears grinding, and they bucked and shuddered out of the parking lot and onto the street. Picking up speed, he managed to grind it into third and they were off to a neck-jarring start.

In a few minutes, Walter was shifting smoothly. He marveled at how he remembered after all those years. It was thrilling to hold the wheel and glide along. Walter checked the car clock. It was only ten p.m., yet the road was virtually empty. He rolled along with such immense enjoyment that he forgot to ask Scarlett where she lived. She, looking out the window at the passing houses, was so silent that it made Walter uncomfortable. He was about to say, 'a penny for your thoughts', but it sounded so awfully corny that he censored himself.

"Say," he finally said. "How about that drink? There must be a little place along here somewhere."

"Okay," she said, making his heart beat faster again. "But just one."

In twenty minutes Walter and Scarlett were seated in a booth in the backroom of a cocktail lounge. Out in the front room the bar was nearly filled with couples watching *Gunsmoke* on the TV mounted on the wall above the mirror. From the jukebox in the corner, Sinatra was singing *"High Hopes"*, his latest hit. His lyrics were interrupted by occasional gunshots or hoof-beats from the TV. It was a truly cozy atmosphere; the TV out front, Sinatra's voice, and the hushed talk and laughter of the other couples in the booths blended into a pleasant chorus. They sat in silence—but this time a comfortable silence—nursing their drinks.

"By the way," she said, "excuse me for the way I snapped at you outside the banquet place."

"I snapped at you, too. God, if anyone had seen us, they'd have thought we were some old married couple."

Scarlett laughed and rested her hand on his. He reached over with his other hand and held hers. His heart came close to bursting with joy when she made no effort to pull away. It was the first time they had really touched, or *purposely* touched, and there was something special about it, he felt. As though a dam had burst; their conversation flowed in a rush; unceasing, animated, gay.

58

They were at that magic stage in a relationship when they knew next to nothing of each other, when each of them could search into the past and pluck baubles of humor to delight the other. She told him about her goofy Sociology prof who wore orange ties and purple shirts. He laughed, and told her about a funny company commander in the Third Infantry Division who looked exactly like Lou Costello. She laughed, and then confessed about the dental braces she'd once worn; and he laughed, and confessed about how scrawny he was as a child, and told her of the outlandish places he used to hide when the kids played Ringaleevio; and she laughed, and the world existed only in that booth; a cosmos of laughter and sugar-coated memories, bubbly talk and happy eyes and warm hand-squeezings.

"My God, what time is it?" she squeaked, four drinks later.

"Well, lessee," he said, his tongue sluggish from the whiskey. He looked at the clock on the wall. "Says one-thirty, but it doesn't say what day it is."

"Gee, I have to go, Walter."

"According to my calculations, we have, lessee," he tapped the keys of an invisible adding machine, imitating the sounds, and then yanked out an invisible strip of paper. "We've got exactly fifty-five hours before we have to be back in the office on Monday. What better way could we spend that time than just sitting here like this?"

She smiled, not sure what to say.

"Say," he said, "I've got an idea."

"What?"

"Ever seen Cape May?"

"Cape what?"

"Cape May! Down at the southern tip of Jersey. It's on the edge of nowhere, really great. I remember my folks took me there once when I was a kid."

"No," she said, shaking her head. "I really can't."

"But it's terrific," he said, waving his hands.

"How far is it?"

"Oh, just a couple of hours ..."

"*Hours.* But I've got to—"

"You've got to what?"

She shrugged and sputtered. "Truth is," she said, her face illuminated as if by a revelation, "I really don't have to do *anything*." She cocked her head to one side and looked at him. "A person can go along day after day with this nagging feeling that there's *something* you've got to do, someone *undone,* and the real truth is you really don't *have* to do *anything.* She groped for the words, then raised a hand to her temple. "Do you suppose there's someplace along the way that serves coffee? My head is swimming."

2

Gravel flew as Walter swung the car out of the lot and onto the road, southward bound. He was borderline drunk, but charged with enthusiasm. In a few minutes he saw a sign that read, "Garden State Parkway-South", and he veered onto the entrance, pressuring the accelerator. The car responded nicely, moving up to sixty. The northbound lane of the Parkway was obscured by a high grassy bank; the lane heading southward was a single narrow ribbon of light stretching out into black nothingness. A few hundred yards ahead, the road grew wider and there was a line of tollbooths.

"What's this, a barricade?" he said.

"It's a toll station."

"A what?"

"A toll station. They've got them strung out every few miles. You drop a quarter in the box as you pass. Got change?"

"A pocketful." Walter slowed down and flipped the quarter. It bounced off the rim of the receptacle and fell to the ground. Looking and feeling sheepish, while Scarlett muffled her laughter, he got out of the car, picked up the coin and dropped it in the box. The uniformed attendant grinned and made some crack about signing him up for the New York Knicks.

At the next toll stop, Walter barely slowed down as he flipped the coin and it landed dead center, changing the red light to green.

"Two points for our team!" Scarlett yelled, clapping her hands.

Turn-off signs flicked by every few minutes: Westfield … Perth Amboy … Matawan … Red Bank … Asbury Park … Toms River … New Gretna … then a long, lonely stretch until the Atlantic City sign loomed up before them and fell away as they continued south.

Nearly two hours had gone by and Scarlett was curled up on the seat beside him, her face turned towards him, her hair waving with the breeze. Walter felt drowsy as the highway rushed beneath the front of the car. He tried everything to stay awake. He turned the radio up a bit, but not too loud, so as not to awaken her. He opened the side vent and icy air buffeted his face. He dabbed saliva onto his aching eyes. He pinched his inner thigh. He wanted to stop, to turn off the road and go to sleep, but he couldn't. He didn't want the night to end.

He looked down at Scarlett and thought how much he wanted to make it to Cape May, to show it to her. But his eyelids were heavy and the car weaved from side to side. He was sure there were long periods when his eyes were shut, but he would awaken with a start and the adrenalin coaxed out by his fright kept him alert for another few minutes. Then a green sign with white letters ballooned up on his right. *Cape May*.

The fatigue drained from him as he cut into the right-hand lane, turned off the Parkway and pulled onto the narrow road. It was still dark, but not completely black; the sky was a royal blue and the countryside murky gray. He drove along the flatlands, looking far ahead and to both sides at the endless blanket of mist hugging the ground; it was as though they were floating above the clouds. All was silent, almost frightening. The radio station had faded into static, and as he turned the dial and found a local station a loud bass voice announced that it was four-thirty.

A few minutes later, the fog scattered into stray fluffs of dirty cotton and the world around him was a monochromatic landscape of varied shades of gray. The silhouettes of the pine trees were like dark spires jutting harshly into the sky, the white, one-story clapboard houses were rectangular smudges of gray stroked in with a pallet knife. A gas station — still closed — was in shadows except for a ghostly night light inside the front office. An old milk truck, the first vehicle he'd seen in an hour, rattled by with its headlights on. Walter drove slowly along the road, trying to remember, searching for familiar landmarks, but he had been there only once before, and *how many years ago*.

He approached a fork in the road, with the macadam curving off to the right and the straightaway consisting of a sandy trail flanked by low shrubs. Walter guided the car slowly onto the sand, which was firm, and continued for a several yards, climbing a gradual hill until he reached the summit and stepped on the brakes, gasping with surprise.

Stretched out before him in a wide panorama were a wavy strip of sand and an expanse of water reaching to the horizon. They were at the tip of a peninsula. The gray powdery sand was dimpled with windswept footprints, a miniature desert with dwarfish dunes; the ocean was placid and blue-gray, as was the sky now, which was bereft of stars. At the junction of sky and water was a fringe of light. Walter nosed the car into the sand a few feet more and stopped, turning off the key.

"Scarlett. Wake up. *Cape May*."

She rubbed her closed eyes and mumbled something. He put his arm around her as she looked up at him briefly, then fell asleep on his shoulder. He sat still for a few minutes, glorying in the lonely view and the warmth of her body. Sea, sand and air stretched out all around him. Black gulls swooped and soared in coy flirtations with the water. Not a person in sight, not a building. The sun peeked over the horizon and blinked at him.

"Scarlett, the sun ... *look*." She moaned and raised her head, squinting at the beacon of light.

"C'mon," he said, "let's go outside and look around."

Still half asleep, she let him hold her close as they trudged through the sand toward the water. It was cold, but there was little wind and no sound except for the gentle wash of the waves and the shrill, intermittent cries of the gulls.

Scarlett seemed to awaken with the sun, and soon she turned from the serene landscape and half-whispered to him: "Spooky, isn't it?"

He looked down at her. The wind lifted her hair, her face was wrinkled from sleep, but she looked beautiful in the early golden light. He felt deliciously happy. He could recall times in his life when he had been happy, but never before had he realized it at the exact moment of it happening.

"You know," he said, his voice hoarse, "I feel as though … as though tonight has been a real experience we've shared. Just the two of us."

She looked up at him, then averted her eyes. "Wouldn't it be nice if it were summer? We could go swimming."

"We can at least sit on the beach for a while. It's not very cold."

She tucked her gown beneath her legs as she sat down on the sand. He leaned back on his elbows and looked up at her. Minutes passed. Her lips were so close, just inches from his. He wanted so much to kiss her, but he had never in his life kissed a girl in the daytime. He sat up and silently cursed the brightening sky as the sun rose and grew like a flower in bloom.

"We'd better get back, eh?"

"Back?" She looked at him as though he were joking. "But *you're* the one who wanted to get here so badly."

"Well," he said with a weak grin, "We've seen it, right?"

She looked perplexed, but then it struck her as funny and she threw her head back and laughed. "Yes, you're right, we've *seen* it." She scooped up a handful of sand and dropped it into her coat pocket. "A souvenir of Cape May."

First Kiss

As he drove towards the northbound lane of the Parkway, Walter watched Cape May shrink in the distance through his rearview mirror. He regretted leaving; he regretted ending his seaside idyll with Scarlett, yet he felt relieved as a strange malaise swept out of his system. It was a prickly, nauseating feeling; a feeling of being *away* from somewhere, and now, though he disliked it, he was going back. They drove northward for half an hour as the warm sun rose rapidly on their right.

"Are you hungry," Scarlett asked. "I'm starved."

A few minutes later they approached a Howard Johnson's Restaurant on the left-hand side of the Parkway and Walter pulled the car into the spacious blacktop lot. They had both been hungry, and after a hearty breakfast of scrambled eggs, bacon and toast, they sipped coffee and watched the steadily mounting traffic speed by the picture window.

"You know," Scarlett said, "you're one of the oddest people I've ever met. I feel in a way that I know you so well after just these few hours, yet at the same time I feel as though I don't know you at all. It's like, well ... you're hard to pin *down*, if you know what I mean."

"You pin down a butterfly and it can't fly anymore," he said.

"I don't mean pin down in terms of *control*. I'm not like that. I mean in terms of understanding."

"You mean categorizing them? Putting them in labeled cubbyholes for easy reference. For your master's thesis, maybe?"

"I don't mean that and you know it. Forget it."

"Look, I'm sorry," he said, reaching out to her hand. "When I get tired I'm pretty cranky."

"What I really meant was, well, we've talked all night, practically, and yet I don't feel as though I know anything about you, and, well ..."

"How about you? C'mon, you first. What about your family?"

"My mom and dad are still in Pennsylvania. I have an older brother out there, too. He's married, with two kids. Oh, and my sister Eileen, she's married, too. Lives in Akron. That's in Ohio. Okay, mister. Your turn."

"I was an only child," he heard himself begin. And he told her about his parents; a middle-aged Protestant couple of English descent. "Fifteen years ago, when I was twenty-four, and in the service, they died..."

"Oh my God," she said.

Smiling, he recalled, "Mom was very sweet, kind of frail; she liked knitting and listening to the radio. Her favorites were Gabriel Heatter and Judy Canova. Dad was with Public Service in Newark; drove the number 48 bus. After work, he read the paper from front to back, *including* all the *want ads*. It was the Great Depression when I was a little kid, and so many people were out of work. He always said, 'I'm grateful to have a job. It's so important to have a job. *A job. A job*' He kept drumming that into me."

"And how did they die?"

"They were taking a summer weekend drive—a busman's holiday— down Route 35 to Asbury Park. Dad had a black 1939 Ford coupe ... and a giant trailer truck—it was bringing grapefruits up from Florida. He swerved to miss a jaywalking dog and smashed right into their car."

"Oh, how awful." Scarlett reached out to hold his hand.

"The war was on. Just as my outfit was being shipped to the Pacific, I was flown home from San Francisco. My Uncle Ed from Syracuse, he had a big hardware store up there, paid for the funeral. I got home in time to see Mom and Dad lowered into the double grave. They were in their early forties ..." his voice trailed off as he looked down and away.

Scarlett, near tears, petted his hand.

"Then I was flown back to Frisco and stayed there until the end of the war, driving a jeep for the Catholic chaplain. He spent all his time trying to convert me. In some strange way, my parents' death may have saved me from getting killed in action. I often wonder ..." A saddened Walter shook his head, and sipped the last of his coffee.

"Gee, you're all alone in the world," Scarlett said, eying him with compassion. He shrugged.

"I think V-J Day was one of the happiest moments of my life," he said, thinking back to that epic afternoon, remembering the pandemonium in the barracks. "There was this huge Tennessee hillbilly who ran around, hugging and kissing everyone, jumping up and down and pouring 3.2 PX beer down everyone's shirt."

"And after college you came to work for the company?"

"I started right near the top; on the thirteenth floor."

"And you've been there ever since."

"Uh-huh."

Scarlett sat back, disappointed. Oh, how he wanted to tell her. He had big plans. But how could he tell her? Sitting here in this bright, sunny, bustling restaurant; how could he tell her the biggest secret of his life? He wished now that they were back on the beach. There had been a moment during that tranquil, beautiful sunrise when he would have told her anything. But she hadn't asked, and he had run from his chance.

Back in the car, Walter felt drugged from the lack of sleep, and now the bacon and eggs, so he left the landscaped green monotony of the Parkway and turned onto the old highway which hugged the coastline. They passed through a succession of quiet resort towns, their populations reduced to a small fraction of what they once were by the migration of the summer people.

The lush trees and neatly manicured lawns faded into open highway, bordered on both sides by pasture-land, then rolling acres of suburbia with thousands of identical, Monopoly-game houses set in precise rows. A few miles further and gray factories belched grime from their tall chimneys. A giant trailer truck hurtled by in the right-hand lane, leaving a cloud of acrid fumes in its wake. The magic was gone. They were going home.

It was just before eleven in the morning when they reached the outskirts of the city.

"Where do you live, Scarlett?"

"No," she said. "I'll drop you off at your place."

"I can take a bus."

"That's silly." she said, eyeing him like he was crazy.

"Uh, well, look, drop me by the library. I just remembered that I've got to pick up some books I ordered. Then I can take a bus from there. Leaves me right at my door."

"You know," she said, "you really *are* an odd one." But she said it with such endearment that it warmed his heart. And when she parked in front of the library she didn't even shrink back when he pecked lightly at her cheek. Their first kiss. It seemed so natural. He took the wide marble steps three at a time, and when he stood at the summit he waved to her. She turned the corner and was gone.

2

As long as I'm at the library, Walter thought, I'll check to see if any interesting books have arrived. Intrigued by Scarlett's comments, he checked out a book by James Thurber that included the story, *"The Secret Life Of Walter Mitty."* For an hour, he sat in the reading room, chuckling over the "escapades" of the hapless dreamer of his almost namesake, Walter Mitty. My God, he thought, this guy Thurber is *hilarious*.

He decided to get some sleep. Book in hand, he walked outside. During the eight block jaunt to the SIC building, Walter felt a rising sense of uneasiness about his relationship with Scarlett; their feelings towards each other seemed to have taken a hundred different turns during the long night and then, despite the kiss at the end, there had been her look of disappointment about his career with SIC. He couldn't let things go at that. She *must* understand. He stepped into a drugstore and opened the phonebook. Her name wasn't in it, but Information had a record of a newly installed phone.

"Hello?"

"Scarlett?"

"Yes?"

"It's Walter."

"*Walter*. Are you still at the library?"

"No. I'm at a drugstore nearby."

"Near my house?"

"No … near the library."

"Oh. Did you get the books you were looking for?"

"Yes. Look, Scarlett. What are you doing tonight?"

"Tonight? Listen, Mister, I'm going to hit the hay now and nothing, not even an *earthquake*, is going to get me out of bed until tomorrow morning. I'm beat."

"What about tomorrow night?"

"Walter, I've got to devote some time to my homework this weekend. Besides, we've got to be in the office early the next day."

"How about Wednesday?"

"I've got a class Wednesday night."

"Say you're busy next Friday, and …"

"*Ha*. All right, Friday it is. What've you got planned?"

"Oh, I don't know. There must be a good movie playing."

"Anything but another ride to Cape May."

"Still got your sand?"

"Yes, in my coat pocket, in the closet."

"I'd like a little of it, too … as a souvenir of a wonderful time. See you tomorrow night?"

"Sorry. I have to study this weekend, for an exam. I'll see you *Monday*, in the office, *Mister Mott*."

"Ah, yes, *Miss* Kosciusko. Well, sweet dreams."

"Same to you."

"Scarlett…don't hang up."

"I haven't."

"I just want to tell you; remember at breakfast we were talking about how long I've been with the company?"

"Yes, what about it?"

"Well, it's not what you think."

"What do you mean?"

"I mean that I … look, I'll tell you about it when I see you."

"All right, Walter. Get some sleep. You must be dead after all that driving."

"Okay, boss. Bye."
"Bye."

3

On Sunday afternoon, Walter took the train from Newark's Penn Station to

Penn Station Manhattan. In the bustling lobby, he walked into a store, bought a pack of cigarettes, and asked to look at a local phone directory. The clerk pulled it from under the counter and handed it over. On the inside back cover of the James Thurber book it said that the author had moved to Greenwich Village back in 1927. That was more than thirty years ago, he thought with considerable consternation. Could he still be there? I *have* to know. He flipped through the pages, and sure enough there was a James Thurber listed in lower Manhattan. He jotted down the address and hurried down the steps to the subway.

Walter emerged from the No. 9 train at Sheridan Square and walked several blocks over to a quiet, tree-lined street. *There it was.* He stood staring with fascination at the old brownstone building just across the street. The front door opened. A man in his mid-60s, gray hair, moustache, thick glasses, slowly descended the steps, holding a cane. *God. It must be Thurber.* The man ambled in a slow gate down to the corner, and disappeared into a nearby store. Walter stood there, frozen. Should he approach him? Ask him how the devil he came up with the name Walter Mitty? The man came out, bearing a small paper bag with some groceries. He climbed the steps and disappeared back into the house. Walter remained there for another ten minutes, torn between crossing the street and knocking on the door, or leaving. He walked away. Perhaps some other day, he thought, regretting his cowardice.

4

"Well, Walter," Mister Furey said on Monday morning. "It was one helluva party, but where did *you* disappear to?"

"I was there for most of it, but I got a headache and went home a bit early. Had a nice time, eh?"

"*Boy* did I have a time. Wilma was in top form, hanging out all over the place. By one a.m. she was hugging and kissing everybody in the cocktail lounge; *in*-cluding yours truly. Lucky thing Miriam stayed home."

Walter smiled. They both looked outside at Wilma who was seated at her typewriter. Irwin Kemp was perched atop her desk, apparently telling her a joke while he peered down the front of her blouse.

"Sometimes I envy Irwin," Furey said. "He's really got it with women. He must've danced with every gal at the party. Even here in the office, when he's not at their desks they're over at his. He probably kicks one out of bed every night. Do you think it's because he's skinny?"

"Skinny?"

"I think girls are more attracted to skinny guys. They don't take me seriously at *all* when I flirt with them. Being the boss here, I can't be *too* open about it, but I've let go some pretty broad hints and they laugh them off. They just don't seem to take portly people seriously." Frowning, he patted his belly, which looked like a massive tumor.

"Say ... you haven't heard about my wound yet, have you?"

"Your wound?"

"This weekend," Furey said, "a bunch of us went hunting deer out in the back woods. Bow and arrow, of course; only sporting way. Just bought a bow last month and this was my first go at it."

Walter remembered how six months ago Mister Furey had been all excited about foreign sports cars. He'd traded in his Buick and bought a slightly used Jaguar. Then he developed an elaborate care and feeding program for the car. He rambled on about torque and camshafts for months; he even parked the Jaguar in a downtown garage and called at least once a day to see if everything was all right. But finally he'd tired of it and re-exchanged it for another Buick.

"Did you shoot anything with the bow and arrow?"

"Didn't even *see* a deer," Furey said with a snort. "Something about being upwind, or downwind, or something."

"Then how'd you get wounded? Someone hit you with an arrow?"

Furey put on a sheepish smile. Color flushed his cheeks. He opened his suit jacket, then his vest, then his white button-down shirt, and pulled up his T-shirt. There was a round discoloration on his hairy abdomen; it looked like a rotten section on a cantaloupe.

"From my handwarmer," he said. "It's a metal disc with something inside that you light up. Burns all day and you keep it in your trigger hand when it's very cold out. I had it lit and hung it around my neck. Must've been defective, because 'round about noontime I began to feel this *heat* on my gut. Damned thing burned right through my wool hunting shirt."

Mister Furey spent the entire morning showing the wound to anyone who entered the office. Even Wilma Tannenbaum touched it and recoiled with mock fright. Mister Furey wore the hero's mantle with magnificent stoicism. At noontime, one meek little stenotypist standing next to Walter in the elevator asked her girlfriend if she'd seen Mister Furey's tarantula bite.

5

Irwin Kemp joined Walter, Marty Shaw, Ray Lang and Charlie Phelps in the lounge after lunch.

"Did you guys see the news on TV last night," Ray Lang asked. "They said two of our soldiers, a major and a sergeant, were killed in Vietnam."

"Where? Marty Shaw said.

"Vietnam," said Ray. "They were stationed as military advisors."

Marty asked, "Where the hell is Vietnam." "It's way over in the Far East somewhere," said Charlie Phelps.

"What the hell are our guys doing over there?" Marty said.

Shrugs all around. Irwin felt in good spirits because during the morning he had caught Scarlett's eye and they'd exchanged a few winks.

"Boy, did I pick a winner last *night*," Irwin said.

"The trotters?" Marty Shaw said.

"No; a *woman*. I'm going to art classes on Wednesday and Sunday nights at the school up the street."

"Since when?" Charlie Phelps said, yanking the pipe out of his mouth. Charlie thought he had the culture market cornered as far as his luncheon group was concerned.

"Oh, the last month or two," Irwin said, basking in Charlie's chagrin with casual aplomb, "It's a good way to kill spare time; and I'm really learning. Now we're sketching live nude models."

"*Now*, we know why you're going," Ray Lang said, with loud chuckles.

"No, really, it's a funny thing. When you're holding the pad and pencil and concentrating, you don't even know the model exists in that way. Honest. But after the session, she's standing around in a kimono and drinking coffee with us, and *that's* when I get the hots for her."

"So what happened, Casanova?" Phelps said, biting his pipestem.

"She mentions that she lives in Greenwich Village." The *Village*. Walter wondered whether she lived anywhere near James Thurber.

"So," Irwin continued, "I make up this story about having to meet someone there later on and I offer to give her a lift. She's sort of thin, but got good knockers; only her face is a little pimply and I didn't know she wore glasses until she comes out all dressed. Anyway, we've driving slowly through the Holland Tunnel in my car, talking about all kinds of things, and she comes on all of a sudden with these stories about peyote—"

"*Peyote*. Did you try any?" Phelps said, deeply interested.

"What the hell's peyote," Shaw asked.

"It's a drug that produces fabulous dreams," Phelps said, recalling and reciting an article he'd read in *Esquire*.

"Yeah," Irwin said. "She tells me she takes it all the time. And listen to this. She gets it from Mexico by *mail*."

"Wait'll Sears Roebuck hears about *this*." Phelps said.

"So what happened?" Lang said. "Did you take any?"

"Will you let me *tell* ya?" Irwin whined, pausing until they all relaxed back in their seats. Walter was curious, too; but he kept silent because he knew from long experience that taking part in the lunchtime discussions promised nothing but indigestion.

"Well," Irwin continued, sounding like a Boy Scout at a campfire, "we get to her door, a real crummy neighborhood and I ask if maybe she could make me some coffee."

"How original," Phelps said. "Why didn't you ask to see her etchings?"

"Go on, Irwin," Shaw said, anxious to hear the end.

"So she says, 'Okay,' and we climb five—no, *six*—goddamn flights and we go inside. What a rat hole. All bare wood floors and naked light bulbs. And she's rigged up a few bookshelves where she's got things about Oriental philosophy and art. There's even one of those scrolls hanging on the wall. All she's got in the room is a bathtub, a refrigerator, a big table filled with bottles of paint and crazy things she's scribbled on wrapping paper."

"No bed?" Phelps said.

"Are you kidding? She sleeps on a *mat* on the floor, right below the scroll. Just a quarter of an inch of straw between her and the cockroaches," he said, indicating the width with his fingers.

"So what *happened?*" Lang said.

"We drink coffee for a while with this awful Preem stuff. Then she shows me her paintings; crazy black brush marks on the wrapping paper. So I say, 'that's nice, that's nice, that's nice.' Just to be polite. And damned if she doesn't roll one up and *give* it to me. Then she changes back into her kimono, lies down on the floor with her back to me and curls up."

"And," Lang asked.

"I left," Irwin said, shrugging his shoulders.

Phelps, Lang and Shaw chorused: "You *what*?"

"I figured she wanted to sleep."

"Some student of feminine psychology," Phelps said in a measured, sarcastic tone.

"So what would *you* have done?" Irwin said. "Maybe she was high on this peyote stuff. How do I know? What am I supposed to do? Screw a woman who's high on peyote? Who's all drugged up? What do you say, Marty? Would you?"

"Why, I don't even …"

"Ray?"

"Well, I hardly ..."

"What about you, Walter?"

"Unthinkable."

Irwin glared at Phelps with disdain. "Geez, how low can you get? A person's gotta have *standards*."

Several wordless minutes passed as they glanced at their magazines.

"Say," said Marty, who abhorred silence. "Any of you guys see the All-Star Show on Channel Two last night?"

"I saw a couple minutes of it," Phelps said.

"Did you hear Belafonte," Marty asked.

"No, I turned it off after a few minutes. I rarely watch TV. It's a real wasteland," Phelps said.

"Boy, he sure did a terrific job with *Hava Nagilah*," Marty said. "He had the whole audience clapping. He does it better than anyone I know, except maybe Connie Francis.

"Connie Francis," Irwin yelped. "Better than Belafonte?"

"Yeah," Phelps barked, leaping into the fray. He was still smoldering from the peyote episode. Shaw's and Lang's heads swiveled from Irwin to Phelps like spectators at a tennis match.

"She's not even Jewish," Irwin said.

"But she grew up in a Jewish neighborhood in *Newark*."

"How the hell do you know?"

"I *read* it somewhere, okay? And since when is Belafonte Jewish?"

Irwin yelled back, "But he's a *folk* singer. Besides, he's *been* in Israel; he even lived for a while in a kibbitz."

"*Kibbutz*, stupid."

"Listen to Mister Phelpsowitz." Irwin said, and laughed.

"I've got *friends* who are Jewish. Anything wrong with that? What are you? A goddamn Nazi or something?"

"No, but I still say that Harry Belafonte can sing *Hava Nagilah* better than Connie Francis. Even *Elvis Presley* could sing it better than Connie Francis," Irwin said, rising to his feet.

"How can you argue with a stupid statement like that," Phelps asked, falling back into his seat and throwing his hands up in disgust. "Walt, what do you think?"

"I don't have a TV," Walter said, trying to stay out of it.

"Ray?"

"I think they both deserve a lot of credit for learning a foreign language."

"Marty?"

"I guess it's a matter of personal preference. It's ... they each have a special style. After all, who can say which is the right way? A Hebrew maybe."

"Have you ever *heard* her sing it?" Phelps said.

"No. But I think an artist as popular as Connie Francis is entitled to a certain recognition and respect."

Irwin's eyes narrowed to slits, and he spoke with slow, savage force: "Connie Francis sings the worst *Hava Nagilah* I have ever heard in my whole ear."

Her Fleshy Buttocks Rose

Late Wednesday night, after the library and his visit to the diner, Walter strolled into the Latino Casino. For the past few nights he had tossed about on his wall-bed, yearning for Scarlett. All day long in the office he had caught glimpses of her. It was excruciating, and Friday seemed an eternity away.

"Well, if it ain't ol' Doc Kildare," a tipsy Stormy said, looking up from her crème de menthe. She tottered on her stool like one of those round-bottomed punching toys that never stay down.

"Hi, Stormy. How's the dancing going?"

"Fine. You jus' missed my act. Picked up ten dollars, and t'night was a slow night."

"Stormy, I'm sorry about the other night. I was pretty silly."

"I don' know if I should forgive ya," she said, with girlish coyness.

"I was pretty crude, I guess."

When he felt the bone-crushing dig in his knees he knew all was forgiven.

"Say," she said, "you never did read me that po-et-tree by that hunchback Pope whatsisname."

"I brought the book," he said.

Stormy's room was furnished in what one might call Early American Goodwill Mission. In one corner, an efficiency kitchen was closed off by curtained French doors. There was also a small, Formica-topped table, a battered portable TV and a massive puce corduroy couch which sounded like an opening drawbridge when it unfolded into a double bed. A floor lamp with a fringed shade cast an ocher hue upon the walls, which were painted a Scraped Skin Pink.

Seated next to Stormy on the couch, Walter cleared his throat and began to read from *The Rape of the Lock*.

"What dire offence from amorous causes springs,
        What   mighty   contests   rise   from   trivial   things   ..."

He nodded and read on, while she fixed her crème de menthe and his Seagram's 7 rye whiskey and water. She handed him the drink, curled up next to him on the couch and gazed at the ceiling.

"Say what strong motive, goddess! Could compel
        A well-bred lord to assault a gentle belle?"

Walter stopped to take a sip. Stormy smiled at him and fluttered her lashes. She reached over and took a healthy slug of his rye whiskey.

"What guard the purity of melting maids,

In courtly balls, and midnight masquerades,
Safe from the treacherous friend, the daring spark,
The glance by day, the whisper in the dark,
When kind occasion prompts their warm desires,
When music softens and when dancing fires?"

Stormy was lost. She looked at Walter, half-listening, the crème de menthe and whiskey swirling around in her senses. She rose, took the glasses and refilled them. After putting the fresh drinks on the rug next to the couch, she went to a tall cardboard wardrobe and turned her back. She took off her blouse and black bra and buttoned on a silk shortie nightgown. Then she stepped out of her dress and slip. She gave Walter his drink, balanced hers in her hand and sat down on the couch. He continued reading. She leaned back against the arm rest, faced him and lifted her long legs atop his lap. He raised the book some to let them pass. *"Stormy"* ..."*Stormy"* read the tattoos on her moving thighs.
"When Florio speaks, what virgin could withstand
    If gentle Damon did not squeeze her hand ..."
Stormy drained her glass and put it on the rug. She reached out and stroked the back of Walter's neck. The hairs bristled. Yawning, she stretched her arms and arched her torso, straining the huge mellow breasts against their flimsy veil. Her fleshy buttocks rose, then grazed against his thigh as they ebbed back into the soft cushion.
"This casket India's glowing gems unlocks,
    And all Arabia breathes from yonder box ..."

2

At four-thirty a.m., his volume of Pope in hand, Walter tip-toed out, leaving Stormy snoring contentedly on the couch. With his special key, he entered the small side door of the SIC building and zoomed up the service elevator. By chance, he reached into his breast pocket and felt the MAD time card. He remembered that he'd fallen behind on punching out at midnight in Machine Accounting, and the cards had to be sent to Payroll in the morning. He stopped at the eleventh floor. Working by moon-glow, Walter pried open the time clock with a penknife, set the hands for midnight and punched out for Monday, Tuesday and Wednesday, bringing himself up to date. After resetting the clock, he closed it and walked up two flights to his office.

Walter closed the Venetians and drapes, lit the neon desk lamp and opened the lock to his secret wall. He pulled the bed down and undressed in haste, throwing his wrinkled clothes behind the bed. He set the alarm, slipped beneath the covers and fell asleep in no time, floating serenely into a glittering pinkish dream-world of guardian sylphs and lap-dogs, ombre and billet-doux.

It was torture getting up in the morning. But Walter managed to stagger through all the hygienic formalities, plummet down to the street in the service elevator at 8:05 and be back in the office at 8:27 with his *Times*, lifesaving toasted bran muffin and coffee dark, two sugars. He half-dozed at his desk until ten a.m., when he could no longer keep his eyes open. So he gave Wilma the old excuse about business in another department, shuffled to the men's room, locked himself in his favorite stall, and fell asleep. At noon, a boisterous group of workers came in to wash their hands and awakened him.

In the dining room, Walter was in no mood for talk. Marty Shaw took a seat opposite him and announced that Raymond Lang was out with the flu, which Walter acknowledged with a porcine grunt. Irwin Kemp, spying the vacancy from his nearby table, picked up his plates and came over smiling. Just as he sat down, in walked Charlie Phelps. Lovely, thought Walter.

Phelps was seemingly undaunted by yesterday's encounter; he wore a parturient expression, as though he were about to begin a new gambit. "Well," he said, "the old genius has done it again."

"Gee," Irwin said, "you mean you found your way down here aw by your iddy biddy self?"

Phelps ignored Irwin. "What is it, Charlie?" Shaw said.

"Let me begin by asking: what's the one thing most families have in common?"

"Bills?" said Shaw.

"Togetherness?" said Kemp.

"No, you asses. *Kids.* Loads of kids they have. And what does every father have on his mind when he has a new little kid?"

"Bills?" said Kemp.

"Putting him through college?" Shaw said, with caution.

"Give that man sixty four thousand dollars," Phelps said, motioning with his pipe stem. "So here's my idea. Am I right in saying that it's a natural link: kids-college, college-kids?"

Kemp's mind raced for a wisecrack, but Phelps followed up quickly. "Here's the gimmick. We, the Security Insurance Company, get in touch with one of those big companies that makes baby layettes and things. You know; what every family buys for a new baby. And we and them figure out a tie-in."

"A what?" said Shaw.

"A tie-in, a cooperative sales promotion," Phelps said, biting his pipe stem. "My idea is this. Inside every one of those layettes we put a small SIC certificate; not an insurance policy, but a certificate that *looks* like one.

If the parents send in the certificate and let's say a one dollar premium, it pays for a small endowment policy in the kid's name. Not for much, maybe worth fifty bucks when the kid's eighteen and ready for college."

"That won't even pay for his freshman beanie," Kemp said.

"That's not the point, idiot. The kid's on our *books*, got it? We've got a record of him. So we let the local SIC agent deliver the policy. Half of those damn agents are scared shitless to knock on somebody's door. That's their biggest obstacle. Hearing the word 'no' murders 'em. This'll give them *confidence*, because for once they're giving something, not selling it. So they visit the home. They deliver the policy for the kid's stinky little endowment. Then, once they're in the door, they begin to talk it up, and *anything* can happen."

"Especially if the wife's home alone," Kemp said.

Unheeding and elated, Phelps continued, "Once he's in the door, all *kinds* of opportunities pop up. More college insurance on the kid. A mortgage policy for the house. *Anything.* It opens up a whole new horizon; don't you guys see it?"

Walter didn't want to see or hear anything. He rushed through his meal so he could doze for a while in the lounge. Shaw, absentmindedly curling a few strands of spaghetti on his fork, nodded agreement with Phelps.

"Say Charlie," Irwin said. "You know those little machines they got in men's room all over?"

"The hand dryers?"

"No, the ones that say, 'If the presence of this machine offends you, visit our state insane asylums or institutions.'"

"Oh, you mean the ..."

"Right. We can make a tie-in there, too. We put a tiny certificate in each package of rubbers, right? Maybe we could call it SIC's New Double Protection Policy. If the thing breaks and a kid's born, at least he's insured, right?"

"You Actually Live Here?"

1

Two days later, after work on Friday afternoon, Walter waited for Scarlett at the entrance to a parking lot near the SIC building. He felt a bit sheepish about suggesting the semi-clandestine rendezvous, but he knew that a great swarm of rumors would arise in the ennui-ridden office if he were to nonchalantly take Scarlett's arm and walk out the door with her. Except for a frequent exchange of surreptitious smiles and winks, plus a few scribbled communiqués via the intra-company mail system, they had said nothing to each other since last Saturday morning in front of the library.

Since then, of course, Walter had paid his visit to Stormy and now, as he waited, he wondered how this would affect his future relations with Scarlett. Wondered, because Walter was not one to plunge recklessly into a state of mind without first wriggling his toes about to test the temperature.

Try as he might, Walter suffered no knot of agonizing guilt over his mid-week spree, yet he knew that, in a sense, he had betrayed Scarlett. To feel guilty or not, then, was the question. Walter arrived at a verdict via a rather circuitous route of rationalizations. First, who was Stormy but a companion in time of need? Theirs was a friendship, not a love affair. After all, he told himself, his feelings towards Scarlett transcended mere sensuality. She was the first girl, the very first, with whom he could honestly say he was in love.

But Walter had no way of knowing how *she* felt towards *him*, and he feared that rushing things, clumsily pawing her, would frighten her away. Perhaps his night with Stormy (he liked to think of it as his Stormy Interlude) had netted a good result after all. Now, he told himself, with his Heavy Bear sated on Stormy's convertible couch, he could approach Scarlett on a more ethereal plane; his overtures toward her could be inspired by motives higher than his belt buckle.

When Scarlett crossed the street toward him, her golden pony tail bouncing playfully as she ran to beat the changing traffic light, he strode out to meet her, wearing his best smile, feeling pure as a young lad with the Communion wafer stuck to his palate; yet his knees trembled with apprehension over what the evening held in store for them.

"Well, stranger, long time no see," she said, wrinkling her nose and squinting into the sunlight which poured over his shoulder. Palm outstretched, she held out the ignition keys, like a little girl offering a gumdrop to her kindergarten beau.

As the car inched along in tedious downtown traffic, they entertained each other with the trivia of the past week. In a few minutes they reached the suburbia-bound highway where the going was less congested, but still heavy; a mile-long caravan of metal creatures bearing their masters homeward.

"I wouldn't take a house in the suburbs if they gave me one," he said. "Can you imagine fighting this traffic every day?"

"That's treasonous talk for a SIC executive," she said with a wink and a kidding tone.

"There you go, generalizing again," he said. It disturbed Walter that Scarlett should, even when joking, group him with the other executives. He wanted so much to tell her how different he was; how he was planning to escape from it all. But when, where and how could he ever begin to explain it?

They found a comfortable looking roadside restaurant and were soon seated opposite each other in a booth by the window, sipping cocktails while their entrees were being prepared.

"Excuse me for staring," he said, "but I missed you."

"What'd you do all week," she asked.

"Think about you."

"My, aren't we getting romantic."

Walter felt empty after that bit of wordplay, which he'd been rehearsing all week. And somewhat foolish, too, because he hadn't the vaguest idea of how she felt about him. He picked up the newspaper at his side and unfolded it atop the table.

"Let's see where there's a good movie," he said, turning to the Amusements Page. "Look, there's a revival of *On The Waterfront*."

"Is that the one with Brando?"

"You've seen it?"

"No, I missed that one."

"It's great. I saw it when it first came out. It won an Academy Award, I think. At least it should have."

"Where's it playing?"

"The drive-in on Route twenty two."

"Oh."

"Anything wrong with that?"

"A drive-in's not exactly the best place to enjoy a movie."

"Really? I've never been to one."

"Either you're the smoothest operator that ever lived, or you've just dropped in for a short visit from Venus."

"*Honest.* I told you, I don't own a car."

"You've *never* been to a drive-in? Ever?"

"Cross my heart."

"My God, where have you *been* all these years? Do you know what most people go to drive-ins for?"

"Well, I've heard … you mean …"

"*Yes*. The one you refer to on Route twenty two is popularly known as 'The Passion Pit.'"

"Scarlett, I didn't know, or at least I didn't think … look, if you prefer going to see some other picture, I mean, in a *real* theatre, we can look—"

"No, that's all right. I think it'll be fun taking you to your first drive-in." She lifted her glass in a toast, "to your first drive-in."

"And to *our* first together," he added, lifting his glass.

2

A full-four-course dinner and three cocktails later, they drove up to the drive-in ticket booth and Walter paid the attendant. He switched down to his parking lights in compliance with the sign posted at the entrance and edged slowly into the immense dark plain. Hundreds of cars rested on dirt embankments, looking like rows of low-trajectory missiles tilted towards the screen, where a gigantic cat chased after a nearly-as-gigantic mouse in startling Technicolor.

They drove slowly along the outer aisle for a few rows. Scarlett pointed. "Look, there's a good space right in the center, and far back." Walter turned in, maneuvered the car between two other vehicles, rolled up onto the mound, and right down the other side. Grinning, he put it in reverse and backed it up on the hump of packed gravel.

"Three-point landing," she said. "Now, take that speaker out there on the pole … that's it, and hang it on the inside of the window." Walter fixed the speaker, raised the window, adjusted the volume and settled back, trying to find space for his feet between the clutch, brake, and gas pedal.

They sat in silence, watching the cartoon, then several commercials by local merchants, then a newsreel, first about how a new sensation—Barbie Dolls—was sweeping the country and drawing long lines at department stores, and then dramatic first pictures of Earth taken by the Explorer VI satellite.

Then it showed President Eisenhower playing golf, while Vice President Nixon received Fidel Castro, the young Cuban rebel leader. There had been rumors that Castro was a flirting with the Soviet Union, but Nixon assured a crowd of reporters that, while Castro was "naïve," he was "not necessarily a Communist."

Scarlett sat well over on her side, intently watching the screen. Walter wanted to put his arm around her, but didn't dare. He glanced at the car next to him. There appeared that no one was inside it, although he'd sworn he'd seen two heads when they pulled up. In the car on Scarlett's side, he thought he glimpsed a bobbing male head, but he wasn't sure.

Floodlights ringing the field blazed on, and the screen flashed a series of slides advertising candy and refreshments.

"I could go for a Coke, Scarlett. How about you?"

"Okay. It's in that low building up front towards the center. See the light?"

"I'll find it."

Trotting between the cars, Walter came close to garroting himself on a speaker wire, but he soon learned to hug the right side of each car, where there were no obstructions, and reached the snack center, with no further mishap. It was a chaos of children and adults storing up on popcorn, ice cream, soda and beer. After fifteen minutes of elbowing his way to the counter, he finally got two waxed cup containers of soda and emerged perspiring from the snack center.

He meandered in a half-right direction towards the car. There were dozens of cars that resembled Scarlett's and he peeked into them all, only to find them either empty or occupied by shiny-faced couples with mussed hair and wrinkled clothes, smoking cigarettes and apparently marking time until the lights were dimmed again. Finally, he spotted the car and yes, there was Scarlett inside. He opened the door and collapsed into the seat.

"God, what a time I had," he said.

The girl, a plump creature with a page boy cut and menacing dental braces, broke into a piercing scream, as though she'd just been accosted by a bloodthirsty band of Huns. A heavy hand reached inside the car window, gripped his shoulder and screwed the padding of his suit jacket into a deformed lump. It took Walter a few touch and go moments to placate the fellow, a cretinous six-footer with a varsity football sweater, but he finally beat a hasty, thankful retreat, letting the girl's cry of, "old lecher!" roll off his back as he scooted away.

The lights dimmed and the credits for *On The Waterfront* began rolling over the screen. Walter continued zig-zagging all over the lot, spying briefly upon one blood-boiling tableau after another until at last, his soda cups half empty and leaking steadily from their bottoms, he found the car, looked inside first to double-check, and sat down in the driver's seat with a sigh.

"Next time I'll stay thirsty," he said. Scarlett laughed so loud when she heard what had happened that there was a cry of protest from a nearby car, where it seemed someone was actually watching the picture.

They settled back to finish off the little of the remaining Coca-Cola and watch the film, but Scarlett kept erupting into fits of muffled giggles. Walter's arm slithered over towards her, then he shifted his body to her side and soon they were snuggled together, watching Marlon Brando get acquainted with Eva Marie Saint.

He kept stealing quick looks at her. She was enrapt in the picture; her face, silvered by the screen, was beautiful in profile; the tiny upturned nose, the wide open eyes staring ahead, the brushed back golden hair. Like a young goddess captured in marble. He wanted to lean over and kiss her, but he felt wary of upsetting things, so he simply squeezed his arm a little tighter around her and nuzzled his nose into her hair.

It began to rain. First in slow syrupy drops, which splotched the windshield, then in a steady torrent. Walter tried the wipers, but it was necessary to turn the motor on. Rain splashed in the windows, and he closed them tight. In ten minutes, with the motor running and the windows closed, it was uncomfortably stuffy and they were perspiring.

"God, it's hot in here," she said.

"We either suffer or turn off the motor and listen to the sound," he said.

In one fluid, graceful motion, Scarlett shut off the motor and turned to him, her eyes glowing. The windows immediately clouded over with steam and vibrant rivulets of rain.

How little we know of each other, Walter thought, how little we really know, as he pulled Scarlett close and felt the faint flutter of her heart and the wetness of her lips.

The screen was a dull white rectangle outside the fogged windshield and the rest of the world around them was an impenetrable gray mass, as though they were all alone, miles from anywhere or anyone. After several minutes, Walter dared and his heart raced faster as her thighs parted to welcome his timid, searching hand. The next few moments were like a wild dream as Scarlett moaned and writhed, seizing him tightly and releasing him, arching herself forward as he balanced her soft bottom in his palm. She pulled away with the roar of several hundred motors starting up.

The movie was over and the cars began to file out. They sat still, hugging each other, their hearts thumping violently, watching the parade of passing headlights. Walter moved back to his side of the seat, turned the key and they rolled into line.

3

Getting a room at the Garden State Motel on Route 22 was easier than Walter had anticipated. Inside the office, the bored clerk collected eight dollars in advance, gave Walter the key and pointed towards the cabin down at the far end, without so much as looking outside at Scarlett. Walter had been unsure when he first turned off the highway and up the drive to the motel; he would have zoomed right by and back onto the road had she offered the slightest objection, but she said nothing, simply staring ahead, her face flushed, her parted lips showing the glint of her white teeth.

But once inside the room Scarlett's features turned wooden and she eyed him stealthily as he turned on the bedside lamp. She sat in a corner chair; Walter sat down on the bed and looked at her.

"What's the matter?" he said, unsure of himself.

"It's no good."

"But why?"

"Twice we've gone out. Just twice. How do I know who you really are?"

"What do you mean *who*? You work right in the same office with me."

"I mean, who are you really? What am I to you? Just some weekend pickup? God, how do I know for sure you aren't married? How do I know? Why did I have to drop you off at the library last Saturday? Were you afraid your wife would be looking out the window if I took you to your door?"

Walter shook his head. How ridiculous this all seemed.

"Maybe you think I'm being silly," she said. It was *uncanny* the way she deciphered his thoughts. "But a woman's love is all she really has to offer, and I don't believe in just throwing it around."

"Scarlett, do you see a wedding band on my finger?"

"How do I know you don't take it off?"

"You mean I take it off when I go to work, too?"

"Oh, I don't know," she said, lowering her head and shaking it from side to side. "I just don't know."

He reached out for her hand. "C'mon."

"Where?"

"I wanna show you something."

4

Half an hour later, they staggered up the deserted downtown Newark street, bent over against the chilly air currents that rushed between the tall buildings. Only the staccato of Scarlett's high heels punctuated the whistle of the wind.

"Where are you taking me?" she yelled.

"You'll see in a minute!"

The wind was like buckets of ice water in their faces. They came up to the SIC building, which towered ominously above them, disappearing into the black sky.

"Walter! This is the office!"

"You should've majored in geography!" he said, pulling her by the hand towards the side entrance.

"But Walter, we can't ..."

"Shhhhhhh!" he said, holding a finger to his mouth. He fumbled for his key to the door. In a wink they were inside; he tip-toed and held a finger to his pursed lips; she tittered and followed him. They took the service elevator up to the thirteenth floor. The door slid open.

"*Wal*-ter, this is ...." she held back, standing in the elevator car. "It's *dark* in here."

The moon silvered the floor and made frightening silhouettes of the furniture. Walter pulled her by the hand as they skipped past black desks which squatted like quadruped icons. They went into his office and he closed the drapes and blinds. Then he flicked on the neon desk lamp, turned to her, made a sweeping low bow and flourished his hand theatrically.

"Welcome, mademoiselle, to my humble abode."

She laughed, although puzzled.

"You doubt me, fair maiden?" Holding the key like a delicate teacup, pinkie finger extended, he slipped it into the master lock on the wall, gave it a turn and the bed groaned downward to the floor. He screwed on the two support legs at the foot of the bed, and stood up, arms out wide like a magician at the completion of a trick.

"My *God*." Scarlett stood there, bug-eyed.

Walter opened a bedside file drawer and took out his transistor radio. The sugary strains of a Strauss waltz filled the room.

"With your permission," he said, loosening his tie. He took off his coat and jacket, and put them on the desk. Arms outstretched, he fell backwards, athwart the bed, and expired a loud sigh. "Ah, what a relief to get home and relax."

Scarlett stared at him. "This—this is—you mean ... you actually *live* here?"

"I know the Chrysler Building is a fancier address, but I expect my friends to take me for what I am."

"My God." Scarlett exclaimed, "you *are* like Walter Mitty, with a secret life. But yours is *for real*." She began to sputter, then broke into laughter. She walked around the room, bent over, holding her sides. And Walter thought it funny, too. He lay back cackling, holding *his* sides. Then, as another waltz began on the radio, he bolted upright, walked to the door, and motioned towards the giant outer office.

"This, mademoiselle, is my ballroom." He held out his arm. "May I have the honor of this dance?"

Scarlett dropped her coat on the desk, curtsied and took his arm. He rested the radio on Wilma Tannenbaum's desk and turned it up full volume. It was playing Straus' *Southern Roses*, and Walter thought he recognized Carmen Cavallero's hand at the piano. Walter had once received a twenty-minute lesson in the waltz from a girl at his high school prom, and he also remembered seeing some MGM musical showing a distinguished looking couple waltzing around in a giant, empty ballroom. But somehow, as if by total recall, when he held Scarlett and took the first step, he knew what to do about the second step and the next and so on; as though he could visualize that tuxedoed smoothie in the MGM musical and match every movement.

They glided along the floor which was a shimmering wafer in the moonlight. Around a mammoth pillar, around the battalion of desks, past the photocopying machine which looked like an overgrown pelican with its top lid ajar, past the waist-high trash basket, the stenographic recording machines, the water cooler, the paper cutter, coming together and brushing their lips, then parting, then spinning around and finally completing the orbit back to the desk; where Walter scooped up the radio like a brass ring on a merry-go-round and led Scarlett back into the office, revolving in circles, faster and faster. They collapsed upon the bed in a rumpled heap, gasping for breath.

The radio was now playing *Voices of Spring* and their hearts beat like trip-hammers as they looked into each other's flushed faces. Walter saw in her eyes that now, it was all right. He lowered the volume of the radio, rose and flicked off the desk lamp. He padded back to the bed, kicked off his shoes, lay down and reached over for her.

"Just what the hell do you think you're doing?" she said, looking and sounding testy. She was standing by the desk where she had just flicked the light back on.

"I was tired and thought I'd catch some sleep," he said, lying on his back and wondering how the hell she'd got over there so quickly.

"Nothing else?" she said, raising an eyebrow.

"No, nothing else."

She pointed a finger at him with her other hand on her hip. "I think you're expecting something, and you're pretty wrong if you think what I *think* you're thinking."

"What do *you* think I'm thinking?"

Her eyebrows knitted and her finger wagged at him. "You know *exactly* what I think you're thinking."

"The only thing I'm thinking is that the light annoys me and that it would be easier to sleep without it."

"Well, if you're so *tired*, I wish you'd show me the way out here so I can go home." She was leaning against the desk for support.

"Let's talk then, okay? But for God's sake, put the light out." He was surprised when she obeyed and came back to the bed.

"Now," she said, standing over him, both hands on her hips. "What would you like to talk about?" She had needed just one final spark of rebellion, but when Walter reached his arms out towards her, she didn't say another word.

A Rich Beatnick

Three hours later, the all-night disc jockey had slipped into a Shearing mood. Walter and Scarlett nestled together, sleepless, listening to the muted gurglings of the radio. She hummed the tune and ran her lips over his chest. He rested on his back, caressing the small of hers, and stared at the dark ceiling. He was deliciously happy. Now she knew, he thought, now she knew that he *was* different from the others. At last *someone* knew. His heart opened to her now, and suddenly he wanted to tell her every detail of his life.

"I remember back in high school," he said. "The biggest dream in my head was to get a steady, decent-paying job. But the Army changed me. It gave me twenty pounds, but it took away all my ambition. Maybe it was the dull security of three meals a day and all expenses paid; or maybe it was the crazy bunch of characters I met: engineering students, card sharps, accountants, professional unemployment collectors, truck drivers. Anyway, when I got out I'd learned there was more than one way to skin that cat named life … that's what one colored fellow in my unit always used to say. Funny thing, though, right after the service, the first thing I do is begin to study Business Administration on the G.I. Bill. But after a year of college, even though it was free, I got disgusted and quit to take a job. Then another job. And another. Funny, when I *had* a job, that's when I felt like rebelling and leaving, to be free. And when I *didn't* have a job, I would reach out frantically to get one."

She stroked his chest, toying with his hairs. "You were struggling against your middle class heritage."

Walter felt like telling her to cut out the sociology crap, but they had just finished making love and he had read or heard somewhere that women were in a hyper-delicate mood at this point and required an undiluted diet of affection and tenderness. So he sublimated his urge, giving her buttocks a fierce, but affectionate, squeeze.

"After a year with the company," he said, "just when I was fed up and ready to quit, the director died and I was promoted to manager. It made me ambitious. But in a few months it dawned on me that Mister Furey was only in his late thirties, so I'd be stuck in the same job for the rest of my life. I thought about moving to another company, but they're all the same, aren't they? I finally decided the only answer was to retire. After thinking about it for six months, I had it all figured out. I would live in the company building and save on rent, most of my food and all of my utilities. I remembered seeing one of those wall beds in a boarding house not far from here, so I made a sketch of how it worked. I smuggled a bed up in the service elevator one midnight. I'd stolen a key to the service entrance and had duplicates made. Then I borrowed tools from the janitorial department. I ripped out a space in the wall two file drawers wide and five high. Then I sawed off the drawer fronts and screwed them to the bottom of the bed. I worked out the movable parts with some old door springs, and I put up a broomstick inside the space to hang my clothes. Then I checked the evening cleanup crew's schedule; they were always finished up by seven-thirty in the evening. I tried it out on and off for a few weeks, just to see how it worked before I gave up my apartment and moved in. That was a little more than nine years ago."

"And no one has ever discovered the bed?"

"This wall had the old records no one ever needs; from 1883 to 1919. I've got the only key and I never let anyone but myself open the drawers. I told Mister Furey it was best that way, so we wouldn't lose any of our valuable old files. I just emptied out some of the drawers for my personal things and threw out lots of stuff that wasn't important. For example, who cares about 1904 anyway, right?"

"It's just fantastic Walter. But all this effort of yours ... is it working?"

"Well, I've been living on about thirty dollars a week for the past few years, and banking or investing between eighty and one hundred dollars from this job alone ...."

"From *this* job?"

"Oh yes, I also work—or at least I'm on the payroll—downstairs in MAD. I figured out that gimmick about five years ago. So that's an extra fifty dollars a week for five years in the kitty. Oh, and I've been investing in the stock market, and rare stamps, too, and doing pretty well."

"It's just too ... and you mean you've never told anyone before?"

"It hasn't been too hard to keep it a secret because I've kept to myself pretty much all these years; almost like a hermit in the city. Then you came along and, well, those things you asked me in the diner last Saturday, I just couldn't let you go on thinking that I was like the rest of the people here in the company. I mean, your opinion is *important* to me. Anyway, I think it's about time to cash in and start living. I've just about reached my goal. Nearly a hundred fifty thousand."

Scarlett was amazed. *"A hundred fifty thousand?"*

"Until now I had no reason to cash it in. The truth is, I've been pretty comfortable living like this. I've actually grown accustomed to it. But now, knowing you, I don't want to go on like this alone. With just the *interest* on my money I can live comfortably; I've got it figured out to the penny.

"But what will you do if you don't work; be a rich beatnik?"

"A *beatnik*. Me? Ha! The *real* beatniks are the slobs who stay in this company. What is a beatnik anyway? I once read a definition which said: 'a person who has given up on life, who refuses to compete in society, who retreats to the safety of inaction.'"

"You're forgetting the beards and smelly T-shirts," she said.

"That's just window dressing. I'm talking about the so-called beat attitude. Believe me, these white collar people have got it. First, how could anyone who *hasn't* given up on life decide to stay here? Where the hell's the taste, the *adventure* of life? It's so safe and sterile in here you couldn't even catch a cold. They hire you and you could practically set fire to the president's office—or take a crap on his desk—before they'd sack you. You sit there mothered and smothered by the good old company through sickness and health; your social affairs arranged, your lunches free, your insurance paid for. And when they're done with you, they pat you on your gray head, nudge your creaking carcass out the door and send you a pension check. Is that a life? It's *worse* than being a beatnik. At least a beatnik—the one with the smelly T-shirt—at least he *smells* life. You know what I smell in this building? Formaldehyde, that's what. This is a goddamned fourteen story ...," he snorted in contempt, "... charnel house."

Walter stroked her back, moved her off to the side, got up and stalked to his desk. He put the lamp on and held up a stack of papers. "Paper. Paper carries some of the greatest thoughts ever created by man. But *these* papers? Know what these are? This is the heroin of the white collar worker. A fellow sits down with a pile of papers in the morning and turns himself on. Hour after hour, thumbing through the pile, numbing himself into nothingness with ciphers and plus and minus signs."

He lit a Pall Mall and flicked off the lamp. Then he lay back down in the bed, a red beacon in the darkness. "I suffered through all this for nearly eleven years because I had a goal. 'Security' isn't a dirty word. There's nothing evil about knowing where your next meal's coming from. But God, it's evil to pay such a price for it; to rent your body and a corner of your brain for the privilege of living out your life in pensioned peace."

She steadied his wrist with her hand and took a drag on the cigarette.

"I thought you didn't smoke," he said.

"I don't, usually. But one tastes good at a time like this."

"What was that a fellow once said? 'The three best things in life are a martini before and a cigarette after."

"You," she squealed, mussing his hair.

He chuckled and took a deep drag.

"You still didn't answer my question."

"What question?"

89

"About what you're going to do if you don't work."

"I know what I *won't* do. I'll never be a worker ant like these people. What has society done in the last century? It lifts the masses from the muck of ignorance, feeds them enough know-how to keep the machines running and to get the reports filed and then drops them into the mire of organizations and systems. In nature, a worker ant is stuck for life, but one advantage of being human is that if you've got enough guts—or luck—you can get out of it all. I'm getting out."

Scarlett sat up in bed. "Walter, that's absolutely ... *ahistoric.*"

"There you go with your sophomore philosophy course," he moaned, putting his hand to his head.

"But it *is.* Don't you feel as though you *owe* anything to the human race? Don't you feel part of the mainstream of history? Don't you feel any obligation to keep things going?"

"I don't *like* most of what's floating in your mainstream of history. So I'm going to sit down on the bank of that crappy old stream and *splat.* I'm going to fish out the few things that are worth hooking. Like you, for instance." He put his arms around her.

"To me that sounds like running away."

"No. To *me* it sounds like *amputation.* When I came into this world, I didn't ask for everything that was dumped into my lap. Now that I'm old enough I'm going to perform a little surgery. I want to be *free.* It's like a yoke around my neck. Systems ... forms ... reports ... if Columbus ever tried to discover America today, they'd probably send a committee ahead to draft a feasibility report."

Scarlett began to cry, soft.

"Did I say something wrong?"

"No ... it's just that I'm so happy."

"I'd hate to see you when you're blue."

"I ... I have a confession to make to you, too."

"What?"

"I ... *some* people, it doesn't make any difference to them. But people have all sorts of ideas about morals and—"

"But what *is* it?"

"Well, this may hurt you; you may not ever want to see me again, but I think it's better to tell you now. You're not the first to ... to *have* me."

He stared at the ceiling and said nothing. The silence had a ringing sound.

"Four years ago I was going steady. His name was Danny. I ... loved him very much; we were going to be married. Then he got drafted, and while he was in basic training he used to come home weekends. What wrestling matches we used to have on the living room couch after Mom and Dad went up to bed. He had his two-week leave before shipping out overseas and we ... well, I just *couldn't* deny him; he was shipping out for we didn't know how long. Then he got sent to Korea. We wrote each other twice a day. But six months later the letters stopped. Danny met someone while on leave in Tokyo and came home with a Japanese bride. That's why I left Scranton and came east."

Walter loved her even more now. His little Sociology major. He nibbled on her ear as she continued her confession in the dark. He loved her, and yet he thought it all so hilariously maudlin. He muffled the temptation to say, 'Now put a dollar in the poor box and say fifteen Hail Mary's.' Instead, he stroked her forehead, gently running his fingers through her blonde hair.

"So," she said, "it doesn't make any difference to you?" He took her in his arms.

2

When the alarm rang at seven-thirty, Scarlett started up in bed, bewildered by the strange surroundings. Though the window drapes and blinds were closed, light spilled through the door from the outer office.

"Walter," she said with a gasp, "It's *morning*."

He had never slept so well, even if it had only been two hours. He sat up and scratched his head. Then he looked at her and grinned. She covered up, ashamed of her nakedness in the morning light. He snuggled his head against her, sighed with supreme contentment and closed his eyes. She lay back, stroking his face, staring worriedly at the speckled white cork ceiling.

"If I'm caught here," she said, "I don't even want to *think* of it."

He looked up at her with one open eye. "Do you realize what day this is?"

"It's ...."

"Saturday. Unless you plan to make love with me until Monday morning, I don't think anyone will come in and catch us."

She laughed and lay back in bed. At eleven a.m., Walter said, "Boy, I could sure go for some breakfast."

"Me too."

"Let's eat in that nice diner a few blocks from here. It'll mess up my budget, but what the hell."

Wrapped communally in the white bedsheet, their clothes draped over their shoulders, they shuffled to the Executive Rest Room. "We'd better share the shower," he said as they entered. "I don't know if there's enough hot water in the heater." Half an hour later, both were fully dressed and Walter combed his hair while Scarlett applied her makeup.

At the diner, they wolfed breakfast and drank an extra cup of coffee as they talked, still caught up in the joy of their union. Scarlett was concerned that her landlord might worry about her. She lived in a rented room in a private home. She decided to call and say that she'd gotten sick at a party, slept over one of the girls' houses, and might stay the weekend.

Despite his fatigue, Walter felt as though he were eighteen years old. "Do you know what one of my greatest ambitions has been?" he said, as she sat down after the phone call.

"We will *not* try for forty-eight consecutive hours," she said, smiling.

"I've always wanted to see the inside of President Jennings' office."

3

Mister Jennings' office was on the fourteenth and uppermost floor of the SIC building. They passed through an imposing ante room, then another room for Mister Jennings' private secretary, then tried the heavy oak door leading to the innermost sanctum. It opened. There, near the window, was Mister Jennings' desk. It didn't have *anything* on top of it. Walter felt a chill race up his spine.

Mister Jennings was President of SIC, the third largest life insurance company in the world, outstripped in assets only by Megalopolitan and Providential. Mister Jennings had even been interviewed by Vance Packard, and was subsequently referred to as "an influential source in insurance circles." Once, a *Business Week* correspondent caught him in a rare jocular mood—minutes after having survived a near-collision over Idlewild while flying in from a board meeting in Chicago—and quoted him as saying, "If the three major insurance companies ever declared war upon the United States, we would win because of our superior dollar-power." Mister Jennings, even at his giddiest, was not given to wild exaggeration.

Like many of the business leaders of the epoch, Mister Jennings began as a corporate lawyer and worked his way to the top, largely because it took a legal background to comprehend the gibberish in the company's insurance policies. As President of the SIC empire, he received $450,000 a year. One uneventful day, perhaps a year ago, Walter pecked away at his adding machine and discovered an awesome statistic. Based on a five day, forty-hour week, President Jennings earned $216.32 an hour. By stealing just ten minutes for a trip to the toilet, Jennings cost the company $36.05.

With a sobering fact like this to ponder, Walter understood why *his* photo of the President was unsigned. Mister Jennings' time was so carefully plotted that he had established a strict policy of limiting autographed photos of himself to SIC senior management, presidents of companies listed in the Dow Jones Stock Average, and members of his immediate family.

Walter had never seen Mister Jennings. Nor had anyone else at his rank level; or, at least, anyone that he knew. At Christmas time, an Executive VP by the name of Alan Gibbs—the chief's personal emissary—came around to shake hands with the management folks. It was said that Mister Gibbs spent almost all of his time with the President. Each time you saw a photo of Mister Jennings in a newspaper, there, always lurking in the dotty background, was the spectral image of Mister Gibbs. Last Christmas, when Mister Gibbs came by to convey Mister Jennings' sincere Yuletide greetings, Walter was gripped by a thought-provoking insight: *I may be shaking the hand that wipes the president.* After all, he reasoned, at $36.05 every ten minutes, one can't afford to waste time.

Hand in hand, Walter and Scarlett approached the imposing desk with caution and confronted the empty leather chair. The office's oak walls were bare except for a Jacques Louis David print in a baroque gold frame to their left. Below it was a bookcase filled with leather-bound texts, one of which said, in gold letters on its spine: *"Joe Miller Jokebook for Afterdinner Speakers."* On the other side of the room was an ebony leather couch; presumably where Mister Jennings took those refreshing mid-afternoon siestas which Walter had read about in *Business Week.*

Walter inhaled deeply to steady himself. He went around to the other side of the desk and sat down in the chair. The leather squeaked some. Walter slowly opened the desk drawer. It was absolutely empty except for ... yes, that's what it was. What else could it be? He held it delicately between his thumb and forefinger, as though it were a precious pre-Colombian relic, and examined it. Just an ordinary Yo-Yo, painted canary yellow and chipped in a few spots. He took care in putting it back.

Looking up, he saw a small door at the opposite end of the room, adjacent to the entrance. He went over and opened it. Mister Jennings' personal bathroom, gleaming with porcelain, chromium and emerald green tiles.

"Excuse me a minute, Scarlett."

Walter went in, as though entering a shrine. Here, he realized was the sanctum where President Jennings cost the company $36.05 for each ten-minute retreat. Walter's theoretical ramblings were now face to face with reality. He noticed a curious apparatus embedded in the wall next to the roll of tissue. There was a row of buttons and a microphone suspended from a hook. He took the mike in his hand and pushed a button labeled "playback." First there was a goofy Donald-Duck-ish garble. Then out came the voice of President Jennings, with occasional thunderclaps in the background.

"Letter to Emil Walker, sales director, Los Angeles regional office. Dear Emil: I note with pleasure that your area's whole life sales over the past three months have increased six point three percent ...." He pushed the "dictate" button. Holding the mike to his mouth, Walter bellowed in a magisterial tone, "Charon! Charon Franklin Jennings! This is God speaking. Keep up the fine work; and persevere at your Yo-Yo, Charon. We're well stocked on executives, but a good Yo-Yoer is hard to find. Bless you. Over and out."

Going down in the elevator, Scarlett turned to Walter with a puzzled expression. "They'll never believe this in my Masters thesis."

4

It was a balmy day. They strolled along the downtown streets, hand in hand. As they sat on a bench in Military Park, Scarlett was full of questions about the future.

"And where after England?"

"France, probably. Then maybe we'll take a look at Italy for a year or two."

"A *year* or two? Won't we lose our citizenship just bobbing around the world like that?"

"Citizenship, schmitizenship. This world would be better without governments."

"*Some*body's got to run things, Walter."

"Run what? Wars? Know what I'd do if I had the power? I'd get rid of *all* governments. I'd replace them with people just to run the really important things. Like garbage disposal. Do you realize how miserable it would be without garbage men? They're the most important people we've got. I wouldn't have presidents. I'd have a *garbage man* as leader of each country. There'd be elections for Head Garbageman, then Vice Garbageman, and so on. They could pick a cabinet; one man to head the highway department, one to head the light company, one for the water company, then a few others for things like phones and trains. After that, who needs anything? Who needs Defense Departments and all that other jazz? Just take away my garbage and leave me alone."

"You're kidding me, as usual."

"I'm dead serious." He stood up on the park bench, raised his fist in the air and shouted, "Down with government! Up with garbage!"

A woman wheeling a baby carriage looked at him and scurried away. Scarlett pulled him down.

They loafed all afternoon, then took in a movie at the RKO Proctor's and went to bed early. Sunday morning, they got up and went out for breakfast. Afterwards, since Scarlett had a few things to do at home, Walter walked her to her car, which was parked a block away. She poked her head out the window and blew him a kiss.

"Up with garbage!" she shouted, waving to him as she pulled away.

A Strange Itching Sensation

1

At the public library on Monday evening, Walter felt a strange itching sensation in his crotch area. Reaching under the reading table, he scratched a few times. But it persisted. It was maddening; almost as though something were biting him. Then it hit him: *Damn. Stormy and the Merchant Mariner.* Trying to look nonchalant, he strolled into the men's room. Two minutes later, he bolted outside, past the surprised check-out clerk, and down the block to a pharmacy.

A middle-aged woman was making a purchase. Walter browsed impatiently at the pocket novel rack. When she left, he approached the counter and whispered to the druggist, a bent old man with scrotal jowls.

"What do you have for ... er, body lice?"

"*For* 'em, or *against* 'em?" the old man said, breaking into a phlegmy cackle. "You mean *crabs*, dontcha?"

Walter looked around, and put his finger to his mouth, to shhhhh him.

Gravely, the old man nodded his understanding, reached beneath the counter and produced a small orange-colored cardboard container with blue printing that read, *"Thompson's Blue Ointment"*. On the back side it had a drawing of a multi-pincered nightmare which was identified as: *"Body Louse (Pubic Pediculi), Enlarged 16 Times."*

At the office the next day, feeling raw but relieved, Walter carried some correspondence over to the filing section. Scarlett was seated at her corner desk, typing address labels between furtive swipes at her privates.

"Oh no," Walter moaned. He scribbled a brief note and slipped it in front of her: "Urgent! Tonite. Library, 9 p.m."

She came into the reading room at eight forty five p.m., a troubled look clouding her face. "Can't stay long," she whispered. "Must get back home early tonight." She scratched herself under the table.

"Why? Feeling itchy?"

She turned crimson.

"Look, darling, don't be ashamed. That's why I called you. There's such a thing called body lice—""Shhhhhhhhh!" hissed a toothless old man at the far end of the table, glaring from behind his *National Geographic.*

Walter whispered into her ear, "There's such a thing called *body lice* ...."

She drew away from him, seeming on the verge of hysteria. He seized her arm and pulled her close.

"Don't panic," he hissed. "I must've got 'em somewhere. Sometimes you can catch them off *toilet seats*, even. Then, when we were *together*, I guess you caught them from me."

Scarlett looked bewildered. A tear welled at her left duct.

"Listen, I'm *cured* already. Take this bottle." He slipped it into her hand. "It's half full; just follow the directions and you'll be okay in the morning."

The tear rolled down her cheek.

"It's *nothing*, honey. You'll be rid of them by tomorrow. I promise. Did you use the girls' room in the office?" She nodded, her chin trembling.

"My God, I used the men's' room, too. The whole *department* will have them. Look, from now on use the girls' room downstairs until we're sure the place is clean." Suddenly, he remembered his visit to President Jennings' private chamber. He tried to think of some way to warn the poor Chief Exec, but it was useless. He held Scarlett's chin and looked into her moist eyes. She scratched herself again.

"I'm sorry, honey," he whispered. "But I didn't know. Cheer up, they'll be gone tomorrow. C'mon, I'll walk you to your car."

2

It was ten p.m. when Walter went up to his room. Inspired by his daemon, and some verses of Robert Service he'd read that evening, he lugged Wilma Tannenbaum's typewriter into his office and rested it upon his desk. He pulled down the bed and hung up his jacket and pants. In his shirt, shorts and socks, he sat awaiting the Muse.

Half an hour later, Walter jumped when all the lights in the big office outside went on. He scrambled to the bed and pushed it up into the wall. There were footsteps. "My pants!" he yelped, panic-stricken. *No time.* He ran behind the desk, sat down and continued pecking at the machine, his bare knees trembling.

A man peeked in.

"Yes?"

"Oh, hi. I'm Bill Ryan from the eleventh floor. I heard the noise while I was out in the hall and got curious 'cause I know there's no night shift up here. They got you at the grindstone, too, eh?" He smiled, puffing on a pipe.

"Yes," Walter said. "I've got a rush report that must be ready in the morning."

"Say, haven't I seen you someplace before?"

"I don't know."

"I work in the MAD nightshift downstairs. I could swear I've seen you eating in the cafeteria with us."

"I eat there once in a while if I'm working late."

"Oh, that must be it. Say, are you Mister Mott?"

"That's right." Walter's knees were really trembling.

"Then you're my *boss*. I read all your circular letters. Gee, it's a pleasure to meet you." The man came close to the desk and extended his hand. Walter remained seated with a limp smile and offered his hand, which the man took and wrung with vigor.

"I've worked in MAD for four years now and this is the first time I've ever met you. Funny world, eh?"

"Yes, very funny."

Walter looked with alarm at his bed, which was sticking out of the wall about an inch. He hadn't had time to lock it. A tug on a certain file drawer handle and it would come down. The man looked around the office.

"Boy, look at all these files." He walked along the wall, reading the labels. "1910 … 1908 … 1895 … *1883*." His voice elevated with excitement. "Say, that's the year the company was founded."

At any moment he would touch something. Walter, panicking, got up, walked around the desk and right past the man, out to Wilma's desk. He opened a drawer, took some carbon paper and started back to his desk, passing in front of the man, who gaped at his gray and white striped boxer shorts and blue socks.

"I needed some carbon paper," Walter said over his shoulder. He stopped, looked down at himself and faced the man. "Oh, excuse me; I always work better in my undies. Feels lots more comfy. You should try it sometime," he said, raising an eyebrow. "It's *mar*-velous." He minced back to the desk and sat down. The man edged backwards towards the door.

"Going so soon?" Walter said in a lilt.

"Well, uh, I'm on my ten-minute break. Gotta get back … or they'll come looking for me."

"Give my best to all the boys," Walter said, winking.

The man was gone. Dank with perspiration, Walter rushed to the bed, pulled out his pants, put them on and locked the bed tight in case the man came back. Then, back to his daemon. Three hours later, after hunt-and-pecking a clean original and two carbons, Walter put the original manuscript into a large manila envelope, addressed it and dropped it into his "Out" box.

3

In the morning, Walter searched for signs of scratching among the employees. Nothing. Perhaps they were still in the incubation period. He walked over to Scarlett's desk and felt relieved when she looked up and lifted the corners of her mouth in a quick, private smile. He left some papers with her and slipped a small note on top of the pile: *"Important business tonite. See you tomorrow, 8 p.m. Library. Movie later? Love, William Shakespeare."*

Walter went to one of his banks at noontime and withdrew $300 in clean, slick hundred dollar bills. Tonight would probably be the last time he ever saw Stormy again, and he wanted to leave her something as a token of his appreciation. After the library that night, and after his usual coffee and English muffin at the diner, Walter went to the Latin Casino. Stormy wasn't there. In fact, the place was deserted except for Jimmy, the owner, who was wiping glasses while he watched Johnny Ray singing, *"The Little White Cloud That Cried"* on TV mounted on the back wall.

"Have you seen Stormy?"

"Whatcha wanner for?" Jimmy said, in his frog-croaky voice.

"Just want to talk to her. You remember seeing me here before, right?"

"Oh yeah, now I remember ya, pal. Stormy wuz in here 'bout half hour ago. She was by her lonesome, den in comes dis guy who looks like a good touch. Buys tree, maybe four rounds, dey talk and out da door day goes. Maybe she left him carry her *books* home," Jimmy said, cockling half of his face in an exaggerated slow-motion wink.

Walter thanked Jimmy and headed for Stormy's place a few blocks away. He *had* to see her tonight. He might be too busy the other nights before he left. He came to the building, a scarred, three-story brownstone, and opened the hall door. After the crisp evening breeze, the thick, cooking fat-saturated air was suffocating. He walked up the narrow, dark stairway and found her door; a pale light shone from below it. He tiptoed up, pressed his ear against the door and listened for a few seconds. Nothing. He tapped on the door. It creaked open a few inches and Stormy peeked out.

"Honey. Whatcha doin' here?" she whispered, surprised.

He slipped in, closed the door behind him and began to speak, when he heard the toilet roar like Niagara. Stormy raised her finger to her lips and frantically looked about for a place to hide him. She pointed at the open cardboard wardrobe in the corner and herded him inside before he could protest. Just as she shut the door behind him there was a voice from the bathroom, slightly echoed by the tiles.

"What was that?"

"Nothin' honey. I'm just openin' up the bed."

"Could you dim the light a little? I'm coming out."

"Don' tell me you're bashful, a big man like you," she said in her best ante-bellum accent. "Okay honey. I'll put it out. But you leave the light in the john so's we can *find* each other, huh?"

The living room lamp went out. Walter peeked through the quarter-inch opening of the door. He caught a glimpse of a fat man in boxer shorts barefooting his way towards the couch. Walter decided to make himself comfortable. He settled back and nearly yelped aloud as a spiked heel dug into his rump. Slowly, he dislodged the shoe and sat down on the floor of the wardrobe. He was still wearing his overcoat and hat and felt soaked with perspiration. He removed his hat and fanned the hot air in his face.

The bedsprings groaned. There was silence for several minutes, except for the sporadic squeak of a spring, or the rustle of the sheets.

"Gee, I'm sorry," the man said. "I don't know what it is, but I can't seem to ...."

"That's okay, honey," Stormy purred. "We got *plenny* o' time, y'hear? Relax. Jus' relax. Say, wouldja like a little drink first? Sorta t' warm ya up?"

"Maybe that'd be a good idea."

He heard Stormy pad by, click on the tiny kitchenette light, get some cubes from the refrigerator and mix the drinks. He felt thirsty. It was *hot* in there. She came back and the springs squeaked again. The springs that *he*, Walter, had made squeak once a week for five years. A surge of lava-like jealousy coursed through him. He reached into his coat pocket and pulled out a long white envelope. He removed two of the hundred-dollar bills, crumpled them in anger and jammed them into his pants pocket, leaving one in the envelope.

"Ah never *did* catch your name, honey."

"It's Leonard ... Leonard Franklin."

"Ah don't b'lieve I've ever seen you before in the Casino, have I?"

"I'm from out of town. Just here on business and felt like having a little drink before heading back to the hotel. I admired your dancing, then you came up and ...."

"An' *here we are*," she said.

"That's right, here we are," he said, laughing.

Silence.

"Does that feel good," she asked.

"Mmmmm."

She cooed and said, "Whyn't we try again, Leonard?"

The springs groaned and there was no more talk for ten minutes; just squeaks and heavy breathing.

"Woweeee!" Stormy finally said. "You may *start* slow, Leonard, you sure are one to catch up. Like 'nother drink? *I* sure could use one."

She went back into the kitchen. Walter was boiling with anger. It was *hot* in there. Stormy returned with the drink. He could see her nude silhouette as she passed. Her bare backside had glowed momentarily like a moon crescent from the bathroom light behind her. The springs sounded again.

"Whatcha thinkin', Leonard?"

"I guess you know that I'm a married man."

"I sorta figured. But I don't b'lieve in pryin'."

"I mean, I don't go around like this *all* of the time."

"I kin see that ya don't. Got any kids?"

"Just one. A boy. He's fourteen now. I'm already trying to get him lined up in a good college."

"That's very smart."

"Do you know that some of the colleges have waiting lists for five *years* or more?"

"Is that right?"

"A man's really got to plan ahead for his kids nowadays."

"I guess so."

"What I meant to say before, Stormy … I haven't had a time like this since the first year I was married. I mean … well, I don't know what it is that *happens* to people after they're married a few years, but in our house we're just bored *sick* of each other."

"Whyn't you try writin' to that Ann Landers lady in the newspaper? She's always full o' good advice. I read it every day and she's got an answer for *every*thin."

"What I mean is, my wife's all right. She's *very* attractive and she runs things smoothly at home. We go to a lot of social affairs, you know. We just moved into a new house not long ago and that's important. She even plays golf with me. We won the Husband-Wife Handicap Cup last year at the club. A real pal, but God, a man's gotta have a little *excitement* once in a while, don't you think?"

"You mean like grabbin' a woman by the behin' once in a while?"

"*Exactly*. I was thinking, Stormy. I come to town almost every week on business … and I just wondered, couldn't we try, I mean, could *you* try reserving a night for me? Say every Tuesday night? I know I don't have any right tying you *down* like that, but …."

"Why not at all; I think it'd be kinda fun."

"And the same money, of course."

"Oh, don' worry 'bout that, Leonard. I sorta *like* ya. 'Course, a girl's gotta *live*, but anytime you got the hots an' your a bit light in the pockets, don' you worry yourself. Li'l ol' Stormy'll take care o' ya."

"Stormy, I really appreciate that. Hell, I'd like to stay longer tonight, but I do have to get going. Very early business conference in the morning. I'd better get dressed and head back to my hotel."

The bed creaked again. Walter saw the man's bulbous silhouette pass and then go out of viewing range into the bathroom. The bathroom door opened again and Walter could see that the man had his pants and shoes on. He stood in the light of the bathroom. Stormy was by the kitchenette, rinsing out the glasses.

"Why *Leonard*, what on *earth* you got on your *stom*-ach."

"This? It's nothing ... just a little hunting accident. Almost all gone now."

"Musta been *terrible* at first."

"Oh, wasn't anything really." The man chuckled.

Walter could see her hand patting the round belly.

"Now you-all take good *care* o' yourself, honey. I wanna see more of ya."

The man was dressed and at the door a few minutes later. "Don't forget," he said with cheer. "Next Tuesday night, same time, same place."

"Ah'll be there, Leonard. Now you take good care o' yourself, here? No more huntin'." She blew him a loud smack of a kiss. The door shut and heavy footsteps faded down the stairwell.

4

Walter rattled the wardrobe door and heard Stormy approaching, too slow for his liking.

"I'm comin'."

Stormy finally opened it. She was wearing her shortie nightgown and her hair was mussed up. Walter slowly stood erect, grimacing and holding his back. He took off his coat and jacket.

"Wow, that's an oven in there."

"I'll fix ya a drink, honey. You must be *dyin'* o' thirst, poor baby."

Walter sat down on the couch, which had been folded out to bed-size. She came over, straightened the sheets out and sat next to him. She took a sip of her drink, put the glass on the rug and leaned back against the pillow, smiling like an office receptionist.

"Stormy," a sober sounding Walter said. "I've got something very important to tell you."

She blinked and propped herself up on her elbows.

"My company has ... transferred me to California."

She took it without flinching, like a real champ. "Gee, I guess that means better pay for ya or ya wouldn' be goin'. Well, I sure do wish ya luck, ya know that."

He had felt angry before, but the way that she looked at him, so sincerely, so full of compassion, he melted. He reached into his pants pocket and straightened out the two crumpled hundred-dollar bills. Then he got up and went to his coat, took out the white envelope and slipped them back in with the other bill. He sat down, holding the envelope in his hand.

"I just came to tell you how much you've meant to me all this time, Stormy."

She lowered her head. "Aw Christ, honey …."

He rested the envelope on her lap. She opened it and saw the three hundred-dollar bills. "Aw honey, I don' really …."

"Look, this is no pay-off. I don't think of you in that way. It's just a little something to put away for a rainy day."

"Gee, I don' know what …."

"I also have a *special* gift; a poem I wrote about you."

She sat up. "About *me?*"

"Not exactly. I mean it's necessary to use what's called poetic license, which means to change things around a bit just to make them more dramatic. But the main character is *you.* And I'd like you to have a copy of it to remember me by." He pulled a folded carbon copy from his pants pocket.

"Oh, *honey.* Nobody ever wrote a *po*-em 'bout me. Why that's like you were tellin' me about '*Rape o' the Luck*' when this crippled little fella—"

"Alexander Pope—"

"Yea, the pope. When he wrote a po-em for that lady. Could ya read mine t'me?"

"Sure. But first I want tell you that it may be published someday. I sent it in today to *Reader's Digest.*"

"No foolin'? *Reader's Di-gest?* Maybe my fam'ly in Louisiana'll read it. They *always* get it. 'N my brother in the state pen, too. He gets it there *all* the time. Ah can't *wait* to hear it."

"It's an honor," Walter said, crackling the three typewritten sheets with importance and clearing his throat. "*The Ballad of Pubic Pediculi,*" he said. And went on.

> "My story begins one cold night
> When I yearned for some carnal delight;
> I discovered a dive
> That was jumping with jive
> And habitues hardly contrite.
> The first local talent I spied
> Was the type whom by all had been tried.
> 'My name's Staw-mee' said she,
> As she slinked up to me;

'And yours?' A pseudo (of course) I supplied.

Walter paused, sipped his drink and looked over at Stormy, who sat up at the edge of the bed, her hands clasped sedately on her lap. She smiled and said, "Is that it?"

"No. There's more."

"Finish, *finish*." she said.

"A garish tattoo on each arm
I noticed with pop-eyed alarm;
These dermal stigmata
In bright terra cotta
Did much to enhance her sweet charm.
Phenix City, St. Louie, St. Paul;
She'd set hearts athrob in 'em all;
Her torrid gyrations
Earned loud acclamations,
Her champions could fill a great hall!
She'd given up peeling last year;
'Had to,' said she, 'stripped a gear.'
Now's she's living her life
Where sin is quite rife
And the small talk consists of 'one beer'.
To get on with my tale of disaster,
I leaned close and proceeded to ast 'er;
'How about a cool ale
My splendiferous quail?'
She accepted, and quaffed like a master.
Her lids drooped with a coquettish flutter
As she gave me a nudge with her rudder;
She asked me to dance,
I jumped at the chance,
And we soon were awaltzin' each other.
On the dance floor my peach was a tease;
'Tween us two there lacked space for a breeze.
She maneuvered her torso
In a way men adore so,
At a glance we were twins Siamese!
To make a short story much shorter,
I did what I shouldn't had orter.
I invited her up
For a night-capping cup
Of coffee . . . or maybe a 'snorter.'
Her mascara'd orbs brightened wide
As she eyed me both out and inside;

She approved in a minute,
But asked me, 'What's in it'
If 'Yes' is the word I decide?'
That just when I should've backed down,
But playing the role of dumb clown,
I blindly persisted,
She hardly resisted,
And soon we were driving uptown.
To describe what occurred in my suite
Would neither be right nor discreet
I'll dispense with the gory,
Get on with my story,
But I must say: 'twas really a treat!
When my one-night amour from me faded,
And I lay 'neath my quilt tired and jaded,
I turned o'er with a sigh,
To fond sleep did I fly,
Sans a thought for what I'd perpetrated.
The renascence of sunlight soon came,
Seemed a day like all others the same;
But there at day break,
I jumped up with a shake,
Lilliputians were gnawing my frame!
I immediately commenced an inspection
Of a rather unmention'ble section;
You can guess my surprise
When I saw with my eyes
That I'd picked up some type of infection!
There cavorting upon me with glee
Was a horrible species of flea!
Upon subsequent careful research
At a drugstore I learned with a lurch
'Twas the dread Pubic Pediculi!
Now, except for the experts in labs,
The rest of us folks call 'em CRABS;
Those tiny crustaceans
That lurk in bus stations
And oft in the rear seats of cabs.
In my own particular case,
The cause I could easily trace.
Though I hate to name names,
Or to fix folks with blames,
It was Stormy who fostered the race!

Oh, they bit and they hatched
While I grimaced and scratched;
Oh, they multiplied quicker
Than rummies drink likker!
Yes, to me they were fondly attached!
Upon the sage druggist's advice,
I purchased a cure for the lice;
I made my anointment,
A tube of Blue Ointment,
To say that it worked will suffice.
Now that I'm clear of the curse,
I can't say I'm any the worse,
I've learned a great deal
From my 'awkward' ordeal;
And I'll sum it up now with this verse.

If ever you're plagued by ennui,
Invite Stormy to a nocturnal spree;
She's always quite willing
For anything thrilling,
But beware of the dread Pubic Pediculi!

Walter handed the three typewritten sheets to Stormy, who held them in her hands and gazed at them like a pajam-ed cherub on Christmas morn. It was the greatest of possible gifts, Walter felt, glowing inwardly.

"Ah'll *never* forget this," she said, hugging the paper to her mammoth bosom. She squeezed his hand and looked into his eyes, her own eyes welling with tears.

Walter was moved. "I'm so glad you liked it, Stormy ...."

She hugged him. "Ah guess you know that I've seen all kinds o' men. But one thing I can say 'bout you, baby. You could *always* get it up. I don' know what's the matter with some o' the boys nowadays, but you, honey, you could *always* get it up." She lay back against the pillow, a warm smile adorning her face. "Like another drink?"

"I can't Stormy. I've got to pack and be ready early in the morning." He stood up.

"See whut ah mean?" she said, pointing triumphantly at his crotch.

He reddened. "I've *really* got to go, Stormy. Stay right where you are; I want to remember you like this." Her eyes turned misty. He leaned down and kissed her on the forehead, then lightly on the lips.

Stormy sat quietly on her bed, scratching herself and staring at her poem. "*Reader's Dahgest*," she said, with reverence.

107

Walter noticed her scratching. "Stormy?"

"Yeah, hon?"

"I brought you another little gift." He pulled from his pocket and gave her a small orange-colored cardboard container with blue printing that read "*Thompson's Blue Ointment.*" On the back side it had a drawing of a multi-pincered nightmare which was identified as: "*Body Louse (Pubic Pediculi), Enlarged 16 Times.*"

He turned and went out the door, a lump paining his throat, and tears blurring his vision, as he walked down the narrow wooden stairway.

A Soviet Plot?

1

Two days later, it seemed as though the inhabitants of a flea circus had broken loose in the Agency Records File division.

For the first time in Walter's memory, Irwin Kemp stayed glued to his desk, writing with one hand and scratching himself with the other. There was barely any traffic or conversation in the entire ARF division. Out in the hall, the coffee-break lady was on the verge of tears; her urn was four-fifths full and seventy-five jelly donuts and assorted Danish remained unsold.

All the workers remained at their respective posts, head down, writing or typing or punching adding machines, and furiously clawing themselves beneath the desks. Wilma Tannenbaum entered Walter's office without a word, dropped the letters in front of him and sneakily ground her belly against a sharp corner of his desk.

At nine-thirty, Mister Furey came striding in; his free hand plunged deep into his overcoat pocket. Walter walked over to meet him in his office. Furey put away his briefcase and coat and sat down; he was red-eyed and had cut himself on the neck while shaving.

"Morning, Mister Furey. I came right in because I have something important to tell you."

"Mm? What's that, Walter?" Furey slipped his right hand beneath the desk and Walter could hear his long, polished executive nails scratching at the Dacron trousers.

"I'm handing in my two weeks' notice," Walter said, producing a white envelope from behind his back.

"But Walter," Furey said with an incredulous air, "aren't you just about to complete eleven years here? You've got a fine, promising career ahead of you." There was that scratching sound again. "Besides," he whined, "I *depend* on you." He leaned forward and spoke in a confidential tone. "Money trouble? I could probably swing a raise." Walter noticed that, by observing the twitching of Mister Furey's right shoulder he could tell when the scratching was hardest.

"It's not that, Mister Furey. An aunt of mine in California died last week ...."

"Oh, I'm deeply sorry to hear that, Walter. I—"

"And she left me a substantial sum of money."

"That's *wonderful.*"

"Oh, it's not much," Walter said, "but enough to get by on for a few years and give me a chance to concentrate on my ... translating."

"Your translating?" Twitch-twitch went his shoulder.

"Yes ... I'm going to translate a novel."

"So you're gonna be a writer, eh? Sounds exciting. I used to be a reporter, you know. On my college newspaper. I also wrote all the funny captions under everybody's picture in the graduation yearbook. Everyone told me I should follow through in that field," he said, almost to himself. He turned to Walter again. "Whatcha gonna translate?"

"The novels of Jaroslav Miklas. Do you know his work?"

"Mmm. I *think* I saw something about him in the *Times Book Review* section once."

"It's possible. He's considered the Mickey Spillane of Yugoslavia."

"Is that so? Walter, I just want to tell you that I'd do *anything* to make you stay. But *c'est la vie*, eh?" He twitched again.

"Also, Mister Furey, if you don't mind, and this is up to you of course; but since I work so closely with the people here I was hoping my opinion would be considered. I'd like to recommend that Irwin Kemp replace me."

"Kemp? Hmmm. He clowns about a too much, but I often see him at his desk working away like a madman, too. To tell the truth I've never seen *anyone* get so deep in paperwork as him." His shoulder violently twitched, thrice. "Offhand, I can't think of anyone *else*. Tell you what; I'll think about it and make up my mind by tomorrow. And if there's anything you need during the last couple of weeks here, or if there's anything bothering you, let me know. Fair 'nuff?" That scratching again.

"Fair 'nuff," Walter said, feeling glad over the nice way Mister Furey was taking the news.

Furey pulled his right hand out from beneath the desk. He started to extend it, stopped, then put out his left hand. Walter, who had raised his right hand, pulled it back and offered his left. They shook on it, just as the phone rang. Furey picked it up and listened for a moment.

"Yes, sir," he answered. "We'll be right there."

He turned to Walter with a confounded expression. "That was Mister Gibbs from the President's office. There's an emergency meeting down in the tenth floor auditorium. He said to drop everything."

2

When Walter and Mister Furey arrived, the auditorium was filled close to capacity with SIC's two hundred top executives; from manager's rank up. Here and there, among those in attendance, one could see men scratching furiously at their privates. Everyone was talking, presumably trying to guess the reason for the emergency meeting.

Two minutes later, the last group of men had arrived and been seated, and the mammoth oak doors were swung shut and locked from the inside by an executive. Walter spotted Ray Lang and Martin Shaw a few aisles away. They nodded, looking grim; he noticed their right shoulders jerking.

He also recognized six of the company's top brass seated in a row of folding chairs on the stage, together with an elderly fellow who held a wooden cane. Only the president himself seemed to be missing. Mister Gibbs, second from the left, looked grim and drawn; as though he hadn't slept for days.

Herman Turner, another top executive, lumbered up to the speaker's podium. Turner, an All-Southern Conference tackle in the 1930s, was a jut-jawed behemoth with a gleaming dome wreathed by gray sideburns. During World War II, Turner had risen to the rank of Major General in the U.S. Army Artillery. He was now a colonel in one of the local anti-aircraft reserve units, in addition to being Executive V.P. in Charge of Personnel.

He gripped the speaker's stand with his banana-bunch hands, leaned into the microphone and cleared his throat. It sounded like the MGM lion. All the executives shushed each other and silence fell over the auditorium. Walter winced, waiting for Turner's first words. He had spoken with him on the telephone once, and Turner's voice was so rasping and strong that it had nearly split Walter's eardrum.

"Men," Turner barked, his face a mask of determination. "I won't beat around the bush." As he said, "bush," his right hand reached down to his crotch with a ferocious scratch. "Men, the company is faced with a crisis; a serious threat to the well-being of every employee and every employee's family. But before I reveal the nature of this crisis, I must remind you that this is a *top secret* matter; a matter of the utmost delicacy, which, if ever made public, could besmirch the good name and future of the company."

"Men," he boomed again, "at some unascertained time in the recent past, someone in this building became infested with a certain species of body louse, more commonly known as … *crabs!*"

There was a stir in the audience when Turner uttered the word; and a wave of revelation swept over the worried faces of the scratching assemblage.

"Men, I assume this happened because some individual—presumably one of the company's employees—although I find it difficult to believe—became infested. I also haven't discounted the possibility that some subversive elements in our society, possibly in cahoots with the Soviet

Union, are responsible, in order to demean and discredit our democracy and our free enterprise system. It seems a strange coincidence—very *strange*—that this crisis should befall us, just at a time when the Soviets have launched the first missile to reach the moon.

"Either way, this thing is catching and *very* prolific. So much so, that in the space of a few days it has spread virtually all over the company. Presumably, the original carrier used the company's toilet facilities. Then the person after him became infested, and so on. All it took was for one member of one department to use the toilet in another department to cause the thing to spread. This morning, after visual reconnaissance, I would estimate that perhaps twenty-five percent of our five thousand, eight hundred and thirty-five employees are casualties, and it could jump much higher in the next few days."

Every man in the audience warily eyed his neighbor. Each time Walter caught someone's eye he assumed an indignant, outraged expression and scratched savagely at his crotch. He glanced sideways at red-eared Mister Furey who slumped deep in his chair, staring at the floor, his beefy, sloping shoulders bearing the guilt of five thousand, eight hundred and thirty-five co-workers.

"Men," Turner continued, "I now hand over the podium to Doctor Mortimer Smolen, of the New Jersey College of Medicine and Dentistry, a world recognized authority on this plague, who will brief you on relevant details."

Doctor Smolen, a short, slender, bespectacled man, with sparse gray hair, rose with some difficulty from his seat next to the top executives. Bent over, assisted by his wooden cane, he made his tedious way to the podium. He nodded to an assistant down below, who turned on a slide projector and the gigantic multi-colored image of a crab popped up on the screen behind him, causing gasps in the crowd.

Smolen was suddenly erect, rejuvenated. Smiling, he pointed with his cane at the image. "This is the kind of crab that we eat."

He nodded to his assistant, who clicked, and another huge crustacean creature appeared alongside the first one. "And this is the kind of crab that eats us!"

A murmur in the audience.

"Crabs have a long history," he said. "Early Creation theory is that around the time mankind was ejected from Heaven, God created crabs to attack mankind's temptation of lust. Proponents of intelligent design dislike crabs, because they see no use for them in the great scheme of things. I first became acquainted with these hungry little creatures many years ago, during my undergraduate days at Syracuse University. A bunch of us got a bit tipsy on whiskey at the frat house and then visited a house of ill repute. I was a virgin at the time ...."

Turner loudly cleared his throat, a clear signal to get to the point.

Smolen pointed to the image again. "After that unforgettable personal experience, I decided to devote my career to the study of these voracious creatures. My graduate thesis was devoted to the very same subject. It was later published by Rutgers University Press, under the title 'Itching For Trouble'...."

Another loud throat clearing from Mr. Turner.

Pointing at the image on the screen, Smolen continued, "Pubic lice, unlike their tasty, edible 'cousins', weigh only about two grams. As you can see, they have six legs, but their two front legs are very large and look like the pincer claws of a crab, which is how they got their nickname. Although, I should add that others have referred to pubic lice as 'crotch crickets' and 'muff berries.'" Doctor Smolen chuckled and went on. "In fact, Oscar Wilde, the gifted Irish writer, is said to have referred to crabs as 'a fine example of why I stay away from muff.'"

Turner again made a loud clearing of his throat.

"In order to survive, lice bite through the skin and feed on blood, which causes terrible itching, particularly in the genital area.

"This little fellow," he pointed again, "is found most commonly in pubic hair. It can also be found in eyebrows, beards and moustaches, particularly among those who engage in French style oral fornication."

Mr. Turner harrumphed, and began impatiently tapping his right foot.

"The individual louse can survive for about twenty four hours apart from its human host. In addition to sex and foreplay, crabs can be transmitted by sharing clothing or bedding, and even by sitting on a toilet seat, although the crabs do not last very long on hard surfaces. They can't live long away from the human body."

Doctor Smolen smiled broadly and gazed out at the scratching crowd. "Cheer up. Crabs are rarely fatal and they are easily killed with a pediculocide, commonly known as Blue Ointment. It is available without prescription at your local pharmacy. Just follow the directions on the bottle. Also, dry clean any clothing that is not machine-washable. Do not have sex until treatment is complete. Repeat treatment in seven to ten days if lice are still found. If you are careful, and follow these instructions, I am sure you will, as I did, rid yourself of this annoying infection. Good luck."

Doctor Smolen nodded, and turned to leave. He suddenly remembered. "Oh. In the event any of you are interested, I later revised my thesis into a somewhat racy memoir, published in paperback by a small house in Paris." He looked off, as if dreaming, into space. "I'll never forget that first time in Syracuse. I was so young ... she said her name was Peaches ...."

Turner let loose with a thunderous cough, rose, and began to loudly applaud. "Thank you, Doctor. Thanks. That was great!"

Doctor Smolen nodded and wearily tap-tapped his way back to his seat.

Turner gripped the podium. "Men," he bellowed, "this situation must be arrested immediately. But, to tell all our employees would not only create a chaotic situation internally, it would surely reach the scandal-hungry press. You can imagine the repercussions; the effect upon SIC's reputation; especially since this type of infestation is associated with the lowest type of conduct. Our agents won't be able to get in a door from coast to coast. Thus, because of the base action of one employee—who I'm sure has by now cured himself—the whole company must proceed with utmost discretion." Walter gave himself another fierce scratch, in case anyone was looking.

Turner stared straight ahead with his steel-blue eyes. "After careful consideration in a top-level emergency conference last night, we have decided to adopt the following plan of action. "First and most important," he said, drumming his fist upon the stand, "we must clean up all infested sites; namely company latrines—rest rooms, that is. However, to employ the services of an exterminating company, or even allow our own janitorial staff to do the job, would certainly result in a leak to the press. Because of the emergency, I have taken the liberty of appropriating a sum from the company's Recreation Fund, which will be listed under 'Miscellaneous' in our annual report next year. With these funds, a company executive acting under an assumed name has purchased a quantity of industrial-size insecticide sprayers which you see behind me on stage; all in cardboard boxes and plain wrappers. Each manager will be given one upon leaving this room. Tonight, after all employees leave, you are to *personally* go to the men's and women's rest rooms and spray everything thoroughly; especially the toilet seats. This should kill all existing lice immediately."

Turner paused and took a sip of water. "With this problem overcome," he continued, "we are still faced by the fact that perhaps two thousand or more employees are already infested and may have even infested their wives, children and neighbors." He hastened to say, "I speak, of course, of neighbors using the toilet in employees' homes or vice versa." We can only hope that these people will learn the truth and cure themselves. I have been assured that this infestation will run its course in a month or so. If one of the employees should come to you and seek advice, you are to act surprised, then compassionate, and then offer a solution *without* letting it be known that this problem is prevalent throughout the company. I repeat, you are to act as though," he slammed his fist against the podium, emphasizing each word, "it is *strictly a departmental problem and nothing more.*"

"As for you officers, or executives, you will be *certain* to use only the executive rest rooms, which you will spray at the start and end of each work day. Thus, we can eliminate this problem immediately among the management ranks. Also, inside of each of the packages, you will find a small bottle of lice killer for your personal use. I suggest that *all* of you make use of this since you may be infested without knowing it."

Turner stood more erect now, his jaw jutting out even further. "Men, I need not remind you how important it is to keep this secret. Our company has a reputation to maintain; a reputation as a leader in the business world; a reputation as a fine, wholesome place to work." His voice rose more. "A *clean* place to work."

From where Walter sat, it looked as though Mister Turner's eyes were a tad cloudy. Turner spoke slower now, raising his eyes and fixing them on the ceiling.

"Let me assert my firm belief right here and now that the only thing we have to fear about this is fear itself."

He looked down at the faces below him; the sea of gray, grim countenances perched atop gray, three-button suits. He opened his jacket and hooked his thumb into his green checked vest.

"Let us brace ourselves to our duty," he said, in a paternostral tone. "With confidence and unbounding faith I predict that we will gain the inevitable triumph, so help us God." After scratching his crotch, he raised his right hand and pointed at the boxes behind him. "We have given you the tools, and it is up to you to finish the job. Good luck."

There was a shuffling of feet as the two hundred managers and executives rose and headed toward the stage in a single file. Mister Turner stood by the pile of boxes and handed one to each manager. The other executives simply walked by and shook his hand. Walter, scratching himself for effect, thought about his high school graduation ceremony as he inched along in the line.

Finally, he was face to face with Mister Turner, who thrust the box of crab killer into his left hand with the fierceness of a T-formation quarterback and shook his right hand with vigor. "Good luck," Turner said, his eyes glinting and hard.

As Walter marched across the stage, down the far stairs, out of the auditorium and into the hallway, he heard a stirring tune ringing in his ears; it was *"God Bless America."*

3

Furey barely heard Mister Turner's speech. He was thinking about the night before last with Stormy; not about the paramount pleasure, but about how he had crept into bed next to his softly breathing wife at two in the morning, and how during breakfast he had avoided her eyes and responded to her questions about his evening out with a noncommittal grunt.

It had all started the night before he saw Stormy. Furey was in their cellar den, watching television with his wife and son. He felt bored with the life of a country squire. When a commercial came on, he climbed the stairs to the kitchen and took an orange from the refrigerator. Then he entered the study, where he idly leafed through a paperback on home carpentry which he'd bought the week before. Perhaps he could while away the weekday evenings by doing something constructive. But he would need saws, a drill, lathes; all sorts of tools. And how could he make such a ruckus while everyone else was watching TV?

Furey had lived in the city almost all of his life; even for the first two years of his marriage. He had two brothers and a sister; there was always something to do in the house, always someone to gab with. And when he had been younger, he would trot down the block after supper and spend the hours arguing about sports with his friends. After he and Miriam were first married, their dream was to escape from their tiny garden apartment and into a home in the suburbs.

The Friday that Furey came home and announced his promotion, that now they could buy the house, they'd celebrated at dinner with a bottle of French wine. What a celebration it had been. But just when they were settling down in their new house, it instantly seemed too small; and soon they were scanning the real estate pages. So here they were, in Shangri-la Pines, where the homes were centered on an acre of neatly manicured grass and a neighborly visit involved phone call negotiations. He looked out the window and could barely see the lights of the nearest house through the tall shrubs lining the driveway.

Then the idea to have a little excitement, to go out on the town, suddenly materialized. He fabricated a tale about a group of SIC executives who bowled once a week. When he went back downstairs and sat next to Miriam in front of the TV, he mentioned casually that the first meeting was tomorrow night. She swallowed the story without blinking. After work the next day, he enjoyed a nice, quiet meal in a downtown restaurant and plotted what he would do with the rest of the evening, which was stretched out before him like a blank piece of paper.

It was still early; he would go to a movie. As he entered the nearly empty theatre on Branford Place, Furey spotted a woman wearing a kerchief, sitting by herself. He sat down directly behind her. He wanted to plop down right next to her, but he feared that she might be waiting for someone. At the picture's end, the girl—still alone—rose and cast him a quick glance from the dark sockets of her eyes; exposing a vile scar which cut a jagged furrow from the ear lobe to the bottom of her caved-in right cheek. Furey ducked down, feigning a search for a lost billfold.

Later, roaming the cold, silent streets, his pride dangling between his legs like a plumb bob, Furey passed the Latin Casino. The musky sound of Oriental music wafted out toward him, beckoning like The Sirens. He opened the door and saw a half-naked Amazon writhing about in the center of the dance floor, her sweaty body gleaming in the spotlight. Before he knew it, he was in line waiting to add his dollar to the scattered bills which circled her like fallen leaves.

There *is* a God, Furey decided; and he *does* punish people. Not only had he caught some filthy, loathsome thing on his own self, but he had infested his fellow employees. And who knows if right now his own son wasn't scratching away in Plane Geometry class; or his poor wife, perhaps, as she strolled amongst the cornucopian aisles of the Shangri-La Pines Grocery Shoppe.

4

Back in his office, Walter noticed the scratching had intensified. The workers twitched about like actors in an old silent film. For the rest of the week, attendance was at an all-time low as clusters of employees disappeared for a day. Then they would return, itchless, and silently resume work. Within a week's time, though no one dared talk of it, it seemed that everyone had caught on. The scratching ceased. And just in time, because Walter's insecticide spray was empty.

Walter worked hard those last few days in a diligent attempt to clean up all possible details in the office. Furey agreed to Irwin Kemp as the next manager and Personnel had approved the promotion. Walter groomed Irwin with astute care, showing him how to open all the letters and always be sure to leave a few for Mister Furey.

Walter saw Scarlett virtually every night. They would go to a movie, or sit and talk over coffee in some diner; then repair to the office where they made love, talked some more, and then made more love. Walter wondered what he had ever seen in Miss Modess. Scarlett brought up a small suitcase so that in the morning she could change, go downstairs and come up again, just like Walter.

Late one evening, when Scarlett went home after work because she was studying for a night school exam, Walter's curiosity drove him upstairs to the fourteenth floor. It was midnight when Walter tiptoed into President Jennings' bathroom. He flung open the medicine cabinet.

Shaving brush, lather, razor, blades, mercurochrome, toothpaste, Listerine, aspirin and...a tiny, orange-colored cardboard box with black printing. *"Thompson's Blue Ointment."*

There, on the front of the box, was the frightening sketch of that magnified crustacean. Fumbling, he opened the box and found the jar half used. *The dread Pubic Pediculi had ravaged the presidency.* Walter slumped down, overcome by the immensity of the event. He broke into a cold sweat. Slowly, he reached out for the microphone on the wall and pushed the "dictate" button.

"Charon, Charon Franklin Jennings!" he boomed, his voice ricocheting off the tile walls. "This is God again. I have cast a plague upon you and your house because ...." and he turned the machine off.

5

The following night, Scarlett sat talking with Walter in his office-apartment. They had just come from seeing *Pillow Talk* in the Branford Theatre down the street.

"But what do you plan to *do*?" she said.

"You'd better get your needle fixed. I've been hearing the same question every night for a week." Noting a fleeting hurt look in Scarlett's face, Walter said, "Remember the time I told you about not being a worker ant ever again? Well let's stay in the realm of nature and I'll put it this way." Seated next to her, he folded his arms and crouched in a fetus-like posture. "For the last *eleven* years I've been just like this ... like inside a cocoon: work, the library, a movie, staying by myself most of the time. But now," he said, standing and spreading his arms high and wide, "I can feel it, I'm ready to spread my wings and start flying ... like a butterfly. And with the money from the dividends I can pretty well fly where I please so long as I keep a budget. Film festivals in France, theatre festivals in England, skiing in Switzerland, tulip-picking in Holland, nose-picking in Istanbul, statue-gazing in Italy; why there's *all of the United States yet to explore.*"

"And after you're done playing Christopher Columbus?"

"But that'll take *years*."

"And you've got years to play with. You're *only thirty-nine*. It's got to end sometime. And then?"

"Will you please stop asking ultimate questions like that? The whole fun of the idea is that I don't know exactly what I'm going to do; and that I do know what I'm not going to do."

"You're answering in riddles."

His voice rose in exasperation. "But you're *asking* in riddles."

"Don't you have anything specific you plan to do?"

"Is there some law that says I've got to do specific things? Is there any law against not wanting to be in the middle of the rat race? What's wrong with just setting out to make each day a delightful one? Just wandering around a park can be fun, can't it? Who knows? Maybe I'll even try my hand at writing. Can you imagine what a delight it will be to know that I don't have to sell what I write; that I can just write to please myself?"

"You've got it all figured out," she said. "A nice idyllic hike in the park, watching everyone else struggle by on the street outside."

"Is that a sin? Is my job here at the company so damned crucial to the survival of the human race? Isn't it possible that a person with a taste for the good life may have been borne into the world by the wrong family? What about all the poor people who bet every spare cent they've got on the lottery? Or the old ladies who play the Daily Double or throw a buck on the numbers? They want the same thing as I do, except that I'm being a bit more systematic about making my fortune."

"But don't you see?" she said, standing up and clenching her fists. "What you're saying is all wrong. Don't you see that the struggle *is* life … that without the struggle, there is no life?"

"Gee, that would make a nice book title," He said, dripping with sarcasm. He rubbed his chin. "No, it's too long."

She rolled her eyes. "You're impossible."

"Now, now … tell you what. We'll see how it turns out in about ten years. Then you can shake your finger and say, 'I told you so.' Meanwhile, let's not argue, okay? I got a new shipment of books a few days ago. Maybe you'll want to borrow some."

Walter climbed up the ladder by the wall near his bed. He opened a file drawer and pulled out four books. "Here's the new arrivals. All the current best sellers." He showed them proudly. "*Exodus … The Manchurian Candidate … Hawaii … Goodbye Columbus* …."

"You just bought all those?" Scarlett said, looking up at him.

"Not exactly. I got them from book clubs."

"To which clubs do you belong?"

"All of them. You name it and I'm in it. Record clubs, too."

"Doesn't that get a bit expensive?"

"I don't pay for them. You know all those free offers you see in the magazines? Clip this coupon and send it in? Choose all these books or records as advance bonuses? I clip them and have the books or records sent to a box at the post office that I took under a pseudonym. No investigations that way."

"Don't you have to buy a certain number after the free offer?"

"Some people do, but I just keep changing my name every few months and sending in for the new trial offers. I've joined the Book-of-the-Month Club *four times*. I even get the coupons free from the magazines downstairs in the Rec Room; and the envelope and stamps are from the office."

"Is that so? What books have you got?"

"I must have over a thirty now, most of them in these drawers," he said, sweeping his hand along the wall. "I just keep throwing out company files to make space. Got rid of 1907 yesterday." Walter looked down at Scarlett. She stood there, hands on hips, glaring at him.

"You," she said, narrowing her eyes to slits, "are nothing but a spineless, irresponsible, parasitic … *nothing*. To think of going away with you! I'd be ashamed to. Do you realize," she said, shaking her finger in his face, "that there are thousands of people who buy these books and pay for them? They pay to enable these clubs to exist, so that you can steal from them."

"I think it was Edgar Guest who said once, 'God helps those who help themselves.'"

"Goodbye!"

"Scarlett!"

"Don't worry," she said, "I know what's running around in your little brain. I won't expose your sneaky scheme here in the office. It's a better punishment to let you get away with it. A few years from now you'll come to your senses; if you've got any." She shook her head a let out a loud huff. "But I'm not sticking around to find out."

She yanked open a file drawer, pulled out a jumble of personal things—undies, pajamas, toothpaste, her diaphragm—and threw them into a small suitcase. Tromping towards the door, she turned for a moment, spat out her words, "Good luck, you'll need it," and disappeared.

Walter stood ten feet above the floor, holding *Exodus* in his hand. He hooked one arm around the ladder and leafed through the pages. He didn't feel in the mood for pleading forgiveness. Besides, forgiveness for what?

Ice Cream Salesman

On Walter's next-to-last day with SIC, he received two letters from the sixth floor Personnel Department. One was for him, asking that he report at his earliest convenience for "a termination chat." The other was an identical request addressed to "Nill, Wilbur" which Walter was supposed to forward to the MAD night shift on the eleventh floor. When Walter tendered his resignation, he had thoughtfully typed up a resignation note for Nill, too, and sent both to Personnel.

Walter browsed through a dog-eared copy of *Business Week* while he waited in the Personnel Department's reception area. It was a year-old issue; the one bearing President Jennings' portrait on the cover. He noticed several copies of the same edition strewn about the tables in the waiting area. The story was titled, "SIC's Jennings Leads Sleeping Giant Into Bright New Era."

When a man came out of one of the six small cubicles along the far wall, the receptionist went in with the letter Walter had left on her desk. She came out again, shot him a spastic smile, and gestured that it was his turn. He tapped at the door to the miniature office.

A slender man in his mid-forties with a crew cut and black horn-rimmed glasses sat at a desk poring over a long printed form; a manila file folder was at his elbow. The man removed his glasses, rose and turned on a bright smile which seemed to sail past Walter's right ear. He engaged Walter in a knuckle-crunching handshake, hooked his left arm around Walter's neck and guided him to the chair.

"How are you, Mister Mott? I'm Phil Gumpert, your personnel advisor."

Gumpert went back around to his own chair, sat down, put on his glasses again and scanned the printed form. Then he took the glasses off and chewed on one of the ear rests.

"Hmmm. I see that you're leaving us," he mumbled.

"That's right."

"Mmmmm."

"Pardon?"

"You realize, of course, that this makes a lot of paperwork for us here in Personnel."

"Oh. I'm sorry."

"Just kidding," Gumpert gushed, baring his gleaming enamel. Walter relaxed, thinking Gumpert seemed to be a nice guy. "Didn't mean to burden you," Gumpert said. "Truth is, though, "SIC pays a lot more attention to its people than they realize. For example, we've got your whole life story here." He patted the file folder.

"Is that so?"

"Want to hear it?"

"Sure."

"Mott, Walter. Born April twenty first, nineteen nineteen in Newark, New Jersey. Served U.S. Army nineteen forty three to nineteen forty four. Honorable Discharge. Rank of Corporal. Studied under G.I. Bill, one year, at Rutgers, Newark campus. Joined SIC, ARF Division, October five, nineteen forty eight." His eyes and voice rose. "*Say*. There's been a *goof*. At this time last year, we should've sent you your ten-year service pin, and I don't see it noted." Gumpert shook his head and looked rather distressed. "Terribly sorry. We've been very busy up here."

"That's all right."

"One year as filing clerk," Gumpert said, reading from the record again. "Promoted to manager November fourteen, nineteen forty nine. Mmmm. Some hefty jump."

Gumpert closed his file folder and learned forward. "Now ... let's be frank, Walter. You're among friends. Anything you didn't like about the company? To leave after all these years with us, something must be bugging you. This is off the record, of course. Be frank now. You can be frank with me, Walter."

"Well—"

"The lunches?"

"The what?"

"The free lunches. Anything wrong with the food?"

"No," Walter said, looking up at the ceiling. "Nothing I can recall."

"Any trouble at the lending library?"

"No ...."

Lowering his voice, Gumpert said, "Any of your superiors giving you a hard time?"

"No. Everyone is very nice."

"You can be frank with me, Walter."

"No, really, Mister Gumpert; everyone is very nice. I've just decided to leave. That's all there is to it." Walter smiled and shrugged his shoulders.

"What are your career objectives, Walter?"

"Pardon?"

"Your ambitions, Walter. Your plans for the future."

"Oh. Well, I guess to eventually settle down, and ...."

"I mean your professional objectives, Walter; the kind of work you plan to do."

"Ah. I really don't know."

Gumpert tried again. "On the Termination Chat form sheet there was a definite blank space for Career Objectives. For example, Walter, what did you study in college?"

"I was thinking of majoring in Statistics."

"Why was that?"

"Because I liked Statistics."

"And?"

"I don't like them anymore."

"I see," Gumpert said, scanning the report for any previous notations about mental instability. "Tell me, Walter," he said in a patient, pleasant tone, "whatever induced you to come with the company eleven years ago?"

"Well, I was walking down the street one day. I'd just quit a job in a factory ...."

"Factory? That's strange. I don't see that on your record."

"I just worked there a few months. I used to stand in front of a big machine that rolled scotch tape onto tiny cardboard cylinders."

"Yes?'

"I got tired of that."

"I see," Gumpert said, anxious now to get the interview over with. "Well, Walter, the procedure calls for us to fill in some plans for the future. With your ten-plus years of management experience here at SIC, I'm sure there some spot in industry for you. Do you have any idea where you're headed next?"

"I was thinking of taking an outdoors job for a while. You can put down 'Good Humor Ice Cream Salesman' if you like."

"Suppose we just put 'Ice Cream Salesman,'" Gumpert said. "Just in case you go with some other company."

"Well, I would prefer going with Good Humor."

"I see. Well, suppose we put 'probably' with Good Humor?"

"I would put 'almost definitely'."

"Uh-huh," Gumpert said, nodding, and writing it in.

"And I don't care if it's a bike or a truck ...."

"Uh-huh."

"So long as it has a bell."

"I see," Gumpert said, writing it all down.

"Anything else, Mister Gumpert? I really must get back to the office. There are several major policy matters that must be settled before I leave. There's a big mess about whose turn it is to empty the waste baskets. I've had it three days in a row now. I know there's a janitor," Walter continued, as Gumpert tried to interrupt, "but he's an old fellow, and so nice, too. So we all pitch in and empty the little baskets into the real big basket by the paper cutter. That way he doesn't have to stoop down so many times."

2

After lunch, Walter returned to the sixth floor and stepped into the men's room. He hung his jacket in one of the toilet stalls, removed his necktie, and rolled up his shirtsleeves. He wet his hair and parted it down the middle, then donned his thick-rimmed reading glasses; the ones the company doctor had prescribed for him, but he couldn't stand wearing.

When he entered Personnel and dropped the letter addressed to Wilbur Nill on the secretary's desk, she looked at it, gaped at him, checked the letter again and pointed toward the same cubicle along the right-hand wall.

Mister Gumpert looked up, adjusted his glasses and looked again, opening his mouth in the grinning shape it assumed when he strained to see something. "Mmmm," he muttered, "I could swear ... well, we get so many here I'm going punchy." He flashed his bright smile, rose and reached out to shake Walter's hand. When he tried to hook his left arm around Walter's shoulder, Walter ducked down as though he were doing a deep knee bend.

Gumpert, taken by surprise, looked down at Walter cringing near the floor. "Thawt ya was gonna hit me 'cause ahm leavin'," Walter drawled in a thick Southern accent.

"Hit you? Ha-ha. Why no. I'm Phil Gumpert, your personnel advisor. I just called you in to ask a few questions. Please sit down."

Walter sat. "This is quite embarrassing Mister Nill," Gumpert said, as they sat opposite each other. "But we don't have any record of you since you started with us except for the letter of resignation you sent us two weeks ago."

"Is thet right?"

"However, I checked with Payroll and they say you have been with us all right, and earning your check every week for eight years."

"Ah shud say so," Walter said in a huff.

"Just for the record, sir, I wonder if you'd mind helping me to fill in this personnel report for our files."

"Whut fo'?"

"Just for our records ...."

"But ah'm leavin' ...."

"I know, but—"

"'Spectin' me tuh come back fo' sump'n?"

"No, but ...."

124

"Ef you fellers cain't keep track uf a feller fer all the eight years he's been toilin' n' sweatin' for ya—"

"I assure you, Mister Nill, we appreciate every minute that you worked for us. Now, could you please help me fill this in? Please."

In a few minutes, Gumpert had the vital information.

"Now. Let's read it back to make sure it's correct. Nill, Wilbur. Born Greensboro, North Carolina on April fifteen, nineteen twenty. U.S. Army nineteen forty one to forty five. Honorable discharge, rank of Corporal. Series of factory and office jobs until starting with MAD nightshift in nineteen fifty one as Computer Keypunch Operator. Is that right?"

"Yup."

"Now," Gumpert said, pleased that he had something on paper. "Why don't you tell me frankly why you're leaving after eight years."

"Well …."

"The lunches?"

"Never got no lunches."

"Oops. Ha-ha. That's right. You ate the supper meals. How were the suppers?

"Cain't complain."

"Ha-ha. Well, was there any trouble at the library?"

"If theah was, ah didn' hav nothin' tide wife it."

"I mean, did you have any trouble with the service at the library?"

"Don't read much."

"I see. Well, there must be something. You can be frank with me."

"Name's Wilbur, not Frank."

"Yes, I know. I mean that you can be frank with me Wilbur. Absolutely honest, direct and to the point."

"Don't know ef ah shed say."

"Listen, Wilbur, perhaps what you say will make this a better place to work for your fellow employees."

"Well …,"

"Believe me, this is strictly confidential."

"It's the niggers."

"The who?"

"The niggers you got workin' heah, that's who."

"Mister Nill, we have no niggers here," Gumpert said in an indignant tone. "We do have a few colored people, but …."

"Call 'em whatcha lahk. Would you want one o' them colored people marryin' yoah sis?"

"First of all, for your information, I don't have a sis."

"Only chile, eh?"

"Yes, if you must know."

"That explains it."

"Explains what?" Gumpert said, exasperated.

"Why you lahk niggers."

Gumpert gasped and slapped his desk. "Mister Nill, I don't like any-body."

"Then why you got them niggers workin' heah if you don't lahk 'em?"

"Sir, jobs at SIC are not awarded because we like people. Experience, skill and initiative are the controlling factors, regardless of race, creed or religion."

"In otha words, you're sayin' that a nigger kin mop the floah as good as any white man, right?"

"Sir, our janitorial staff is completely integrated. We have whites, colored, Puerto Ricans and even a few Cuban refugees on our staff."

"Next thing y'know they'll be workin' up in the offices in them suit n' tie jobs. With people lahk you doin' the hirin' it's a wondah they ain't up theah already."

"Mister Nill, there is not one negro working in our offices. Of course, we don't do anything to stop them, but I guess they realize that we're more like a big happy family than a company. I guess they wouldn't feel comfortable mixing like that at birthday parties, farewell dinners and things."

"Ah don' know," Walter drawled. "Ah figgered theah was a bunch o' good white Christians running this' company. That's a big reason why ah joined up. Next thing ya know, they'll be goin' out on *dates*, like that Sammy Davis Junior, got himself a blonde white girlfriend! Real pretty, she is. Turns mah stomach. What's this world comin' to? Got a good mind t' cancel mah policy; an' when ah get home to Greensboro, don' you think foah a minnit that ah ain't gonna spread the word aroun'."

"Now Mister Nill," Gumpert said in a purr, "there are only a few old colored people here who wash the floors. These few harmless old fellows couldn't possibly be reason enough for you to leave. I can't believe that a man like you would—frankly, I have a feeling you're holding back on me." Gumpert was thinking about his departmental rating, which was calculated according to the average longevity of the employees he serviced.

"Well, ah was jus' comin' up t' the important thing."

"What else, Wilbur? Be frank now."

"Cain't really say who, but theah's a feller in mah department who's not right."

"How do you mean, Wilbur," Gumpert asked, straining forward with curiosity.

"Well, one o' the fellers who works wif' me is a bit diffrunt, if y'know what ah mean. He kinder looks at me all th' time, an' when ah goes home, he follers me ...."

"Ever try anything?"

"Nope. Not yet. But he's allus got this funny grin. I git home 'bout twelve-thirty and sometimes he's outside mah winder at one in the mawnin'. Just lookin' up."

"You mean ...."

"A goldarned fairy, is whut ah mean."

"Can you tell me who—"

"Mistah Gumpert, since he ain't done nothin', ah caint go pointin' him out. But you'd know him all right; jes' lookin' at him."

"I understand what you mean about rash accusations, Wilbur. There are quite a few men in your department; but we'll find him. We don't want this kind of element in our ranks. This company is a clean, wholesome place and we mean to keep it that way. We'll plant someone in your job and weed out this rotten apple, don't you worry."

"Ya really orter. Ah was jus' readin' in the papers las' month 'bout one o' those fairy boys in Englund who run off t' the Commies wif' a bunch o' secret documents. Fer all ya know, this feller in mah department might be feedin' secruts t' Providenshul."

"Highly possible," Gumpert said, solemn. "Well, Wilbur, I can't thank you enough for being so frank with me. And I want to wish you the best of luck wherever you go. By the way, what do you plan to do after leaving us?"

"Well, ah got some o' mah G.I. Bill still comin' t' me an' ah figgered a little learnin' wouldn' do me no harm. So ah might fin' me a part-time job, maybe pumpin' gas, an' get me a col-ledge degree."

"That's *mar-velous*. Where do you plan to study?" Gumpert said, poising his pen over Career Objectives.

"Ah was kinda leanin' towards Howard University."

Walter got up and left. Phil Gumpert fumbled for a vial of tranquilizers in his desk drawer. He popped two into his mouth, then washed them down with a gulp from the water fountain outside the office. He closed the door behind him, sat back down at his desk and dialed an outside number on the phone, feeling irratible.

"Ralph? It's me, Phil. I don't care if I woke you. Listen, I can't talk now, but let me tell you, mister, I'm boiling mad. Here I pull all kinds of strings to get you this night job and you start cruising the help already. *Christ*. What do you *mean* what am I talking about? I just got a complaint from him personally. Thank God he's leaving the company. What does he look like?" Gumpert bit his lower lip and said in a malicious hiss, "How many are you chasing, you bitch?" "The guy's an absolute maniac, but he couldn't make a thing like that up out of thin air. Listen, Ralphie, don't get upset; I just wanted to warn you, that's all. We'll talk later, okay? And oh yes, if you're gonna drink all the milk, will you please buy a bottle before you go to work? I got home yesterday and had to drink my coffee black. *Ciao amore.*"

Lady Day

1

Walter was depressed. And lonely. He and Scarlett were no longer speaking, and he had already made his farewells to Stormy. What to do tonight? After leafing through books at the library, he stepped outside and decided to take a stroll. It was late. Perhaps he could pick up tomorrow's *Times* at the newsstand at Broad and Market. After that, newspaper under his arm, he strolled along Broad Street, past Peddie's All-Night Pharmacy, and approached Fusari's Bar, just across the street from City Hall. As a loyal patron of The Latin Casino, Walter had never entered Fusari's.

The owner, Charlie Fusari, had been a fair welterweight whose claim to fame was lasting 15 rounds with, and losing to, "Sugar Ray" Robinson in a world title fight. Charlie had retired several years ago and decided to try his luck with the bar. After all, Jack Dempsey was drawing celebrity clients at his joint in Manhattan. And up in East Orange "Two Ton" Tony Galento held court behind the bar at his place, cigar clenched in his teeth, and pointed to the wall behind him, showing a huge blow-up photo of him, after a lucky punch, standing over the floored Joe Louis. Tony neglected to mention, of course, that Louis quickly got up and beat him bloody and senseless.

Fusari's was a dark, narrow place. It was a slow weekday night. Fusari wasn't there. A white couple sat at a small table in the rear, holding hands, sharing quiet talk. A black man, middle-aged, was the only customer at the bar, sipping a whiskey.

Behind the bar, on a narrow raised platform, a black man nicely dressed in suit and tie appeared, sat at the piano and played a soft, sad tune. From behind the curtain came a black woman, in a silken gown. She stood beside the pianist, clinging to a microphone, her slender hand trembling. She was gaunt, so gaunt that Walter felt concern for her. And her voice was ever so weak. There was such sadness in her voice as she sang, *"I'm a fool to want you."* Walter sat at the bar, not far from the black man, and whispered to the bartender, "Seagram's Seven and water, please." A minute later his drink arrived.

As he sipped his drink, the woman began to sing, "Southern trees bear strange fruit, Blood on the leaves and blood at the root ...."

Watching and listening to her, Walter could barely contain the tears. The woman looked, and sounded, vaguely familiar, but no, it couldn't be.

He leaned over towards the man next to him and asked, "Who's the singer?"

"Pastoral scenes of the gallant south ...."

The man, never taking his eyes off her, whispered, "Lady Day."

"Billy Holiday? Here?"

The man shook his head, sad. "She fallen on hard times ...." He held an invisible needle in his hand, and jabbed it into his forearm.

Walter finished his drink and in silence headed for the door, as Lady Day sang, "Here is the fruit for the crows to pluck ...."

He desperately needed some fresh air.

2

Two days later, Mister Furey's unexpected invitation was strikingly opportune; cocktails that evening at the Furey household in Shangri-La Pines; a sort of pre-going-away party. The real party, the official one, was tomorrow night at Glenwood Manor; an obligation that Walter had tried to avoid, but busybody Irwin Kemp had already reserved the hall and collected everyone's money.

Not once in eleven years had Furey invited Walter to his home; not even when the Fureys lived in a modest ranch in the more accessible outskirts of the city. Walter had met Miriam Furey a few times at company functions. When she shook hands with the employees, he noted, she behaved like a countess—tall, gracious and cool—among a band of awed, grubby peasants. Now he was invited into her palace, but ... he couldn't understand why there was this sudden surge of interest in him.

It was five forty-five and Mister Furey had said that things got started around eight p.m. Walter decided to grab a bite somewhere and kill time until the seven p.m. train left the downtown station. He couldn't go upstairs to change and shower; Hannah, the cleaning lady, was undoubtedly emptying ashtrays and feather-dusting his desk at this very moment.

He walked the downtown streets, guarding the brim of his hat against the strong breeze. It was getting dark already and street lamps bloomed on overhead like nocturnal flowers. He stopped in front of a restaurant with a large, haphazardly lettered sign taped to the inside of the front window: "4 the best STEAK U ever 8, try our SPECIALITY-$2.95 with potato and green vegetable." Walter wondered why they made such a thing about it being a green vegetable, unless even their carrots were green; but the price seemed attractive and he walked in.

Near the entrance, on the right-hand side, there was a bar, and Walter sat down for a rye whiskey and water before dinner. Sipping it in tiny draughts, he gazed out the window at the passing traffic and reminded himself that only tomorrow in the office separated him from freedom. Reminded himself? How could he forget? For so many years now it had been a cherished but impalpable dream.

Less than twenty-four hours from now, at four-forty p.m. on Friday afternoon, he would walk through the revolving doors of the giant main entrance of the SIC building and look back at those polished brass letters for the last time. Walter salivated at the prospect of it. But now that freedom virtually stared him in the face its visage intimidated him. The rest of his life with no place he had to go; *nothing he had to do*. For a brief, dreadful moment he felt adrift; as though he had just been born in the world—naked, toothless, bewildered.

The company—the good old Security Insurance Company—was a safe mooring mast; but the lines were being unraveled and tomorrow he would be free as a bird. He shivered over the unfortunate analogy, recalling his mother's pet finch. He was ten years old at the time. While he was changing the water in the cage one day, the tiny bird hopped along his arm and flew out. It became so elated over its new-found freedom that it dashed its brains out against the spotless living room window.

But he would be smarter. Yes, after eleven years of shuffling papers, tapping adding machine keys, scrutinizing meaningless statistical charts, dozing over hieroglyphic reports and getting along with the other members of the happy, ever-smiling SIC family, he was starting from scratch.

Not quite. There was a difference; a difference of nearly $150,000. And, nine years ago, he had embarked upon an intensive study program; a pursuit of knowledge which was prompted at first by the need to occupy his spare time and which soon became an obsession to feed his voracious curiosity. Literature, history, language; the monkey of revelation squatted upon his back. But in his limbo-state of new-bornedness, not a single jot of it crossed his mind. Quick, he prodded himself mentally, who was...who was Richelieu? He clawed vainly at a blank, amnesic well. Who cares? Who cares? Here, on the brink of devoting his entire life to the pleasurable pursuit of self-education, he faltered. Was this it? Was this the way to ... to what? Bewildered, he waved for another drink. Steady, he told himself, downing half of it in a throat-searing gulp. No use worrying. The important thing was freedom. First things first. Never again would he have to clutter his mind with the inane minutiae of commerce. He sat, enjoying the lights and sounds of the passing traffic.

Later, not feeling hungry any more, he paid for his three drinks and walked outside. The church clock across the street chimed as the huge golden hands joined at six-thirty. Walter headed towards the railroad station several blocks away, feeling lightheaded and carefree from the liquor sloshing about in his empty stomach.

As he walked, he chuckled, recalling once more his time as a young draftee at basic training in Fort Dix. How Sergeant Sigler would burst into the barracks at sunrise and yell, "Okay guys, drop your cocks an' grab your socks! Time rise n' shine!" And when they were lined up outside and some poor, shy recruit would raise his hand and ask permission to go to the toilet, Sigler would shout, "Okay! Be quick about it! Piss on the way there and shake it on the way back!" Then there were those arduous hikes, and Walter began to count cadence in a low growl. *Lef', raht, hreep, hawrp, lef' raht, hreep, hawrp ....*

He tried to recall the words to that funny, multi-versed marching song about Jody that the Army recruits used to shout all together, but couldn't; so he *hreeped hawrped* all the way to the station, bouncing along past bent, bat-gray vagrants who haunted the downtown streets after sunset. He entered the Broad Street station at six-forty, bought his ticket and decided to have a hot dog and a coke at the quick lunch counter. Then he stuffed a second hot dog into his mouth. After that, he felt like another soda, and he was just finishing it when the loudspeaker in the cocktail lounge crackled and exploded: *sevenpeeyemtraintomillburnmadisonmorristowndoverandpointswest ... allboooooooooooooord.!*

3

The car was empty except for a few dozing commuters with briefcases on their laps. Walter gave up trying to read the newspaper he'd found on the seat. He closed his eyes as the train lurched into motion, picked up speed and was soon whizzing by the gloomy silhouettes of factories, warehouses and office buildings; chugging inexorably westward and upward into the hilly countryside; past brooks and forests and highway discount stores; up into the clean, crisp, exalted ozone which enveloped Shangri-La Pines.

A polite uniformed guard halted Walter's cab at the wrought iron entrance gate and asked his destination. Excusing himself, the guard stepped into a tiny gate house, made a phone call and leaned out to wave the cabbie forward. After a few minutes on the rollercoasting asphalt road, with houselights winking at him from behind the rows of pine trees, Walter was in front of the Furey household; 14 Whippoorwill Lane; an imposing, white colonial structure with, he guessed, at least ten rooms.

Walter paid the cabbie, crunched up the gravel walk to the porch and peered through the bay window into the living room. About two dozen people were inside, all standing up, all thoroughly involved with each other, all sipping from cocktail glasses.

He was somewhat tipsy, but sober enough to care about appearances. His pants were wrinkled from sitting at the desk all day. As he reconnoitered his cheeks, tiny cactus spines prickled his fingertips. And though no one but he would know, his big toe was sticking clean through a hole in the sock of his right foot.

He looked again at the noiseless, animated manikins inside the window. Everyone looked chic, correct, and happy. Watching them reminded Walter of his high school science class, when he'd observed Protozoa through a microphone. The people were clustered in small tightly knit groups; standing still with only their heads and arms in motion; like wavy flagella. Suddenly, a member of one group would look about, detach himself, float across the carpet and attach himself to a new cluster of people. At the same time, someone from a different group would drift over to the cluster which had just lost a member. This went on continually, as the number of groups remained constant, but individuals criss-crossed each other's paths, gliding slowly over, drink in hand, to adhere themselves anew. Walter stood there fascinated, wary of upsetting the ecological balance.

No, he couldn't just walk in. He descended the porch steps and tiptoed along the drive to the kitchen door in back. He looked in. A Negro maid had just lifted a copper disk filled with canapés and was apparently heading out towards the living room. He tried the door handle and it was open. He went in.

A man entered the kitchen. He was in his late forties, plump and red-faced with hornrimmed glasses and a gray silk Italian suit which fit him tight. Four fingers of his left hand were plunged into empty highball glasses which he was presumably going to refill. He was most cheerful.

"Hi!" he boomed. "I'm Gardner Lowell. Don't think we've met."

The kitchen's fluorescent glare and this salmon-pink creature with the loudspeaker lungs were too much to take. Tears rimming his bloodshot eyes, Walter squinted at the man, who regarded him with suspicion.

"You are with the party, aren't you?"

Walter said in a snarl, "I'm not affiliated with *any* party."

The man backed away toward the living room, but was stopped short by Lindstrom Furey, who was coming in with two more empty glasses.

"Walter," he roared. "How the hell'd you get in without me seeing you?"

Walter's head and voice lowered. "Through the back door."

Furey turned to the man with the four glasses on his fingers. "This is my *writer* friend, Gardner, the one I was telling you about."

The man nodded, relaxed and smiled, then began to rinse out the glasses. Now Walter understood why he'd been invited. He was Furey's *writer* friend.

"Walt, come into the living room. I'd like you to meet our neighbors." Furey subsided into a between-you-and-me whisper. "This is the first time we're entertaining at our place, and boy I picked the swingingest bunch of nuts in Shangri-La for this shindig. Wait'll you meet them. Ad men, marketing men, engineers, chemists, salesmen, even a magazine editor. But real *swingers*, if you know what I mean," he said, winking.

"Mister Furey, I'd like to use your bathroom first."

"Sure," Furey said, "but look, from now on I'm *Lindy*; that's what everyone outside the office calls me."

Walter entered the bathroom, which adjoined the kitchen, and splashed some water on his face. He combed his hair, inspecting himself in the ruthless bathroom mirror. God, my eyes, he gasped, pulling his lower lids down and unveiling two bloody-looking gashes. His skin, pocked with sprouts of beard, seemed jaundiced. Screw 'em, he said aloud to himself. They came to meet an offbeat literary type, didn't they? He wrenched open the bathroom door and strode into the living room.

"*There's* our author," cried Miriam Furey, raising her slim white arms aloft and floating toward him like an apparition in her fluffy pink cocktail dress. Walter counted twenty people. All held drinks, their bodies faced into the center of their conversation groups, but their heads swiveled sidewards to look at him. Miriam Furey was upon him, lightly pumping his hand before he could retreat to the bathroom. She had quite a bag on; she looked like Blanche Dubois after a tussle with Stanley Kowalski. Transfixed by her perfect, toothy smile, Walter let himself be led toward the others, who gathered together in an informal reception line.

"People, this is Walter Mott, our guest of honor, who is leaving Lindstrom's company to write a book. Walter, meet Harvey Keegan, Alice Williams, Mary Byrd, Oliver Fisher, Cliff Edgeworth, Bill Thompson, Ursula Keegan ...."

"Well," Miriam Furey said with a sigh a few minutes later, "now that *that's* over, what would you like to drink? Martini? Gibson? Daiquiri? Bloody Mary? Scotch?"

"Just some rye and a little water."

"Rye? Rye. Goodness," she said, biting her lip and wrinkling her porcelain brow. "I'm not sure we have any rye. *Oh yes*. There's some in the kitchen we use for cooking. Don't go away now."

Walter stood on the perimeter of the groups, listening.

One guest, the engineer, was recounting with great enthusiasm his recent visit to the New York Coliseum, where a fellow from the Midwest had introduced something called a microchip, that would someday replace huge computers. He raised his right hand, put his thumb and forefinger almost together, and said, "It's smaller than a baby's *dick*." But most of the small talk revolved about art, and family.

"As far as I'm concerned, they can bury *Wozzeck* all over again ...."

"Did you read ...?"

"And on top of that I had to slip the ticket broker an extra five ...."

"Look, if you don't hit them once in a while ...."

"And Greg didn't even know I had the wig until I told him three weeks later ...."

"Did you see ...?"

"Did you hear ...?"

"Look, I flip over abstract art, but in music ...."

"We never hit our little Timmy ...."

"No, the reviews scared me away from reading it ...."

"Absolutely fantastic!"

"Look, you've got to consider the book and the picture as two separate entities ...."

"But you've got to hit them once in a while ...."

"Hi," purred a short, slender man in his late thirties with a balding, ocarina-shaped head. "I'm Harold Lawrence. I live up the hill. Lindy tells me you two have worked together for more than ten years, and that now's the first time he even knew you were a writer. Not the publicity-seeking type, eh?" he said, coyly peeking over his Gibson.

"Some writers talk a good game," Walter said, feeling and sounding terse, "I prefer writing."

"Bravo. I'm in publishing. It's an industrial magazine called *Ball Bearings*."

Three more people floated by.

"Tell me, Mister Mott," said a gushing, slim, intense woman who was either Alice Williams or Ursula Keegan. "What's the title of the book you're writing?"

"I'm not writing a book at the moment, madam. I am translating one," Walter said, calling upon the didactic tone he'd acquired from observing butlers in British films.

"Oh yes. Lindy mentioned something about a Czechoslovakian I think he was," she said.

"I've put that aside for something more urgent," Walter said, not recalling what he'd told Furey.

"Really? A book from what country?"

"From our own United States of America."

"And you're translating it?"

"Yes; into English."

"English," she said, smiling.

"The author, my dear woman, is the leader of the Angry Young Brave movement of the Mahican Indian tribe of the upper Hudson valley. He is so angry that he steadfastly refuses to write in anything but his native tongue; which, unfortunately, is now extinct."

"And he's never been translated before," asked another woman, who may have been Mary Byrd or Millie Edgeworth.

"Well, yes. He himself has translated two of his books into the Powhatan, Pequot and Narraganset dialects; all of which are now extinct."

"But how does he plan to communicate with his audience," asked the first woman in an amused tone.

"Since when," Walter asked, arching an eyebrow, "does an artist cater to his audience? *But,* I have convinced him that he should share his genius with the world. So we are collaborating on his first three novels, which comprise a trilogy entitled *"The Last of the Mahicans."*

"But hasn't that been used before?" asked the second woman.

"That was *Mo*-hicans," Walter corrected. "Which was simply the eastern branch of the *Ma*-hicans; and a very uninteresting branch at that. My friend has never forgiven JFC—James Fenimore Cooper. No Mahican has."

"Where did you meet your Indian friend?" said the second woman. "On a reservation?"

"He's a gas station attendant, though he does keep a few scalps on his living room wall. Keepsakes from his great-grandfather."

"In Greenwich Village, then?"

"My dear woman," Walter said, "the Village is completely passé. The new art colony, the avant garde, has established itself quite unobtrusively in ... no, I shouldn't tell; the place will become a bloody tourist hangout."

"Please," the first woman pleaded. "We'd never tell."

"Well," Walter said, shifting his weight and reluctant, "It's Hoboken. New Jersey. In a section of brownstone walkups near the Tootsie Roll Factory."

"Hoboken?" the first woman said, disappointed. Are there any coffee houses there?"

Walter confided in a loud whisper, "Espresso is out; Tootsie Rolls are in."

"Very phallic," said the smirking editor of *Ball Bearings.*"

"But, very tasty," Walter said, raising his finger for emphasis. "And now, if you good people will excuse me, I have an irresistible urge to take a pee."

The girls let out a shriek of laughter, and one of them ran over to tell the others what Walter had just said.

4

Walter checked his bloodshot eyes in the bathroom mirror again. His mouth was dry and fetid. He opened the medicine cabinet to look for toothpaste, and *there it was*: the little orange cardboard box with the blue printing. *The cure for the pubic pediculi.* Walter looked askance at the toilet seat behind him; it gleamed with menace. He sat on the edge of the bathtub to collect his thoughts, to stop his head from swirling about so. What in hell had he just *said* out there? God, he was getting the balls to say *anything* to people lately. Was this what freedom was doing to him? Or was it just the liquor? No matter, he told himself, he was having fun.

When he ventured toward the living room again, Miriam Furey burst out of the kitchen, took him by the arm and thrust a drink into his hand as though it were a relay runner's baton. "There. Finally found some rye," she said, gasping, as though she'd run into town to buy some. "It was on the top shelf of the pantry."

"Thanks," Walter said, sipping it to soothe his withered throat. He wondered, where in hell do they hide their toothpaste?

Miriam Furey was glassy-eyed; it appeared as though her eyeballs had jumped their sockets and were bobbing about on springs. "Come," she said, extending her hand and gripping his. "I'll show you around. You've never seen the house before, have you?"

She didn't wait for his answer. They tripped up the carpeted stairs to the upper hallway. "This," she said, flinging open the door and flicking a light switch on and off, "is our bedroom. And here," she said, repeating the action by the next door, "is Lindstrom Junior's room. He's staying with his grandmother tonight. And this is the spare room, and this is the upstairs bath." That's where they keep the toothpaste, he decided.

Skipping down the stairs again, they stopped at a middle landing which overlooked the living room. "Beyond the living room," she said, pointing, "is the dining room and the kitchen. And the maid's room is next to the kitchen, and so is the laundry room." She tugged at his sleeve. "The study is over here."

They walked in and there was a large wooden desk with an expensive looking art book open atop it; there was a globe of the world and a full-wall bookcase crammed with encyclopedias and volumes in shiny, colorful dust jackets. The books seemed to be arranged according to color. Out they went with Miriam leading, towing him by the hand, again to the middle landing and down to the living room, skirting the guests, through the kitchen—she snatched a canapé from a tray on the sink in passing—and down the cellar stairs.

"Here," she indicated with a dramatic sweep of her hand, "is our game and TV room."

It had a black and white checkered tile floor; a green ping pong table occupied the center of the room. The cylindrical enclosure for the hot water heater looked like a Parisian kiosk; it was plastered with the same kind of bright-hued airline travel posters which decorated the walls of SIC's recreation room. In one corner, behind a wall divider decorated with tinted vases and Chianti bottles, were the TV set, a battered leather couch, some folding chairs, and a small rattan bar.

"Doesn't it get annoying," he said, "if someone's playing ping pong while another's watching TV?"

"We never do both at the same time, silly." She ducked behind the bar and exclaimed, "My. Here's some more rye. How absent-minded I am." She took the bottle, opened it and moved to pour him another.

"No, really. I don't ...."

"Then I'll try some. Haven't had any in God knows how long. High school, perhaps; and don't you *dare* ask me how many years *that's* been. Lend me one of your cubes, sweet?"

With her long, graceful fingers, she daintily fished a cube from his glass. She dropped it into an empty glass and poured herself a generous double shot. Throwing her head back, she downed it with a long, sustained gulp; like a thirsty child with a glass of milk.

"Aaaaaah. Say, now. This isn't bad ... much warmer than gin."

Walter stood there, unsure of his ground, groping for something to say.

"Like to watch TV," she asked, matter-of-factly.

"But there's a party going on up ...."

"Oh screw them. I see them every day. Or, if you prefer, we can just talk; perhaps about your writing?"

"That might be—"

"Good. We don't need the light for that." 'She got up and turned it off.

Walter shrugged and sat down on the couch, facing the blank, 21-inch TV screen. She sat next to him. They could hear the people scuffling, laughing and talking upstairs, where a sliver of light showed through the bottom of the closed cellar door.

"You know, Walter, with your leaving the company and devoting yourself to writing, it might be a bit rough on you financially."

"Well, I ...."

"I don't want to mix in, but if you like, you're more than welcome to stay with us for a while, in our spare room. There's a desk and no one would bother you; you could write all day. It's very quiet with Lindstrom at the office and our boy off at school."

"Thanks very much Misses Furey, but I don't—"

"Miriam. You think about it. Never make hasty decish ... decisions; not even negative ones." She slumped low in the chair and leaned her neck against the headrest. "You're very lucky," she said, "very lucky."

Walter saw the rye bottle glint in the light as she raised it to her lips. "Why am I so lucky?"

"Because you've got tomorrow ahead of you; tomorrow that's different than today. Me, I'm a prisoner. A prisoner in this house."

"It's a very nice prison," Walter said, trying to inject some levity.

She whined. "But there's nothing to *do*. I've been to every damned meeting of every fund-raising and social organization in this town, but they're all the same. And here in the house, with the maid, I don't have to lift a finger all day. I sit around the beauty parlor with the rest of the girls. We even bring sandwiches and drinks there. I just don't do nothing all day."

"What's so bad about not doing nothing all day," he asked, committing the same grammatical slip by some gallant impulse.

"Try it some time."

"But that's why your husband works; so you don't have to."

"I hardly ever see him," she said, slurring, "and it's dandy by me. Between his job and his hunting and things on weekend ... and now once a week he's got this *bowling* club he belongs to ...." She sighed.

"You don't sound very happy," Walter said, beginning to feel sorry for her.

"I'm *miserable*. I'm *useless*. Sometimes I feel like running away; perhaps to join some religious order."

"Religious order?" Walter said, watching the rye bottle glint in the light.

"Yes. Someplace where people live their lives simply ...," her voice trailed off to a hoarse whisper, "... and spend their time giving to the poor."

"But those charity organizations you belong to. Don't they give to the poor?"

"You don't understand," she said, whimpering, wearily shaking her head from side to side. Suddenly, she sat up and became very excited. "I want to be *among* them, right in the *middle* of them. I want to see and smell and *touch* the poverty, don't you see? I want to give something directly *to* someone; I want to *give* something directly *to* someone."

She stared at the ceiling, her thin arms stretched tautly upwards.

"I must *help* someone!"

"Who?" Walter said, feeling nervous.

"Anyone. *Anyone*." she yelped, leaping on him, straddling his left knee and crushing him against the back of the couch. She was hugging and kissing him on the face. He was so bewildered by the maenadic assault that his first instinct was to push her away. She crumpled to the floor; slowly, fluently, like a ballerina, and sobbed quietly with her face hidden in the fragile basket of her fingers.

"I'm sorry," Walter murmured. "You surprised me." She continued to cry, her frail shoulders quaking. He feebly extended a comforting hand towards her, but it fell short. "I guess I'll go upstairs," he said. "Are you all right? Can I get you something?" She shook her head no.

Walter meandered up the stairs to the living room.

Lindy spied him and said in his vociferous, obnoxious manner, "Walter. Whereyabeenolpal? Boy, that was *some pee*."

"I've got to be going, Lindy, I—"

"Not without one for the road. Whatcher poison?"

"Rye and water."

"Rye. Gee whiz, I'm not sure if we got any. Lemme look." A few more people came over. One woman asked when his translation would be published and said to make sure he reserved an autographed copy for her, which he promised to do. "And do bring the Indian up here sometime; we'd love to have him," she said, envisioning a copper-skinned bearded beatnik with an opulent feather headdress offering an impromptu concert of tribal ululations in her living room.

Miriam Furey entered and wafted right by to another group at the far end of the room. Her face was freshly made up, her hair was combed and she wore a frozen smile. Furey came back with Walter's drink. "*Here*. I found some rye in the kitchen, in the pantry."

5

The party progressed. Walter, feeling too fatigued to continue his role of literary translator, lingered at the fringe of Furey's circle, listening to a roundelay of bawdy jokes. Just before midnight, one of the men said, "I don't know about you folks, but I'm tired," and sat down cross-legged on the living room rug. Another man followed suit and, within ten minutes, the whole group was seated in a circle like a scout troop around a campfire. Someone got up and turned off the floor lamp, leaving just the small table lamp dimly glowing. The stereophonic record player, Furey's pride and joy, which he used to talk about so often in the office — before his affairs with sports cars and bows and arrows—switched to a fervent, but soft, flamenco.

"Let's play spin-the-bottle," a man said with childlike enthusiasm. Another man, holding up an empty fifth of scotch with a look of triumph, said in a bellow, "And *here's the bottle*."

Walter, seated in the circle at Furey's left, was quite drunk now. Each time the bottle spun and a man drew his own mate there was a moan of mock disappointment and the two would exchange a sedate kiss. When a man drew someone else's wife, they locked in an exaggerated embrace while everyone oohed and aahed. The kissing game went on for half an hour, until everyone had been oohed and aahed over at least twice.

Even Walter had spun the bottle and both times drew a mousy brunette, Betty Faulkner, the wife of marketing research consultant Harlow Faulkner. "You're *made* for each other," everyone said. She French-kissed him both times and, after he thought about it for a while, Walter decided her tongue tasted like escargot. What *had* she been drinking? Then he wondered what *his* tongue tasted like, so he excused himself and headed for the upstairs bathroom, where he suspected they had hidden the toothpaste.

When he came downstairs, there was little laughter and the kissing was going on in real earnest. "Do you have Ravel's *Bolero*, Lindy?" a man said. "Just like you," a derisively nasal woman's voice said. "Always seeking artificial stimulation."

"Say," Furey said, "anyone game for a little key swapping?"

He might as well have said baby-drowning. There was a stony, over-long silence. "This is getting a bit too rich for my blood," a man said. His shadowy form rose to a standing position. Slowly, everyone rose except for Furey and Walter. "Just where did you get a crazy idea like that?" an indignant woman said. "What do you think this is, Peyton Place or something?" More silence. The shadows moved off towards the front hallway, pausing at the closet to get their coats. A few limp good-nights floated back to the trio seated in the center of the floor. Then the front door closed.

Walter didn't know what to say; he aimlessly twirled the bottle around in front of him. Miriam Furey sat there, glaring at her husband, who stared down at the floor, his lower jaw slack. There was a knocking at the kitchen door out back, and the door opened. Muffled giggles were heard from the kitchen and a grinning man's head—it was marketing research consultant Harlow Faulkner—popped into view. "Well," he said, "we're finally rid of the squares." As he emerged from the kitchen he was followed by his wife and three other couples. "*Dum vivimus, vivamus*," said the little magazine editor. Soon, there was another camp-fire circle.

"Buck up, Lindy," Faulkner said. "Half of them would have wanted to stay, but they're just shy. The others would have gone home soon if you'd just bided your time a bit. The swingers always stay to the last," he said, grinning.

"Now," he said, as he rose to his feet. "All men; on your feet and keys out!"

He held up his own keys like Perseus exhibiting the Medusa's head. Walter reached into his pocket and fingered the SIC office keys—service entrance, Executive Rest Room, office wall—shrugged and held them up. "Girls ready?" Faulkner said. "Now, when I say go, the fellows drop their keys in the center of the circle. Keys up in the air, ready, set, *go*."

Years ago, in a *March of Time* newsreel, Walter had seen bands of starving Chinese peasants clawing for food morsels thrown from a train. He also remembered films of piranha devouring a live pig in a frothy scuffle on the Amazon. But *never* anything like five giggling, screaming, shrieking women fighting over those keys. In a few seconds they were peeping with excitement: "Whose are these? Whose are these?" Then silence as they paired off. One woman drew her own husband, groaned, and exchanged partners with another without a word. One set of keys was left on the floor. Walter crouched down to see if ….

"No, that's not yours, sweets," Miriam Furey said. "I've got yours."

"Oh no!" Faulkner roared. "*Lindy's* keys are on the floor." A sheepish Furey stood there, forcing a grin, while everyone clucked evocations of pity.

"Now hear this," a booming Faulkner said. "This being a Thursday night and tomorrow being a day at the office, all men will evacuate no later than four in the morning. Boy, what a day in the office *tomorrow's* going to be." He slapped his palm to his forehead.

Further talk seemed superfluous, so the four couples began to leave. As the last one stepped out the front door, Walter went to the bay window and watched them descend the driveway; two by two, hands together. The magazine editor was holding hands with the marketing consultant, while their female partners had found each other, too. The four of them were skipping.

"Lucky draw," said Miriam Furey, who was standing behind him.

Walter turned around. He was alone with the Fureys. Lindy was back on the floor, staring at his keys. Walter approached him and crouched down. "Lindy," he whispered. "This isn't right. Why don't you and Miriam … besides, I don't have a car and couldn't possibly take her anywhere. My room is all the way *downtown.*"

"No, no, Walt," Furey burbled, drunk, wagging his finger and shaking his head. "Fair's fair. We've got to follow the *rules*. That's what they're for. You take the bedroom and I'll take the guest room." Furey sighed, looked at Miriam, then at Walter. "Guess I'll go to bed."

He picked himself up and slumped, crestfallen and forlorn, up the stairs. Miriam Furey stood watching from over by the window, her eyes shining, dangling Walter's keys from her hand like Mesmer. She went to the stairs, stopped at the first step and turned to Walter.

Arm in arm, pitching from side to side in their drunkenness, they went up together. Walter felt queasy. Man, the hunter—*hunted.* It was against nature,! he told himself, stubbing his toes against the carpeted steps.

In two minutes, Miriam was peeled and spread-eagled—a toppled crucifix—in the center of the colonial fourposter bed which loomed in the darkness like a sacrificial altar. "Give," she moaned, "*give!*" Walter, fully dressed, sat gingerly on the bed and looked at her, as though he were ruminating a prize butterfly pinned under a glass, running his gaze along her slender, pervious body; the bud-like breasts where her heart fluttered; the corolla, pink and hairless after dutifully following the instructions printed on the tiny orange cardboard box. The moonlight streaming between the cherry blossom curtains imparted a sallow barium caste to her skin. Walter was gripped by an urge to cover her up.

"I'll be right back," he whispered, the chyme bubbling high in his throat. "Gotta go to the bathroom." He made a motion to pat her thigh, but pulled back his hand and went out of the room, closing the door on her low, funereal moans. He tiptoed down the hall to the guest room, knocked and heard stockinged feet bound to the door. Furey stood there in striped boxer shorts, his hair awry.

"Walter."

"Lindy, I can't go through with this."

"But Walter, the *rules, man.*"

"*Fuck* the rules. Look, Miriam, your *wife,* is in there, hotter than a tamale. How do *you* feel?"

Furey's mouth curled up in a grin. His brown eyes were big and watery, like a grateful bloodhound's.

"Lindy, you've been bossing me around all these years. Now's my turn. I'm borrowing your Volks to drive home, and you can bring it back tomorrow. I *order* you to get in there."

"But—"

"No buts. I *know* you can do it. Make believe it's your honeymoon. Make believe she's someone else. *Anything.* But ... *get your ass in there.*"

Furey gave Walter's arm a firm squeeze and staggered along the hall toward the bedroom door. He turned, lifted a corner of his mouth in a silly grin, and entered the room. Walter was at the bottom of the stairs when Furey called, *"Psssst."* from the top landing.

"What now?"

"She won't," he said, nearly crying. "She keeps raving about *giving* things to people."

"Tell her that charity begins at home," Walter snapped, feeling a tinge of regret now that he wasn't back up there in the bedroom. Furey was gone again, but as soon as Walter had put his coat and hat on and begun to wonder where the Volkswagen keys were, the round, near-nude body appeared at the top landing once more.

"Walter?"

"Already?"

"Not yet. She says okay, but she says she's *sure* that I'm thinking of someone else. She wants *you* to watch for *her* sake."

Furey waited, wringing his hands, at the head of the stairs. He melted into a grin of relief as Walter, his face ashen from fear, liquor, anger and expectation, came trudging up toward him.

Last Night in Captivity

1

At that very moment, precisely 1:09 a.m., twenty-six miles east in the suburban town of Montclair, Raymond Lang of the Accounting Department was heating a baby bottle in the kitchen of his three-bedroom, $15,300 Cape Cod home.

Four miles from Lang's house, in the community of Bloomfield, Marty Shaw of the Actuarial Department scribbled on a note pad in the living room of his $14,700 Cape Cod. Only the small desk lamp glowed; his wife Sharon and his boy Freddy were asleep. Marty had always wanted a separate room for his study, but nine years ago, when Freddy became too old to sleep in their bedroom, they had to put the boy in the other room, and Marty's study was shunted to a corner of the living room.

Earlier that evening, in his second floor garden apartment in Elizabeth, near Newark Airport, Irwin Kemp had sat chuckling on the sofa watching NBC's "The Tonight Show", as Jack Paar sparred playfully with Dody Goodman, and celebrity guest Zsa Zsa Gabor. Now, gazing out the window from his darkened living room, he stared eastward towards the bright lights of Manhattan, yearning for…what?

In a third-floor apartment in Belleville, just fifteen minutes from the SIC building, Wilma Tannenbaum dozed on her living room couch while Tab Hunter and Dorothy McGuire were quietly getting acquainted in a war movie flickering on her TV screen.

In a one-roomer with kitchenette on the third floor of a modern apartment building in Hillside, Charlie Phelps of the Advertising Department was snoring loudly on his Castro Convertible Couch.

Three miles away, in a two-story house in Irvington, dark except for the light of the TV screen in the living room, Johnny Mulligan popped SunMaid Raisins into his toothless mouth as Dorothy McGuire, wearing a USO hostess' uniform, asked Tab Hunter, wearing Army khakis, why he was so shy and nervous.

Still wearing his hat and overcoat, Walter Mott slumped deep in a Bergere chair upholstered in a gay Toul-de-Jouy fabric and watched the tossing, gasping shadows in the bed before him; transfixed as Aretino contemplating Romano's sixteen *Posizioni*, muttering to himself, "This isn't really happening. No, this isn't *really* happening."

In the darkened bedrooms of four other homes in Shangri-La Pines, four couples, unobserved, frenetically approached nirvana ….

Marty Shaw had received a small slip of paper from the Personnel Department that afternoon. It said that beginning in 1986, 27 years from now, on the basis of his current income and projected normal raises, he would receive an annual retirement pension of $8,973, which included his Social Security benefits. *1986*. It stunned him. To think, that in 1986 he would be 65 years old. He was feeling morose; he had expected more from life than $8,973 a year, which would be worth even less in 1986, although there would be adjustments for inflation, of course, and he felt too young to be faced with that distant prospect.

Of course, he might get some big promotion, but Mister Shank, his director, was only five years older than he, and at least three other men were competing for Shank's job. On the scratch pad, Marty calculated the cost of going into the egg business as a sideline. Eggs are a daily necessity, he reasoned. Everyone in his community would prefer getting fresh eggs delivered to their door. He would hire young boys to deliver; just like newsboys. Who knows? It could be a profitable thing; so profitable he would go into it full-time. He had written down all the things necessary: a coop, grain storage, hens, feed; there was plenty of space in the backyard for a coop. Then he wrote down "market" and put a question mark. Some Sunday, he would have to count all the houses in the area. He also put a question mark next to "feed"; he had no idea what this would cost. Frustrated, he resolved to write to the U.S. Department of Agriculture in the morning. They would have some literature on the subject. He rubbed his eyes and sighed, wondering if he would eventually grow tired of the egg business.

Ray Lang, 49, had three children, two of them teenagers attending the local high school. Eleven months ago his wife Harriet announced quietly, almost with awe, that they were going to have a baby. With a wry smile, she reminded him of the night they had both come home tipsy after her brother Mike's birthday party. Now, little Raymond Junior was four months old. Ray had purchased a special pomade to darken his silvering hair because last week, while wheeling the baby in the park, some sweet-intentioned woman had asked if he was the grandfather. For the first two children, Ray had slept while Harriet performed the late-night bottle chores, but now Harriet was taking a longer time to recover from the delivery. Ray pulled the bottle from the pan of boiling water and shook a drop on this wrist; then he held the bottle under the cold water tap for a moment. The baby's maddening wail from the bedroom was getting more urgent. When Ray rushed in, his son's face was creased and red from crying. He put the bottle in the baby's mouth and propped it up on a brown teddy bear which was the baby's favorite sleepmate. The child, relaxed now, sucked busily at the bottle, gaping up at his father with incredibly blue eyes.

Earlier that evening, Charlie Phelps had dined in the home of some married friends and returned to his apartment at nine-thirty. After skimming a John O'Hara short story in *The New Yorker,* Charlie had tried to work up an idea for a story. He concentrated intensely for fifteen minutes, nearly biting his pipestem in two, but he was dry of ideas. He had read about these barren moments in *Writer's Digest,* which he bought regularly. He picked up *The Times,* hoping that some news item would start his creative juices running.

Johnny Mulligan thought to himself that he'd better get to bed because tomorrow was going to be a busy day. Tomorrow evening, he would see all his friends at SIC, because he'd been invited to Walter Mott's farewell dinner. Friday afternoon, before going to the dinner, he would have to pack his bags because the next morning he was flying to Los Angeles to visit his other married daughter who worked as a secretary for a film studio. She had promised to take him on a tour of the movie lots.

On the rug next to the couch where Wilma Tannenbaum lay asleep, there were a half-empty can of Planter's salted peanuts and a highball glass which contained one nearly melted ice cube swimming in an inch of water. There was also an ashtray heaping with butts and crowned by a rumpled cigarette pack.

"This isn't really happening to me," Walter repeated to himself for the twentieth time ....

Marty Shaw wondered what the neighbors would think if he came around peddling eggs at their door. He hadn't spoken to Sharon about it yet, either. He remembered the time many years ago when his parents had taken him on a drive through Southern New Jersey and they stopped at a farm. The owner let him take an egg from the nest, which gave him an immense thrill. He remembered, too, how dirty the chickens were; and how some of them looked half-dead from a disease the farmer said was going around at the time. He was confused.

Marty pushed the pad and pencil aside and picked up the *Diner's Club* magazine which had arrived that morning. He'd joined the Diner's Club a few months ago; he liked to use the card when Sharon and he took their occasional trips into New York City and dined at a fancy restaurant. He didn't even know there was a *Diner's Club* magazine until he'd joined; but it was thick and full of ads. Idly turning the pages, he came upon a story by S.J. Perelman which was about a trip to Africa. He was stumped in the first paragraph by the word "dekko," so he skipped to the next paragraph and was stumped by "abstemious." His dictionary was on the other side of the room, so he flipped the page. He saw a large ad for a "Confidential Pocket Camera" the size of a pen which cost $14.95. The coupon said you could bill it to the Diner's Club account. Marty thought how much fun it would be to always carry a little camera around with him. He reached for his pencil to fill in the coupon, but stopped. His budget was pretty tight for the next few months. The new clutch on his car had seen to that. On top of the mortgage and car payments, Sharon said the washing machine—which still had three payments to go on it—was making funny sounds.

Next weekend, Ray Lang said to himself, "I'll go down to the basement and start on that fallout shelter. Fred McMurray on the radio said a guy can build one for a hundred bucks. I can save a lot of dough that way." But for now he watched his son who was now twenty-one inches long and weighed sixteen pounds. He tried to visualize what he would look like in eighteen years. Ray would be sixty-seven then, he calculated. After some thought, he guessed that engineering would be the best paying profession; the want ad sections were always screaming for more engineers. A young fellow could have his pick of jobs. Yes, he decided, I'll send him to engineering school. "Would you like to be an engineer, Junior?" he said, grinning at his son, who sucked the bottle as if starved.

Charlie Phelps, bored with looking for story plots in *The Times*, drifted to the classified section. First he looked under "advertising", then "copywriter", then "editorial", then "public relations", then "sales promotion", and finally "young", which continued with "young" this or "young" that and sometimes had something to do with what Charlie called the "communications" field.

A frown crossed Wilma Tannenbaum's sleeping, troubled face when the background music turned brooding and turgid as Tab Hunter became involved in one of the many crises he would survive in the movie.

Johnny Mulligan half-watched the same movie while he calculated the cost of his trip to Los Angeles. At least five hundred dollars, even if he stayed in his daughter's house. John had $8,000 in the bank from the sale of the house, and he'd told everyone it was for his grandchildren's education. They can still learn plenty for $7,500, he rationalized.

I can't really believe that this is actually *happening* to me, Walter thought. It's like watching a foreign movie.

Marty Shaw repeated to himself, $8,973 a year. And that's all there would be. He wasn't saving a cent of his $7,300 annual salary. He turned the pages of his *Diner's Club* magazine. "At last, an organizing system that makes sense 365 days a year," an ad said. "The new super deluxe 365-er Executive Organizer." This, too, was $14.95. He flipped the page. "An amazing U.N. wall clock which instantly shows diplomats the time in 70 different places: Tokyo, Darwin, Zanzibar, Casablanca …." He turned the page. "Your own business; start while employed; $9 hourly gross profits." The illustration showed a man cleaning a lounge chair with some type of apparatus. Next to it was an ad for a "radar detector" to warn motorists about speed traps. It clipped on the sun visor and came in either beige, sapphire blue or emerald green. $39.95. "Prime Filet Mignons mailed from Chicago. $33 ... Expense-paid foreign travel; Start big profit home import-export business; Famous world trader shows how ... Escape to an island hideaway in the sun; your site in the Bahamas for only $10 and $10 monthly; Magic Mail Plan - can make you $5 an hour; Learn to play the guitar in 10 days or your money back; Ever get stuck in ice, snow or mud? For a quick start this winter carry a pair of Campbell Traction Klips - $3.99 a pair; Bawdy Elizabethan ballads! Courtly, de-lightfully shocking, flourished with the double entendre."

So many things, Marty thought, so *many* things. To do, to buy, so many things.

Scarlett Kosciusko had finally fallen asleep in her bed. So had Irwin Kemp, slumped on his sofa, the test pattern flickering on the TV screen.

Ray Lang looked over to the far corner of the bedroom where his wife was sleeping. He turned back to the baby who had finished three-quarters of the bottle, waved it aside with a tiny pink fist, rolled over on his stomach and fallen asleep. Ray quietly lifted the bottle out of the crib and put it on the night table. He eased himself down at his wife's side—she was breathing lightly—and lay in the dark, wondering about the best branch of engineering for his son to enter. Chemical? Industrial?

Wilma Tannenbaum's face was placid now as she slept, and dreamed of walking hand in hand in a park, with Tab Hunter ....

Marty Shaw flipped back toward the beginning of the magazine. A full-page ad shouted, "Tap hidden sources of energy—Never Feel Tired Again! Burn up stale energy right in your home or office—without getting out of your chair. You'll sleep like a baby every night in the week once you slip a certain small object under your pillow. $4.95." And the Book-of-the-Month Club asked: "Just for self-appraisal, check the books you fully intended to read and then failed to, through oversight or overbusyness." He looked them over and was dismayed to find that he hadn't read any of them. *And oh.* He'd missed this before: a miniature confidential tape recorder. "Record conversations anytime, anywhere; secretly if you like." *So many things.* "Monogrammed Beer Goblets, set of four, $4.95; When fire strikes, be safe with a Safe-T-Escape Ladder - two-story length, $19.95, three story, $25.95."

Charlie Phelps turned to a Perelman story in *The New Yorker*, and plunged into the middle of it, straining to concentrate. "Exacerbated." He laid the magazine aside. A Thermonuclear Engineer? A Biological Engi-neer? An Aereonautic Engineer? A Metallurgical Engineer?

Wilma Tannenbaum slept peacefully as *The Star-Spangled Banner* waved in the dawn's early light before the station sign-off. Johnny Mulligan got up from his easy chair, clicked off the TV and went to the kitchen to throw away the empty raisin box. Walking up to his bedroom on the top floor—a converted attic—he imagined how his daughter and son-in-law, who were sleeping in the second-floor bedroom, might resent his spending $500 in three weeks. He felt a little sad as he eased himself into the bed. Now, Charlie Phelps also slept, his pipe neatly settled in a mahogany rack he'd bought last week. A pile of mimeographed double-paged resumes lay on the coffee table near his bed. There were also a dozen business-size envelopes stamped and addressed to destinations he'd jotted from the want ads.

A Management Engineer? A Marine Engineer? A Rocket Engineer? "This can't be happening," Walter muttered to himself. "Have these people no shame?" Marty Shaw was now reading a copy of *Playboy.* He chuckled over a cartoon. Sharon had kidded him for subscribing. "It's got the best fiction being published today," he'd snapped back. He came across a story on food and wondered why he didn't make a point of clipping the recipes before he threw the magazines out. Yes. He would buy a loose-leaf notebook and he would paste in the recipes for all sorts of exotic dishes. Their meals would be an adventure. He'd buy some candles at the supermarket this weekend. He glanced at a list of recipes. There was one for "Truffle Stuffing" which called for a 7/8-ounce can of black truffles, minced fine. Truffles, he said, puzzled. Annoyed over having to get up, Marty crossed the room to the bookcase and opened his dictionary. "Truffle, n.1, any of the various subterranean edible fungi of the ascomycetous genus *Tuber.*" He pressed his aching temples. So many things.

Taking the magazine with him, he went into the bathroom and sat down. He opened the magazine to the centerfold; a voluptuous nude girl lay on her stomach in bed, looking directly up at him from a slim volume of verse, a quilt artfully spread across her thighs, just short of the buttocks, and a buff Siamese cat reclining aloofly at her side. Carefully, he rested the open magazine before him on the white tile floor. Blood surged from his heart in bludgeoning throbs. So many things. Marty's burning eyes darted to every part of her, pleading for a miraculous resurrection. Did her smiling lips quiver? Hurrying, fumbling, straining upward on his haunches to meet the sylph's airy charge, he galloped breathlessly towards euphoria.

2

At three-thirty in the morning, Walter drove Lindy's Volkswagen down the wiggly mountainside road, taking the curves in swift, slalom-like trajectories. Still glowing in his memory was the vivid tableau of

Lindstrom and Miriam Furey enmeshed in the throes of mutual rediscovery.

Afterwards, Miriam, her gaze lambent, and proud Lindy, his hairy chest heaving, sat huddled in a bedsheet, sharing a Lucky Strike and babbling uncontrollably as one is wont to do after a titanic experience. When Walter finally rose to leave, they both insisted that he stay the weekend sometime soon.

Below, in the distant flatlands, the city blinked a gentle welcome through a membrane of low-hanging mist. The city; the office — where he would spend his last night in Captivity.

Very Nutritious

1

On the morning of Walter's last day with the company, a Friday, he was about to leave his office for a toilet seat nap in the men's room when he received a visitor; a fiftyish woman with an orchid-hued hair rinse. Were it not for the exotic, stone-encrusted turquoise eyeglass frames, her wrinkle-free powder-pink face was perfect for those grandmotherly pie mix ads.

"Mister Mott?" she said, extending a vein-marbled hand. "I'm Misses Carpenter, the night supervisor downstairs in Machine Accounting."

"Oh yes, of course. How are you?"

"Fine. Yourself?"

"Oh, just fine."

"That's good to hear," she said, smiling.

"Well. Anything I can do to help you?"

"I work evenings as you know, Mister Mott. But I came by this morning because I was downtown shopping at Bamberger's and I stopped by to ask you about one of our people; a Mister Nill."

Walter tensed. "You see," she said, "I received a note from Personnel that a Mister Wilbur Nill was leaving our department today after eight years. Frankly," she said, a worried look clouding her face. "I don't have any Mister Nill on our list."

Walter felt the walls crumbling around him. For eight years he had been pocketing Nill's paycheck; a hefty bit of larceny by any standard. Would he have to murder this lady, in order to protect his secret?

"But I'm sure if there's been an error, it *couldn't* be Personnel's," she hastened to add. "You see, Mister Mott, most of our people are part-timers who work for a few months or a year or two and there's really not the *esprit de corps* that you people have here in the daytime. We never really get to *know* each other as well as you *day* people do." She looked around the office, her eyes opened wide, like a dazzled ichthyologist emerging into the sunlight after six months of hunting cave fish.

"It's very possible an error *was* made, Misses ...."

"Carpenter. Alice C. Carpenter. No, I'm *sure* there must be a Mister Nill with us; and I thought the *least* the night people could do on his last day — or rather *night* — was to make our supper meal a sort of *last* supper for him; you know, we could sing a song or two and wish him luck and all that."

"That's a very lovely thought," he said, relieved that murder was off the agenda.

"And the reason I came, Mister Mott, was that since you're the *head* of our little night group, perhaps, if it wouldn't be too much trouble, you could spare a moment between five and six to sit with us and make a little speech wishing Mister Nill goodbye."

"Well, I …."

"That is, if you don't have anything else *important*," she said, biting her lower lip.

"The truth is, I have to attend a conference starting at five sharp this afternoon, and it might tie me up until quite late. I have an idea. When the meeting's over, I'll see if I can drop by the office and say goodbye to him. And if I can't make it, I would like you to act as my personal representative and offer my best wishes."

"Oh, thank you, Mister Mott. I know he'll be thrilled. We'll have a piece of cake for you, just in case. Well, I must get my shopping done. It's been so nice meeting you. I never realized you were so *young* and, if you don't mind my saying so, good-looking." She crinkled her nose, smiled and was gone, swiveling her head about as she walked out, marveling over the brightness and *esprit de corps* of the day people.

2

At lunch hour, Walter told Mister Furey he was going to take some extra time since he had some of shopping to do. He walked down the street to Bamberger's, where he had a charge account and bought all his necessities, paying them off five dollars weekly. He'd figured it out; about $250 a year times eleven years added up to $2,750—and it was all paid except for a balance of $24.83. Walter decided that it was about time he got his money's worth.

He had always been conservative: a T-shirt, a pair of socks, shaving cream, tie pin; always struggling to stay within his $5 weekly budget. But now he needed traveling clothes. He picked out piles of underwear and socks. He bought two pairs of shoes and a pair of beach sandals He rode the escalator upstairs and impressed the clerk, nonchalantly strolling among the racks and saying, "this and this," to two summer suits— on sale for $34.95 apiece—two pairs of slacks and two sports jackets.

"Thank *you*, sir," said the clerk as he handed the plastic charge card back to Walter.

At a nearby bookstore, he decided to splurge and purchased the Thurber book that he had enjoyed so much the past few days. Out on the sidewalk now, Walter staggered along, cradling the pile of packages in his arms and craning his neck like a Balinese dancer to see where he was going.

"So you've started your new job as messenger boy, eh?"

"Irwin," he said with enthusiasm. Hi; I was just buying a few new clothes."

"For who? The whole department? Here, lemme give you a hand." Irwin grabbed half of the packages, allowing them both to walk in comfort.

"Heading back to the cafeteria for lunch?" Walter said.

"Nope. On paydays I usually treat myself to a meal on the *outside*. Say, since this is your last day, why don't you let me invite you to lunch?"

"Oh no, I—"

"Come on. Look, I heard it was *you* who pushed for my promotion and the least I can do is give you heartburn, right? There's a new health food place over on Halsey Street. Why don't we try it?"

At the entrance to the Ponce de Leon Restaurant there was a sign: "Where the secret of Long, Lasting Life is in every Morsel." The front window resembled that of a delicatessen or grocery store. There were signs announcing: "JUST ARRIVED! Organically-grown fruits from our Jersey farm!", and "Natural honey, from TROPICAL BEES!" Inside, in front of the white marble counter, was a row of bins, each one containing a different variety of dry seed.

The white-frocked proprietor, a tanned gentleman in his sixties with a wild shock of silver hair, was preparing carrot juice in a blender at the counter. He smiled, showing a set of gleaming, even teeth and said something which was lost in the roar of the blender. His eyes were as blue as the sky on a clear summer's day. Walter and Irwin walked to the back of the store where there were several Formica-topped tables and three booths.

They sat down opposite each other in a booth, resting their packages on the seats beside them. The table had a sugar bowl and a salt shaker with a menu propped between. The salt was labeled "natural" and when Irwin lifted the sugar bowl lid the sugar was brown. They scanned the menu. Nothing familiar. At one of the tables, an obese man with a morbid pallor and a three-day beard was shoveling a plateful of brownish-yellow mush into his mouth. The owner approached them, pad and pencil poised.

"What's that?" Irwin asked, pointing over at the mush.

"That's our vegetable protein special; it's a meat substitute for vegetarians. *Very* nutritious."

Irwin wrinkled his nose with distaste. "Say, how about this," he asked, pointing at the menu. "Fresh fruit salad with cottage cheese."

"It's *very* nutritious," the owner said. "All the fruit is organically grown."

"What does that mean?"

"No chemical fertilizers. Everything is *natural*; decomposed vegetation and animal droppings."

"Oh well, Walter, whatcha say we try some of that organic stuff?"

"I'll try anything once," Walter said, smiling.

"You've got a sale," Irwin said to the owner, who wrote up the order and walked into the kitchen. "Well, Walt, how does it feel to be getting out," Irwin asked.

"Pretty good, I guess."

"*Pretty* good. My God, if I was getting out I'd be screaming hallelujah."

"Why don't you?"

"Where the hell would I go?"

"It depends on what kind of work you like."

"That's the trouble," Irwin said. "There's *no* kind of work I like."

Walter smiled. Inwardly, too, because he felt a kinship towards Irwin. He remembered himself eleven years ago.

"You think I'm kidding," Irwin said. "I may play the clown in the office, but I'm serious. There is not *one* goddamn kind of work in this *world* that interests me." He said it so loudly that the fat man stopped shoveling the mush for a moment, glanced over, and then resumed.

"But you can't possibly have tried everything," Walter said.

"At first I got to feeling bad about it. Then I really thought about it one night and said to myself, 'Irwin'—I always call myself by my first name—'Irwin, why in hell *should* anything interest you? Is there some kind of *law* or something? And I'll betcha ninety-nine percent of people are like me. But they *gotta* work, don't they? *Somebody* gotta pay the rent and the car and TV, right? So they clench their teeth and dig in."

He reminds me of me a few years ago, Walter thought.

3

"A few weekends ago," Irwin said, "I drove into the city and parked down by Greenwich Village. It was a Saturday night. I start walking around, just enjoying being there. I take a walk down one street, not sure if it was McDougal or what, and I see four guys, three white and one colored, sitting on a stoop in front of this old brownstone. I come closer, and one of them is this big guy wearing khaki pants, checked shirt. Guess who?"

"I'll bite."

Irwin slapped the table and said with intensity, "Jack Kerouac."

"Jack Kerouac, the novelist?"

"*Yeah*. I've seen him on TV, and on the cover of his book. He's big. I think he played football at Columbia. And right next to him is this guy with glasses and a beard. I think it was Ginsberg, the poet."

"Wow."

"The reason I was absolutely sure it was Kerouac, I saw him a few months ago on "Nightbeat," this late night TV show on Channel Five. He's sitting there in front of this real serious interviewer, John Wingate. Dark room. Spotlight just on them. And Wingate says, 'Mister Kerouac, I understand that you associate with all kinds of people, including homosexuals.' So Kerouac looks at him, very straight-faced, and answers, 'I'm talkin' with you, ain't I?' The screen went blank for about a minute." Irwin rocked with laughter. "They must've had a *fit* at the station. It was *hilarious*."

The fat, pale man at the nearby table erupted an ear-splitting Vesuvian belch, pushed himself up from the table and waddled out; a walking avocado.

"So Kerouac, and Ginsberg and these other two guys, they're just sitting there, hanging out, watching folks walk by, joking around, not a care in the world. They know how to *live!*"

"And what did you do?"

"I hung around in front of the next house for a coupla minutes, maybe twenty feet away, watchin' them. Then I felt funny, so I just waved, getting ready to leave. Kerouac waved back and kinda winked. And Ginsberg, he waved, mumbled something I couldn't hear, and ... he giggled."

"Giggled?"

"Yeah. Then I left." Irwin laughed. "And I walked down the block, saw this little nightclub, heard people laughing like hell. So I go in, order a drink, and stand in the back. Right next to me, there's a coupla cops, looking real upset."

"Upset."

"Yeah. They're looking at this comedian on stage. Guy named Lenny Bruce."

"Lenny Bruce? I think I saw him on the Steve Allen show the other night."

"One and the same. So he's up there, cracking people up, cursing like hell. '*Fuck. Pussy. Cunt. Come.*'"

"My God."

"And the audience is cracking up. And the cops next to me, I could see steam coming out of their ears they were so pissed. But this Lenny guy isn't only dirty. He's *funny*. He got a real big hand. Then they invited anyone in the audience to come up and tell jokes."

"So did you?"

"Are you kidding? I would have shit my pants. But this guy, I think his name was Bob Bletter, he gets up from one of the front tables, holding a drink in his hand, smiling, and he says, 'what's faster, or a bullet?' Nobody knows what the hell he's talking about. So he gives them the answer like he's talkin' to a bunch of retards. 'The higher the fewer!'"

Walter chuckled, recalling Irwin's comedy routine after lunch the other day. So *that's* where he'd heard the gag. "How did people react?"

"They were cracking up. Then he says, 'What's the difference between a duck?' And he answers, 'Each leg is both the same.' People were *howling*. Then he says, 'If all the girls at Vassar were laid end to end in Yankee Stadium ... I wouldn't be a bit surprised.'"

"Now, *that's funny*," Walter said.

"Yeah. I left after a while, and when I was walking back towards train, I see this dark, quiet little bar. Just a couple of people inside. I figured I'd get a nightcap. I go in, order a drink and the bartender puts an LP on the record player. Let me tell ya, I didn't want to leave."

"What was it?"

"It was this tenor, singing Mozart. Man, his voice was like heaven. Listening to him, I felt like crying, and flying at the same time. I asked the bartender to see the LP cover. A young German guy. Name's Fritz Wunderlich. Boy, he is beyond great. That's another thing. I want to learn more about opera and start attending. There's so much to do in New York."

Walter wanted to reach out and hug Irwin. He'd found a kindred spirit.

"What now?" Walter said.

"To me it's all wrong. The whole goddamned system. 'Thou shalt live by the sweat of thy brow.' I could *kill* Adam for eating that sonofabitching apple." Walter laughed aloud.

"Laugh, go ahead. You got it made inheriting that money. But me, I gotta live by the sweat of my brow, or rather by the brown of my nose."

"The only thing to do is make the best of it, I guess."

The owner came with the food. They were each served a big cereal bowl with chunks of fresh fruit: oranges, bananas, apples, pears, peaches, raisins.

"Organic, huh?" said Irwin. "Smells okay."

"It's very nutritious," the man said, returning to his carrot juice blender.

Irwin scooped up a big spoonful of fruit. "Mmmm, good." They both began to eat. When Walter probed deeper with his spoon he found that the bottom half of the bowl was filled with cottage cheese, so he ate vertically, digging deep and taking spoonfuls mixed with both cheese and fruit. Irwin, however, ate horizontally, skimming the fruit off the top.

"Like you were saying about making the best of it, I guess you're right," Irwin said. "That's just what I'm doing. First I had a job with the Tastee-Cola Bottling Company on the other end of town. I was a Bottle Watcher. No kidding. I sat in this chair in front of a moving conveyor belt. Behind the belt was this big lit-up fluorescent plate. On the other side of the room was this cleaning machine where they put all the dirty empties returned from the cellars of restaurants and candy stores. By the time the bottles got to me, they were clean and heading single file along the belt towards the refilling and capping machine. *My* job was to sit there and try to catch anything the cleaning machine missed. It was pretty good at killing germs, but sometimes a big thing, like a clothespin or a mouse, would stay wedged in. You could spot the silhouette of it against the fluorescent light and then pull the bottle out of line. But man, it was *hypnotizing*. I was *always* falling asleep at the chair. One time the plant foreman pulls a bottle out of the line to take a swig and there's a *dead little mouse inside*. That was the end of *me*, let me tell you."

Irwin looked at his plate and curled his upper lip.

"What the hell's this?"

"That's cottage cheese. You ate all the fruit at once."

"Arrrrgggghh." He pushed it aside. "That was a fine dessert. Now, how about some *dessert*, huh Walt?" They picked up their menus.

"Prune whip!" Irwin shouted. "Man, I haven't had that in years. My aunt used to make it for me when I was a kid; a big bowl of whipped sweet cream with just a bit of prune flavor. It's delicious." He motioned to the owner, who wrote the order down on his pad. Walter asked for a cup of tea and honeycake.

"So, as I was telling you," Irwin said, "after they fired me at the bottling plant, I came to SIC. I heard it was one place you could make a living without really working. There's not a *damn* thing interesting going on around here. So, I joke around to stop myself from going nuts. *Industry*. They say industry exists to serve people. I think they've got the wires crossed. Boy, if I could find a way out. I don't care about being rich; just enough to get by on, that's all."

"And if you could, where would you go?"

"Oh, I don't know." Irwin shrugged. "I heard good things about Ibiza."

"Where?"

"Ibiza. It's a small Spanish island in the Mediterranean. I read a magazine article about it. They said it's beautiful ... and cheap to live there."

"How old are you, Irwin?"

"I'll be twenty-eight in February."

"You're young yet. Something may turn up."

Irwin pulled a tattered paperback book from his coat pocket, leaned close to Walter and spoke in a whisper.

"This friend of mine, Danny Rogers, he's in the Army over in Europe. He came home on leave coupla weeks ago, and he smuggled this in, gave it to me."

Irwin showed Walter the front cover: *"Tropic of Cancer. Henry Miller."* He flipped through the pages, continuing in a whisper. "This guy's great. Look what he says, right here on page one. *"I have no money, no resources. No hopes. I am the happiest man alive."*

Irwin looked at Walter, waiting for a reaction. Walter smiled, shrugged.

"That, my friend," Irwin said, "is the way to *live.* I wish I could be like him."

"Miller," said Walter. "Aren't his books banned here?"

"Yeah." said Irwin, flipping through the pages. "Just look at this." He pointed. "He talks about cunts, and pricks, and cocks, and shit and piss, even fucking ... he lets it all hang out."

"Really?" said Walter.

"The guy's a genius. Would you like to borrow it when I finish?"

"Sure. Thanks."

The proprietor was back with dessert. First he served Walter a steaming cup of tea, then a plate with a small piece of honeycake. He went back to the kitchen and came out again, carrying another plate.

"Prune whip," he announced. *"Very* nutritious." He put it in front of Irwin, left the bill face down on the table and returned to the front counter where he began to make a reddish juice in the blender.

"What the *hell* is this?" Irwin said.

There on the plate was a fist-sized mound of prunes which had been pulverized and whipped to a lumpy mashed potato consistency. It glimmered dully with an iridescent patina. A green-winged horsefly buzzed in and settled atop it, making Irwin think of a huge horse turd.

"I wouldn't eat this with *your* mouth," Irwin said, pushing the plate away. "Want it?"

"Nope," Walter said, shaking his head. "I'm sticking to Nedick's from now on." They rose to leave. Irwin grabbed the check.

"Can I at least leave an organically grown dime for a tip?" Walter said.

At the counter, the proprietor rang up the sale and gave Irwin his change. "Well," he said, his teeth gleaming, "how'd you enjoy the meal?"

"Very nutritious," Walter said.

As they left the restaurant, and walked back along Military Park, Irwin glanced at his wristwatch. "We've got a few minutes before we have to get back. I've gotta tell you something." He gestured towards a park bench. They sat.

Irwin looked around, then stared into Walter's eyes and said: "I'm gay."

"I know, Irwin. You always seem so happy ...."

"No. No. *Gay.* I'm a homo. A *queer.*"

Walter was shocked, speechless for a moment. Then he said, "So, all those girls you're always grabbing ...."

Irwin was near tears. "It's an act. If they ever find out about me, I'll lose my job."

Walter shook his head, trying to absorb it all.

"There's something else," Irwin said.

"What?"

"I'm Jewish. My parents, they came here from Poland, changed their name from Kemplowitz to Kemp. So I'm a *fay-ge-lah* and a kike. I don't know which is worse."

"What the hell's so bad about being Jewish?"

"Walter, get real. How many Jews do you see in the company?"

"What about Al Rosenthal? He's a VP in the sales department."

"And?"

Walter rummaged around in his head, trying to think of someone else.

"And?"

"I'm sure there are more."

"Sure, Walter. When you come up with a list, let me know."

"Irwin ... why are you telling me all this?"

"You're someone I can trust. Someone I like."

Walter gave Irwin a look.

"No. Not in that way. I mean, someone I like as a pal, *a buddy.*"

"Okay ... thanks."

After a few moments' silence, Walter asked, "So, now what."

Irwin shrugged. "Nothing. I just wanted someone to know."

"So, the thing about being ... gay. Do you have a ... friend?"

"Nah. I've messed around a few times, mostly in New York. I'm too scared to get involved with someone."

Now Walter felt terrible about complaining to the personnel officer, inventing some "homo" in the night shift. Somehow, he was going to make it up to Irwin. Somehow. "Thanks for confiding in me, Irwin. My lips are sealed."

Irwin turned to Walter. "Oh, Walter, I feel so relieved. You can't imagine how tough it is, living a secret life all this time, keeping it bottled up. It's so fabulous, being able to share my secret with somebody. It's like a thousand pound weight's been lifted from my shoulders."

Walter extended his hand. Irwin shook it, tears brimming in his eyes. Walter wanted to hug Irwin. He looked around, so many pedestrians walking by. No, better not.

These Are Nice People

1

The menu on the occasion of Walter's Farewell Dinner that Friday evening at Glenwood Manor was just like the one for old Johnny Mulligan; right down to the Delmonico Steak and Fried Scallops.

Irwin Kemp, who served as emcee, rose and said, "Walter, now that you're leaving us, I guess you'll be taking a vacation trip across the Atlantic to The Old Continent. Maybe to gay Pa-ree. So here's a little bit of wisdom I heard that may prove helpful."

Folks in the audience leaned forward expectantly to enjoy Irwin's "pearl". He began, *"Zee French zay are a funny race …."* As Irwin mouthed these words, many in the audience, particularly men who knew the old gag, stared at him, open-mouthed, amazed that he would dare to as he continued. *"… zey fight with zair feet …,"* and after a dramatic pause, *"… and zay* eat *with zair face!"*

A moment's silence, and then uproarious laughter. Some of the men and women who didn't know the gag were bewildered, but coworkers in adjacent seats leaned over and explained, which prompted another explosion of laughs and giggles.

Moments later, the audience settled down, and Irwin, beaming, produced a travel clock inscribed: *"To Walter, we're with you wherever you go."* Walter wasn't sure whether he felt touched or frightened by the sentiment. There was also a big greeting card which said, on the cover: *"Hear you're leaving town …"* On the inside, it showed a wild mob in pursuit of a man who was tarred and feathered. *"Good luck!"* said the caption, and everybody in the department had signed it.

Mister Furey then rose and spoke long and sonorously about what a fine fellow Walter was, and wished him good luck in translating the works of that Indian writer, which prompted quite a buzz in the audience.

When Mister Furey introduced him, Walter rose and looked around. Furey, standing beside him, was beaming broadly. Irwin, on the other side, was smiling and crossing his eyes, trying to make Walter laugh. He looked down two long tables and spotted everyone he knew: Paul Horwath, Wilma Tannenbaum, all the little typists and filing clerks, even old Johnny Mulligan, and his lunchtime buddies Marty Shaw, Ray Lang, and Charlie Phelps, who were there by special invitation. Near the back of the room was Scarlett, who looked rather glum.

"Thank you all," Walter managed to say. "It's been a great pleasure working with you and knowing you, and ... I wish you all the best of luck in the future." He wanted to say much more, oh so much more; about how he'd waited eleven long years for this; how he'd sacrificed; how he'd dreamt of this moment; how he'd cursed the company a thousand times.

But no, why ruin such a pleasant evening? After all, was it the fault of anyone here? *Whose* fault was it? Where could he place the blame? He sat down amidst a thunderclap of applause and a serenade of silverware on the drinking glasses. Fighting back tears, he thought, These are nice people.

In the cocktail lounge later, Walter had a good glow on as he chatted with well-wishers and sipped his fourth Seagram's 7 and water. Everyone was curious about that Indian writer he was going to translate. Walter was happy, but very tired after only three hours' sleep the night before. And then that Mrs. Whatsername had stopped him from taking his nap in the bathroom. He put his hand to his face and muffled a yawn.

Scarlett was over in a corner talking with some of the girls. She looked marvelous. She'd be so nice to have along on his travels, Walter thought. If she just doesn't *push* me with the *what are you going to do* stuff, everything will be fine. And she'll love Europe.

2

Irwin, Charlie, Marty and Ray were engaged in an animated conversation at the bar. As though they don't get enough of each other at lunch, Walter mused. He looked around the lounge and saw Wilma Tannenbaum leaning against the far end of the bar, spilling out of her low-cut dress. How nice it would be to rest my weary head upon yon pillowy whites, he thought. Wilma turned, caught his eye, smiled and walked toward him.

"Guess I'll never get rid of those old books of mine," she said, pouting and looking at him with little-girlie eyes.

"I could drop by tomorrow night and look them over, Wilma. It would be a shame to miss out on a rare edition."

"Why not tonight? Morty will be home tomorrow and you'll never have a moment's peace to concentrate and really choose the ones you want. Tonight he'll be at the factory until eight in the morning."

"Fine," Walter whispered. "Why don't you slip out in a few minutes? I'll follow you in a cab a bit later." She gave his hand a warm, moist squeeze and walked away.

Walter walked over to Irwin Kemp, who was railing at Charlie Phelps, as usual, while Shaw and Lang looked on, as usual. The veins in

164

his neck like taut thongs, Irwin shouted, *"Fats Domino* could sing *Hava Nagilah* better than Connie Francis!"

"Excuse me, fellows," Walter said. "Irwin, since you'll be taking over Monday and I won't be around, there's a couple of very important details I'd better fill you in on. Let's go over in that corner for a few minutes, okay?" Walter fished in his pocket for the keys to the bed hidden behind the file drawers.

3

At eight the next morning, a Saturday, sunbeams slanting through the window of his seventh floor hotel room dazzled Walter into wakefulness. It had been an eventful evening. Irwin Kemp had been amazed when Walter told him his Big Secret, about living in the office, and when Walter handed the keys to Irwin, his friend broke into tears and gave him a huge hug.

Walter was still scratching his head, figuratively speaking, of course, over last night's visit to Wilma Tannenbaum. Wearing just a cotton bathrobe and slippers, she had welcomed him with open arms, literally, squeezing him tight to her pillowy breasts. After a couple of drinks and some animated chatter, she showed him her book collection stacked neatly on a shelf. Walter politely scanned the titles but found nothing of interest, until he spotted *"The World's Greatest Short Stories, Written In Munson Shorthand"*.

"That's all you want?" she had said.

"That's all."

They had stared at each other for a moment; then Walter embraced Wilma and kissed her. She had responded, and they'd keeled over onto the sofa, landing in a crunch on a half-opened bag of Cheez-its. Walter had reached inside the bathrobe to her bare breast, and massaged it lightly, causing Wilma to moan. He had leaned closer and licked her nipple, causing her to moan even louder. When he moved his hand lower, below her tummy, she had grabbed his hand, and put it back on her breast. Moments later, after more breast massaging, licking and moaning, his hand had wandered downward again, below her navel, and once more she had stopped him. Walter had looked at her, puzzled.

"I'm a married woman, Walter."

He tried again. *"No, Walter."*

"But Wilma ...."

"If we ever did ... that ... Morty is so devoted to me, I couldn't hurt him."

"How would he know?"

"If we did—that—I couldn't face him."

"So why did you keep inviting me over here? Just to see your books?"

"No ...."

"What then?"

"I ...."

"What?"

"I, well, I enjoy the attention, the *flirting*, but ... I'm sorry, Walter, I just ... can't."

"That's okay, Wilma," he said, rising and backing away.

As he reached for his coat, she grabbed him. "Just when I've found you, I'm losing you." She sobbed.

Walter kissed her gently on the forehead and backed out the door, thinking, I'll never be able to understand women. They are beyond me.

4

After leaving Wilma, Walter splurged and took a taxi to the Pocahantas all-night diner, where he splurged again and ordered a huge slice of cherry cheesecake with his coffee. The horseplayers at the counter—Herbie the Hozzer, Normie The Nosher, Bermuda Schwartz, and Cappy Capodanno—were mildly impressed; they all nodded, to welcome him to the Cherry Cheese Cake Club, and went back to reading *The Daily Racing Form*. Even Rick, the bookie/accountant—and possible hitman, offered a nod and perfunctory smile. As Walter left the diner, there was Leroy, still tootling a jazz tune on his alto sax. Leroy spotted Walter and sang his latest hit tune, *"Ah got somethin' long an' tan, ah'm the last o' the big rah-ah-kin' men!"* Walter dug into his pocket and, instead of the usual dime, as a kind of farewell gift, he pulled out a five dollar bill and dropped it into Leroy's cup, which prompted a big grin and a grateful nod.

Now, lying in bed, he spotted the prized copy of *The World's Greatest Short Stories, Written In Munson Shorthand* atop his wrinkled clothes on the bedside chair; just where he'd dumped everything last night, before collapsing to sleep.

Walter looked around. It felt so strange to wake up in a different place after all these years. It was just an ordinary hotel room, but he felt like a king. On the opposite wall, next to the bureau, were his two large steamer trunks; one held his clothing, the other all the books and records he'd kept stashed in the file drawers, letting them accumulate over the years.

He wondered whether the company would ever miss the files from 1883 to 1907. Walter had smuggled the trunks into the office one evening during the middle of last week. After carefully packing everything away, he'd lugged and heaved the trunks in the service elevator and out the service entrance, where he'd hailed a passing cab. He'd checked into a hotel, just a few blocks from the SIC building, deposited his luggage and returned to the office where he slept through Thursday night.

Walter ran his tongue along his teeth; escargot again. He went to the bathroom and brushed, then walked to the window. Out there, a few blocks away, partially eclipsing the blazing sun was the SIC building; a shadowy, blue-gray obelisk rising in the sky. Good riddance. It was Saturday and the offices were empty, but on Monday they would all be in there at eight-thirty sharp. And at nine-thirty Mister Furey would come strutting in like an old soft shoe dancer. A tinge of nostalgia diluted Walter's disdain.

He called room service for breakfast, and just as he was emerging from the bathroom after his shower and shave, a bellhop wheeled the tray of food in, together with the morning newspaper. God, it's great to live like a human being. He tipped the boy a dollar and sat down to devour the breakfast: a glass of cold pineapple juice resting in a small silver ice bucket, poached eggs and bacon, a pot of coffee, hot rolls and marmalade, and … even a *newspaper*. He thought back to all the bran muffins he'd eaten for breakfast the past eleven years; *thousands* of them.

He glanced at the newspaper, and there on the front page it said that jazz singer Billie Holiday, 44, had been taken to the Metropolitan Hospital in New York, suffering from heart and liver disease, the apparent effect of drug addiction. She was destitute, with just 70 cents in the bank. Walter felt a pang of sadness. So much heartache in the world, but what could he do?

His stomach full and warm, Walter sipped at his second cup of coffee and took deep, heady inhales on his Pall Mall, marveling over the way his life had changed these past few days. On a graph sheet—he still visualized in terms of statistics—it would have been a long, unswerving horizontal line for nearly eleven years, and then, during the last few days, *zoom*.

All those years of self-imposed isolation, of living in a cocoon of inaction, awaiting the metamorphosis. First he'd met Scarlett; then, for some reason, he'd gone completely haywire; raiding Mister Jennings' bathroom, mischievously deciding to rattle that smug Mister Gumpert in Personnel. And he would never forget the wild party at the Fureys, nor last night's brief fumbling encounter with Wilma Tannenbaum. She had actually *cried* over him. And so had Miriam Furey; or at least she had cried over something. Yes, his life was on the ascent; he had burst the chrysalis and was flying free. He bounded out of bed, lifted his arms up and flapped them, skipping barefoot about the room in his pajamas. "Wheee!" he yelled. "I'm a fucking butterfly!" Puffing, he sat back in bed and poured the little remaining coffee into his cup.

He reached over and picked up the James Thurber story collection—he had splurged and bought a copy—and turned to *"The Secret Life Of Walter Mitty."* He read it again, for the nth time, chuckling again. Then, prompted by only God knows what, he rose, got dressed and, book in hand, went outside and walked the few blocks to Newark Penn Station.

Searching For Walter Mitty

1

Less than an hour later, Walter stood outside the old brownstone in Greenwich Village, trying to summon the courage to call on Mister Thurber. Finally, he took a deep breath, climbed the front steps, and with a trembling forefinger rang the buzzer.

After a moment, that elderly white-haired man answered the door. "Yes?"

Walter was taken aback. *Thurber in the flesh.* "Mister Thurber.?"

"Close," the man said. "my name's Burbage."

Now Walter was confused. "Is Mister Thurber here?"

"God no," the old man said. "The Thurbers sold the place to me and moved years ago."

"Do you know where they went?"

"Somewhere up in New England," the man said. "What's it about?"

"I really have to see him. We're related, and ...."

"Really? In what way?"

"It's kind of complicated, sir. Please, if you can help me?"

"I kept getting their mail here for quite a while. Forwarded it to, ah, Connecticut ... a place called Cornwall. *No. West* Cornwall. That's it. *West* Cornwall." The man shrugged. "Sorry. That's all I know."

Walter sat in the coffee shop at Newark Penn Station for a while, thinking. Finally, he murmured to himself, "No more indecision." He went to the ticket window and told the clerk, "Roundtrip ticket to West Cornwall, Connecticut, please."

The clerk, puffing on a cigarette, responded, "No such thing."

"Can you tell me the closest place to West Cornwall?"

The clerk glanced at a map on the wall and said, "Hartford. Then maybe there's a bus, or you can rent a car."

Three hours later, outside the train station in Hartford, Walter entered a car rental agency and asked the counter clerk, "How far to West Cornwall?"

"Oh, maybe forty miles or so. Wanna rent a car?"

"Yes, please."

"I got a nice Chevy, with automatic shift, coupla years old, good price. Whaddya say?"

"How much?"

"Thirty-seven fifty a week, plus eight cents a mile."

"I just need it for one day."

"It's seven-fifty a day, plus the eight cents a mile."

"Fine," said Walter.

"Can I see your driver's license, please?"

My God, Walter realized, *I don't have a license.* He fumbled around in his pocket, pulled out his wallet, searched, and—improvising—told the man, chagrinned and pleading, "I must've misplaced it, somehow."

"I'm so sorry, buddy, without a license, I can't ...."

Walter pulled out a business card. "Sir, *please.* I'm with the Security Insurance Company ... one of the biggest outfits in the country. Been there more than ten years. You can call them. They'll vouch for me."

"Gee, I don't know, I—"

"Sir, I'm a good driver. I promise I'll bring back the car safe and sound." Walter reached into his pocket, pulled out five ten-dollar bills and dropped them on the counter. "Here's forty dollars for the week, and ten for you, for your inconvenience."

The clerk put the forty dollars in the register, pocketed the ten, and stared into Walter's eyes. "You look like a decent guy. I'll keep your card. Don't let me down."

Walter wanted to reach over the counter and hug the guy. "*Thank you. I'll be back today. I* promise."

As Walter drove away, the guy stood by the door, waved and yelled, "Be careful!"

About two hours later, after taking Route 44, to US202, to Sharon Goshen Turnpike, to Wright Hill Road, to Cogswell Road, to Cream Hill Road, Walter arrived in the center of West Cornwall. He entered the local coffee shop, ordered a cup, and asked to see the phone directory. He flipped through the pages, murmuring, "Thurber ... Thurber ... Thurber ...." My God. *There it was.* It had the Thurber address, and even the phone number: *Orleans 2-6557.* Walter jotted it down on a slip of paper. He went outside to a pay phone and was about to dial, then thought better of it. Walter returned to the coffee shop and asked the waitress for directions to the Thurber house.

Ten minutes later, turning off a country road, Walter pulled up in front of the Thurber home, a modest, comfortable looking cottage, sheltered by shade trees, and a neatly maintained garden. .

Taking a deep breath, he approached the front door and knocked.

A pleasant looking, gray-haired woman opened the door. She said, "Yes?"

Walter asked, fidgeting and nervous, "Is this the Thurber residence?"

"I'm Helen Thurber. How can I help you?"

"I'm an admirer of Mister Thurber's writing. I wonder if ...."

The woman smiled and pointed to a suitcase on the floor in the foyer. "We're leaving for the airport later today, to visit friends in Paris. This won't take long, will it?

"Oh, *no*." He held up the book. "Do you think he'd be kind enough to autograph my book?"

She turned towards the interior of the house and called out, "James, dear? Can you receive a visitor?"

"Who is it?"

"A gentleman who admires your writing. Wants you to sign a book."

After a pause, "Sure. Show him in."

Heart pounding, Walter followed Helen Thurber into the dimly lit study. There on the sofa—*at last*—sat James Thurber. He was listening to a Mozart piano sonata, playing softly on the radio.

Helen took Walter by the arm, and led him up to her husband. She smiled, and with her hand silently invited him to proceed, then left the room.

"Mister Thurber?" Walter said, trembling a bit.

"Yes?" Thurber reached over and turned off the radio.

"I'm so sorry. I didn't mean to disturb you."

"That's okay. I can only take so much of Mozart. He's so damn brilliant, makes me feel like a dope. So. How can I help you?"

"I ... I wonder if you would be kind enough to autograph my copy of your book."

"Which one is it?"

Walter glanced at the title. "It's called *My World And Welcome To It.*"

"Ah yes," Thurber said, smiling. "Give it here." He reached out.

Walter remembered reading that Thurber had lost an eye in an accident during his youth, and his vision was quite limited. He placed the book in Thurber's shaky right hand. Fumbling, Walter pulled a ballpoint pen from his shirt pocket.

"Oh, and I have a pen. Here, sir." He handed it over.

"And to whom shall I dedicate it?"

"If you could, please write, '*To Walter Mott.*'"

Thurber smiled. "That's your name? Walter Mott?"

"Yes, sir."

Thurber patted a spot next to him on the sofa. "Please sit down." He looked away and raised his voice, "Helen?"

Helen peeked in. "Yes?"

"Can you make us each a little martini?"

"Sure, darling."

Thurber looked at Walter, smiling. "So. You are Walter Mott?"

"Yes."

"I guess you might've been interested in my story about Walter Mitty."

Helen came in with the drinks, and handed one to each of them. Thurber lifted his glass and said, "One martini is all right. Two are too many, and three … are not enough. *Cheers*."

"A fellow worker, I'm with an insurance company in Newark—"

Thurber interrupted. "Newark? New Jersey? You've come a *long way*."

"Yes, sir, and when I first met this fellow worker, she's a young lady, and I told

her my name, she smiled and said Walter Mott, was amazingly close to Walter Mitty. That made me curious. So I borrowed the book from the library, and read the story. It was *wonderful*. I enjoyed it so much that I later bought the book." Walter held up his copy.

Thurber smiled, took the book, scribbled his autograph and handed it back.

"Thank you so much. I'll *treasure* this." Walter said.

"Some years ago, they made a movie of that story, with Danny Kaye," Thurber said. "He's a wonderful fellow, I met him out in Hollywood, but it was a lousy job. If you haven't seen it, don't waste your time."

"Thanks. I won't. I just was wondering, Sir, how you came up with the name."

"Many years ago, I met a man named Mott."

"Really?"

"I was down in Princeton, visiting some pals. Must've been in the late nineteen thirties. I took the train home from there—we lived in Greenwich Village at the time—and the conductor yelled, 'Penn Station'. With my lousy eyes I got off in Newark, *thinking* it was *Manhattan*. I'm wandering around the station, looking for the ticket office, when this very nice fellow asked if I needed help. He was wearing some kind of uniform, blue, with a cap—"

"My *dad* was a bus driver," said Walter. "He wore a blue uniform and drove the Number 48 bus down to Penn Station Newark." Walter grasped his head with both hands and gasped. "He must've been on his break!"

"My God," said Thurber. "*Small world*. Well, your dad guided me over to the ticket office, and then sat with me in the waiting room for about half an hour, chatting about all sorts of things. At some point I mumbled my name, but he didn't have a clue who I was, just some poor half-blind guy. Then he walked me down to the platform to catch the Manhattan train. I asked for his name and address, wanted to mail him a check or thank you gift. But he wouldn't hear of it. Just said his last name was Mott. Never got his first name."

The Secret Life of Walter Mott

"It was Roger," Walter said.

"While I sat in the train heading back to New York," Thurber continued, "I was thinking about my short story, you know, and, thinking of your dad, such a kind fellow. I almost called the story, *The Secret Life of Walter Mott,* but then decided to name my hero '*Mitty*', pretty close to '*Mott*'."

Walter was thrilled. "That is amazing."

"I had a school pal back in Columbus, Ohio, named Walter, so I chose that first name. The Mitty character I modeled somewhat after my own dad," Thurber explained. "He was a dreamer ... a little clerk sitting behind a desk, wanted to be a lawyer, an actor, was quite often out of a job. But we got by." He turned to Walter. "Was your dad a dreamer, too?"

"Not really, Mister Thurber. Or at least he didn't seem to be. He drove a bus, read the newspaper, listened to the radio, and—since he grew up during The Great Depression—he said he was thrilled to have a job, *any* job."

"I see."

"But I'm a dreamer, Mister Thurber. Almost like your Walter Mitty."

"Really?" Thurber said. Then he lifted his glass and called out, "Helen, dear, can you please give us a refill?" He turned to Walter, most interested. "I'm all ears."

Helen took away their glasses, and soon returned with a refill, as Walter began his account of the past ten years, living secretly in his office, his friendship with Stormy at the Latin Casino, giving the crabs to hundreds of coworkers, investing his money, and winding up with a small fortune.

Half an hour later, when Walter finished, Thurber shook his head and said, "My God, that's *fabulous*. Sounds like something I'd write."

Walter felt flattered, and emboldened. He reached into his pocket, pulled out two folded sheets of typewritten paper and handed them to Thurber. "This is a little poem I wrote."

"Thank you. Tell me, Walter, do you have a favorite poet?"

"I really like Alexander Pope."

"*Very* good choice," said Thurber. "I've spent many an hour basking in '*The Rape Of The Lock.*' Let's see, Canto I ...'*What dire offences from amorous causes springs, What mighty contests rise from trivial things ....*' I once read a marvelous appreciation of Pope's work in a small book by a scholar with the odd name of ... Clement Fairweather—"

Walter's expression lit up and his voice rose. "He was my professor a few years ago at Rutgers."

"Really? It is truly a small world. And what is your poem about?"

173

"It's not at all like Pope's work. It's called, '*The Ballad of Pubic Pediculi*.'"

"Ah, a ballad. Sounds something like one of Robert Service's lively epics. '*A talented Scotsman*'. Poor fellow kicked the bucket last year."

"Gee, I didn't know about his passing. But I was inspired by some of his work. Mine is all about how one night I caught the crabs from my friend Stormy."

"So," Thurber said, "it's all about body lice?"

"Yes, sir."

"I'm just *itching* to read it." said Thurber, and they laughed aloud together.

"What about you, Mister Thurber? Are you still writing?"

"Oh, I eke out a piece or two now and then, but at my advanced age, I've developed inflammation of the sentence structure and a definite hardening of the paragraphs." This made Walter giggle.

Thurber then leaned toward him and asked, "Are you married, Walter."

"No."

"Got a girlfriend?"

"Sort of."

"Sort of?"

"I did, until recently."

"Is she cute?"

"Yes."

"And bright?"

"Yes."

"Do you have feelings for her?"

"Yes ... very much so."

"How old are you, Walter?"

"I'm heading for forty, Mister Thurber."

"After my story was published, a British psychiatrist published a scholarly paper and referred to the 'Walter Mitty Syndrome.' He said it was a clinical condition that manifested itself in compulsive fantasizing. Walter, take some advice from an old fart. Dreaming is okay. But there comes a time to *live* your dreams. Dig deep into your soul and ask yourself, what do I *really* want? Then, *go for it*."

Tears welled in Walter's eyes. "Mister Thurber?"

"Yes, Walter?"

"You were born around the same time as my dad. He and my mom died when I was just in my twenties. Auto accident ...."

"So sorry."

"I feel as though you've given me some wonderful fatherly advice."

"Glad to hear it, Walter."

Helen Thurber peeked in. "James, dear," she gently said, "the car's coming soon to take us to the airport."

Walter stood. "I have to go now, Mister Thurber."

"Okay, Walter … maybe we can get together after Paris."

Walter reached out to shake Thurber's hand. Then he hesitated and said, "May I give you a hug?"

"A hug?"

"My dad used to hug me."

"Helen! Walter wants to give me a hug. What do you think?"

Helen smiled. "How lovely," she said. "Permission granted."

Blinking back tears, Walter leaned over and hugged Thurber, who patted him on the shoulder. Then, book in hand, he left in silence and drove back to Hartford.

"Ever been to Grant's tomb?"

1

That evening, in the Newark hotel room, Walter removed his bank books and stock certificates from the night table drawer and fanned them out before him. Humming, he fondled his assets. Then he thought of Scarlett and recalled the vision of her wistful loveliness at the party last night. She would really enjoy this, he thought. Hell, it's silly for us to be fighting, he said to himself, reaching for the telephone and dialing.

"Hello?"

"Scarlett?"

"Yes?"

"Guess who."

"Walter?"

"Yes."

"Oh, hello."

"Listen, Scarlett, I've been thinking."

"Yes?"

"About those book clubs ...."

"Yes?"

"If that's the only thing that's worrying you, I could pay them off. Scarlett, are you still there?"

"Yes, I'm here." It sounded as though she were crying.

"Scarlett, listen; we have so much to look forward to, *together*. Please, listen to me."

"I'm listening, Walter," she said. Her voice sounded meek, subdued.

"I'm staying at the Robert Treat Hotel, right down on Broad Street. Room four o seven. Come over. Just to talk, I mean. We have so much to talk about. So many plans to make. Things are just the same as before, aren't they, honey?"

"Yes, Walter," she said in a tremulous voice. "They're just the same."

"You'll come then?" he said, feeling ecstatic.

"I'll be over in a few minutes."

Walter hung up and lay back in bed, smiling at the ceiling. He saw himself and Scarlett, hand in hand, shopping at the book stalls in Paris, lolling in the sun at Mallorca, traipsing up the hills of Corsica. It would be so much fun with her along! He got up and paced impatiently about the room, waiting for her knock on the door. He looked out the window at the SIC building, a dark, drab shadow.

2

Half an hour later there was a knock at the door. He opened, and Scarlett stood there, hesitant, tears in her eyes. He smiled, and wanted to take her into his arms. "What's the matter, sweetie?"

"I'm ...."

"What?"

"I'm pregnant."

"Pregnant?"

"Yes."

"How long?"

"Going into my second month."

"You're sure?"

"I'm always twenty-eight days, right on the dot. I haven't had my period for nearly two months. Maybe the diaphragm was in wrong, or something."

He turned away from her and stared out the window.

"The reason I came here, was to ask your advice about ... an abortion. I thought you might know ...."

Abortion. The word made his stomach turn, conjuring up images of Draculan horror chambers filled with screaming women and fang-toothed doctors. Lurid *Daily News* headlines. Scarlett's bloated corpse in the river, his face on the front page, flashbulbs popping.

"No!" he yelled.

"No?"

"We'll feel guilty about it for the rest of our lives."

"But what else?"

"Where's your car?"

"Parked about a block from here. Why?" "Let's go," he said, taking her by the hand as they exited the room.

Now in the car, Walter reminded himself, *I must get a driver's license.* He drove up South Orange Avenue towards Irvington.

"Walter, where are we going?"

"To a very important place."

In a few minutes, they were parked by the Christian cemetery. Walter took Scarlett by the hand and led her to the gravestone of his parents. She stood there, bewildered.

"My mom and dad," he said, pointing at the gravestone, his eyes brimming with tears. "I told you how they died, in a crash."

"Yes, so sad. And they were still so young."

"I wanted you to meet them, and them to meet you. He solemnly took her by the hand. "Scarlett ... marry me."

"Oh, Walter, I couldn't let you ...."

"But I *love* you," he said in earnest, looking into her eyes. "Don't you see? Why else did I bring you here? I couldn't imagine anything like that happening to you, letting those butchers …."

She put her arms around him, leaned her head upon his chest and closed her eyes. Tears glistened on her cheeks.

"We'll get married Monday, first thing," he said, blowing away one of her hairs which was tickling his nose. "No kid of mine is going to get dumped … down a *toilet*." He felt another squeeze around his ribs as she hugged him tighter.

They stood that way for several minutes, and now Walter felt peaceful, content. He dismissed the image of a judge in a powdered wig slamming his gavel and booming, "You are hereby condemned to fatherhood for so long as ye shall live." His heart softened as he imagined a smiling little cherub … *a tiny mirror-image of himself*.

Half an hour later, they were back in Walter's room.

"You're being pregnant isn't so terrible," he said, rubbing his cheek against her. "After all," he said, chuckling, "anything we do now is perfectly safe." He lifted her, let her down soft on the couch and kissed her neck. She giggled and pushed him away.

"Oh, Walter, I love you. But really, not now," she said, caressing his cheek. His blood, which had risen to a quick boil, subsided to a simmer. He looked at her and suddenly she seemed so fragile, so … *pregnant*. They lay silent, staring at the ceiling.

"Walter?"

"Yes, hon?"

"I know how much you want to travel, and believe me, I do too. But I'm worried. I've never had a baby. Do you suppose we could settle in one place, at least until the baby's born?"

"Sure honey. There's plenty of time for travel."

"Just until the baby's born."

"Of course."

"And my college courses … I was hoping I could get my degree."

"Of course."

"Someday that degree could come in handy. I'll be the first one in our family to finish college."

"That's great."

After a few moments silence, he said, "You know, Scarlett …."

"Yes, hon?"

"I was thinking, maybe, just while you're pregnant, since I wasn't counting on this in my budget—the hospital and all—maybe just during those few months I could take a job … a part-time job. Just to defray those extra expenses."

"So long as it's something pleasant, something you'd enjoy. That's so important."

"Say. While we're waiting, why don't we get a little house? We can always sell it later at a profit. Why throw away money on rent?"

He picked up the *Star-Ledger* and riffled through the classified section. "Scarlett. Look at this one. In Nutley, not far from here. 'Well built, six rooms, attached garage, near schools, stores, buses.' Just nineteen thousand."

"Nineteen thousand?"

"Don't worry. We'll get it back and more when we sell. I know a good investment when I see one. And I'll buy it for cash, so we don't pay all that interest."

She peered over his shoulder at the ad. "It certainly looks good," she said.

"Figure another three or four thousand to furnish it up nicely. I've always wanted a really good hi-fi ...."

"Oh, how wonderful," she said. "Drapes and furniture, and do you suppose I could get a sewing machine? I *adore* making my own clothes. That's a real economy, too."

"Sure, I'll get you one. You know, Scarlett, we can really enjoy life while waiting for the baby. And let's face it. Once the kid's born we can't just pack up and leave immediately. Not with an infant. Can you imagine lugging a little tot all around the world with us? God, you can't even trust the *water* in some of those places. What kind of life is that for a kid?"

"There's plenty we can find to keep ourselves entertained right close by."

"With your car—or maybe we'll get a sports car—we could travel all over on weekends; there's lots of places to see right here in the east. Hell, we're right in the middle of football season and all the Ivy League schools are around us. And how about Washington D.C., just a few hours from here. And New York, right across the river. Christ, sometimes things are right under a person's *nose* and he doesn't appreciate them. Like the Statue of Liberty, or Grant's Tomb. Ever been to Grant's Tomb?"

"No, never."

"See? That's just an example. Life is so full, yet people are always running here and there to *other* places ... always other places. All they're doing is running from *themselves,* dontcha agree?"

"That's what I've been wanting to tell you for a long time, Walter, but I thought you'd be upset."

"Say," he said, pointing to the classified ads, "here's an interesting sounding job: 'PART TIME. Office worker needed three days a week. Light pleasant work for mature gentleman.' It's got a phone number.

Wonder if I'd find anyone in on a Saturday," he said, reaching for the phone.

"It can wait until Monday, hon," she said. "Let's enjoy the weekend. Later we can take a ride and look at that house. There's that nice miniature golf course out on Route twenty two. Maybe we can go there. *Oh.* And sometimes we can drive out to Pennsylvania, and Ohio, to visit my family. They'll *love* you."

"Right," he said, with a mixture of enthusiasm and trepidation.

The afternoon sun dipped behind the distant towering SIC building, shrouding the room in shadows.

Scarlett snuggled up close to him. "Walter?"

"Yes, sweetie?"

"I can't think of any place on earth—or in the entire *universe*—where I'd rather be, than with you, right here, right now."

Walter hugged Scarlett. Her stomach, filled with the seed of their child, seemed to be larger already. He felt a sudden urge to tell Stormy about the baby. He was sure Scarlett would like Stormy. Maybe she could be the kid's Godmother. And Irwin could be the Godfather. He could invite Mr. and Mrs. Thurber to the wedding, too. That would be *so* great. If it's a boy, they could name him James. Oh—and he must get that driver's license. It was such a pleasure, both loving and resenting Scarlett. This *woman* who was clipping his wings with houses and jobs and children and sewing machines and family visits to Pennsylvania and Ohio. My God, he thought. All those strange people. What will I say to them? But Scarlett was his, his alone, he realized with tremendous relief and a frisson of dread. At last he belonged somewhere.

About the Author

Kal Wagenheim (born in Newark, N.J.) is a journalist (formerly with The New York Times and currently editor of Caribbean UPDATE monthly newsletter), author and translator of eight books, and ten plays and screenplays. His biography of Babe Ruth was a Playboy Book Club selection and was adapted for an NBC-TV film. His biography of Roberto Clemente, published years ago, will be reissued in 2010 in an updated edition. His plays, "Bavarian Rage," "We Beat Whitey Ford", "Wegotdates.com" and "Coffee With God" have been produced off-off-Broadway. "Coffee With God" has been published by the Dramatic Publishing Co. and is being produced at festivals and schools nationwide. His poetry and fiction have been published in the online literary magazine www.jerseyworks.com. His nonfiction articles have been published in The Nation, and The New Republic. He has also taught creative writing at Columbia University and The State Prison in Trenton NJ. Member: PEN American Center and The Dramatists Guild of America. Film producers may access his screenplays on the website www.inktip.com. Further details on website: www.kalwagenheim.com.

ALL THINGS THAT MATTER PRESS ™

FOR MORE INFORMATION ON TITLES AVAILABLE FROM
ALL THINGS THAT MATTER PRESS, GO TO
http://allthingsthatmatterpress.com
or contact us at
allthingsthatmatterpress@gmail.com

21462001R00111

Made in the USA
Lexington, KY
16 March 2013